C000098819

Owned by a Billionaire

Lovechilde Saga Book 5

J. J. SOREL

Copyright © 2023 by J. J. Sorel

All rights reserved.

No portion of this book may be reproduced in any form without written permission from the publisher or author, except as permitted by U.S. copyright law. This is a work of fiction. Names, characters, businesses, events, and incidents are pure products of the author's imagination. Any resemblance to actual persons, living or dead, or an actual event is purely coincidental and does not assume any responsibility for the author or third-party websites or content therein.

Edited by Red Adept

Proof by Red Adept

AUTHOR'S NOTE: There are elements of abuse, violence, and graphic sexual scenes. The violence and abuse, although not described in detail, could still be a trigger for some readers.

jjsorel.com

CHAPTER 1

Carol

1985

A YEAR AGO, IF SOMEONE HAD told me I'd be sitting in this swish Mayfair bar clutching a crystal glass, admiring the latest Dior and Alexander McQueen designs swanning about, I would have thought them mad. But there I was, in that discreet London bar which oozed old-world sophistication with its mahogany paneling and moody lamps.

I also never expected a room to myself at Oxford, nor to be staying in a swanky hotel during breaks. And it was all thanks to a life-changing meeting with Reynard Crisp, a man I didn't know that well.

I'd just taken a sip from my glass when in strode my benefactor. He nodded at a couple of men in bespoke jackets, lounging back on soft leather under dim, flattering light capturing smoke exiting their self-assured smiles.

They held out their hands as though he were their lord and master. Mm... Funny thing about that. Crisp, with his fiery-red hair, piercing blue eyes, and upright stature, knew how to command a room.

Though Reynard held a certain allure that drew me in, I'd quickly discovered I wasn't his type, despite one awkward night of intimacy that insecurities put down to my inexperience with men.

It wasn't really that, though. Reynard just liked his girls pure, or so he'd admitted after a few drinks.

Like mine, his past was a no-go zone, never to be shared under any circumstances. Not that he admitted that, but I noticed how he would change the subject deftly when prodded about his youth or schooling.

Having an almost unhealthy obsession with books was the only thing he'd disclosed about growing up.

I didn't ask him too many questions anymore. Not since I'd become his *project*, as he put it. All I knew was that Reynard Crisp possessed an enviably sharp mind. His extensive knowledge of history made it seem as if he'd experienced those times.

As he joined me, I stood up and kissed his cool cheek, taking away the scent of his citrusy cologne.

He glanced at my drink and, without asking, ordered me another.

"Distinctions on all your exams. I'm impressed," he said, looking pleased.

Despite experiencing the profound satisfaction a child might at a father's praise, I returned a nonchalant smile.

Showing one's emotions only made one weak, I kept telling myself. Especially when darkness fell and muscle-gripping fear threatened to crush me. Thanks to Reynard's generosity, I'd exorcised that debilitating shadow by becoming cool-headed and pragmatic, determined to make the most of my life.

It was nice sharing how my essay on the birth of the English monarchy had received a high distinction. Missing out on celebrating such small wins, like passing an exam in flying colors, was one downside to not having a family.

I ran away from mine.

I'd had to. My embittered foster mother seemed to blame me for her inability to bear children, and her husband was a drunken slob. Then I reached puberty, and he started to notice me.

That's why I preferred to look forward. If I needed a reminder of life's bleakness, I read Zola or Hardy rather than dwell on my childhood in that ugly council flat in Dalston.

Reynard ordered a single malt then returned his attention back to me, nodding his head and patting my arm. My academic success meant just as much to him as it did to me, it seemed.

He passed me a key. "This is for Notting Hill. The place is yours to do as you wish. The title is in your name."

I stared down at my palm, almost speechless. The key caught the light and glistened as if it was gold and held some kind of magic power.

Waves of anticipation and hope rippled through me. Not that I wasn't enjoying my stay at the five-star hotel off Oxford Street that he'd so kindly paid for. But a place of my own offered so many possibilities. So much freedom.

His motives behind such staggering generosity brought up all kinds of questions, however, because he never gave anything without some kind of expectation. I was already fulfilling a few of those expectations, for which he'd repaid me generously. Or so I thought.

"Rey, I just don't get this. You're being so generous. How am I meant to repay you?"

His eyes gleamed with that sly spark I recognized, a telltale sign that something brewed behind his collected façade. I'd already witnessed that same glint at dinner parties he'd insisted I'd attend, where business became the main course and would often involve me sealing the deal.

So to speak.

The older Swiss banker had been my favorite.

That's what we did. I was the sweetener for Rey's deals. I didn't have to do it. He made that clear. But it surprised me how much I enjoyed sex. Rey knew that. And with curves in all the right places, or so I'd been told, I'd been very useful to my new benefactor.

As I waited for a response, Alice Ponting, a girl I knew from college, waltzed into the bar with Harry, someone I'd only met briefly.

Alice had become a friend of sorts, in that she lived in the room next to mine at Oxford. I kept to myself as a rule—a habit I'd adopted from an early age. One of the few advantages of being a lone wolf was avoiding pesky questions like "What are you doing for Christmas?"

However, lone wolves sniff each other out, it would seem, because I met Rey at a bar one night when we were there alone. He'd even once told me that we were cut from a similar cloth, which prompted my first and last question about his life growing up. His evasive reply, "One's past is best left behind," was something I understood well, having buried my first sixteen years somewhere dark and forgotten.

Privacy and discretion meant possessing a tight rein on one's dignity, Rey would stress. And no one understood this more than I did.

Before I met Rey, I was nothing but a hollow shell, but he taught me the ways of the world. In his eyes, being streetwise superseded any advantage gained from a college education.

College indulged my hunger for books and knowledge, which was born the moment I buried my head in a book as a child. It was my only escape from the brutal reality of living in a council flat and hearing people screaming at each other day and night. In my teens, I found a copy of *Nana* on the school bus and discovered French literature, where I learned about human conditions worse than mine.

That's when I realized the true value of books. They became that non-judgmental friend who not only understood me but made me see that when it came to misery, I wasn't alone.

"You're here." Alice, always the bubbly one, seemed genuinely pleased, which baffled me, considering we hardly knew each other.

She pecked me on the cheek, and despite finding the whole kissing-and-touching thing a little awkward, I went with the flow. Must have been the gin and tonic, but my natural aloofness seemed to thaw after a few drinks.

Before I started rubbing shoulders with the upper classes, I always related touching and kissing as something one did before fucking. My foster parents never hugged each other, or me, for that matter. Bill, my foster dad, only did so once I had, in his words, ripened.

I wasn't much better. I'd refused to hold the baby I'd given birth to all those months ago, despite the look of horror on the nurse's face. Her expression still haunted me on sleepless nights when scenes from that hospital bed careened through my head like an out-of-control car.

"You've met Harry?" Alice asked in her breezy tone. The glitzy blue jacket emphasized her ebullience, while her slender frame seemed swallowed by those horrid shoulder pads.

I nodded while acknowledging her beau with a subtle smile.

Returning a warm and very handsome smile, Harry leaned in close and kissed my cheek. As he withdrew, his cologne lingered, leaving a subtle but pleasant scent of sandalwood mixed with smoky leather—a scent I associated with wealthy males, now that I'd already soaked in it.

"This is Reynard," I said.

He bowed his head in acknowledgment and shook Harry's hand. "We've met on a few occasions."

Of course, Rey knew Harry Lovechilde. He knew every wealthy person in that city, it seemed.

"Well done on becoming dux of the class," Alice told me, her eyes beaming like she was the one with the top grades. She turned to Harry. "Carol got a perfect score on her final-year essay."

Harry looked genuinely pleased for me. When he smiled, his cheeks dimpled and his blue eyes radiated warmth. I felt an instant attraction. He seemed so inclusive, not snobby, like so many of the elites I'd met through Rey.

The satisfaction emanating from my benefactor's gaze also inspired me to succeed—a drive I'd never really known until I met him. Reynard believed that beauty was best served with a well-developed mind.

It was a stroke of luck meeting Rey when I had.

Or was it?

Sometimes I wondered.

I'd done some wicked things for him... but the payoff was worth it. It meant having someone supporting me. Paying my way through college. Not to mention having a new wardrobe of designer clothes and rubbing shoulders with wealthy, well-spoken people who seemed to laugh a lot.

Nothing like that riffraff I left behind in Dalston.

Yes, I'd become a little snobby too. Fraternizing with the *best kind* made sense to me, and I was determined to make my life that way forever. Whatever it took.

I would never again return to a hell that even Dante couldn't have imagined.

Whether driven by ego or sheer need to become someone, I couldn't say. All that I knew was that becoming a woman of substance, as Rey recently described me as manifesting, was all that mattered.

And if that meant fucking rich older men so that Rey could seal some deal, then so be it.

"I've heard about your new enterprise," Rey said to Harry.

"Yes, well, it's early days." Harry sipped his drink. "I've developed this desire to kick-start an investment arm to the Lovechilde brand. My father's not so keen. He believes in land ownership and bricks and mortar. He hates the money market."

"He can afford to carry those beliefs." Rey's eyebrow raise wasn't lost on me. An occasional hint of his modest beginning slipped out now and then. I even sensed that he might have had a tough home life, just from the little things he'd mentioned after a few drinks had loosened his tongue.

That's why, I believe, we connected that first time I met him at that swish bar, despite me not having a penny to my name, determined to seduce my way out of poverty.

It worked.

I met Rey.

Only Reynard Crisp wasn't interested in me *that* way, I quickly discovered. I wondered if he was gay, but I soon learned about his juice, and it had little to do with men or even women. He liked them young and untouched. They had to be at least sixteen, he quickly added, after noticing the shocked look on my face.

Maybe that's when I should have bolted from this entanglement.

But then, I was desperate, and meeting Rey had catapulted me into a glamorous life of possibilities. Faustian bargain or not, only time would tell, but it was a risk that I couldn't afford *not* to take.

With Rey's financial and moral support, I completed my final year of high school. He even paid for a public-school education so I could learn to speak the Queen's English with clipped accuracy.

He bought me a new wardrobe of clothes. All I had to do was turn up to dinner parties as his partner and then fuck some wealthy, nice-smelling older man.

I soon became very popular. I even started affairs with some, mainly for the gifts and weekend stays at five-star hotels by the coast.

All were married men. My moral compass had gone off-kilter the moment I ran away from Dalston. Besides, being nice was overrated. Especially if it meant marrying into poverty and enduring a lifelong struggle.

"So, what are you planning over your break?" Alice asked, brushing wispy blond strands from her eyes.

"I might just hang around London."

She touched my new red silk blouse, which cost the equivalent of waiting tables for a week. "This is nice."

"Couldn't resist it. I picked it up at this quaint boutique on Oxford Street."

Harry seemed attentive as he and Rey discussed some financial scheme. Or it could have been his natural cordiality. It was at that moment that I developed a serious crush and had to take care not to swoon. Whenever Harry caught my eye, my face heated.

Handsome, filthy rich, intelligent, and refreshingly inclusive, he neither patronized nor played the chauvinist card like so many men I'd met. And he was the first to make me blush.

I sensed that marrying a man like Harry would be like winning a lottery that promised a lifetime of bliss.

Alice smiled at me. "Harry asked me to marry him."

I hoped she hadn't noticed me wince in response to her excitable announcement. "How fantastic. I'm pleased for you." Never one to show the kind of overflowing emotion that made women like Alice squeal and lose all sense of decorum, I remained cool, despite a sweeping rush of envy.

Yes, he was a catch, all right. A billionaire who wasn't just pleasant-mannered but also tall, dark, and handsome.

"He hasn't given me the ring yet. But soon, I guess." Her smile was so sunny I had to squint.

Foreign as her excitement was to me, I would have loved a dose of her cheeriness and to feel that pounding-heart arousal that I'd read about in novels. Although I orgasmed easily by allowing my mind to wander into some lusty fantasy involving a big dick and a dangerous situation, I never walked away pining for the men I'd fucked.

"So, what about you?" She side-eyed Rey.

"We're not like that. I'm not his type."

"Wow. I would have thought you were everybody's type. You're so pretty, and you've got the best body."

I nodded thanks. Yes, I'd been endowed with large breasts and an ass that poked out, as evil Bill, my foster father, often pointed out.

Would I have preferred being invisible?

Back then, I would have.

Now that life had taken a nicer turn, however, I enjoyed being desired by the right men. The powerful ones. The rich ones. And on occasion, the sexy ones. But they were only a dalliance, an irresistible dessert I allowed myself on certain occasions. But I would never allow myself to fall for anyone with less than eight zeroes in their bank account.

Despite believing that women could run the world—and do a better job of it, as history had showed—I also appreciated having my physical attractions to fall back on. What else did I have? I couldn't exactly sell myself on wit alone. Not yet.

That would come. Education would see to that.

Speaking of, Alice raised an eyebrow. "What about Ben? He's absolutely besotted."

"He's not my type." I sighed. *If only*. He was as wealthy as they came. "A little too studious for me."

She laughed. "This coming from 'sorry, can't go to the pub—I've got an assignment I want to work on.'"

I had to smile at how wedded I'd become to my studies. They were a gift. I loved being at that hallowed college and absorbing the resonance of brilliance seeping from those chiseled halls. When I first arrived,

I was almost breathless, like some gushing teenager. Only my idols weren't pop stars but former Oxford alumni like Aldous Huxley or Robert Graves.

"Harry's throwing a party on Saturday at Mayfair. You should come. Everyone will be there. It will be such a hoot," Alice said.

Now that sounded like fun.

Rey heard, of course. Supersonic ears and eyes, that man.

Harry smiled. "You should both come. Please do." He looked from Rey to me, and my heart missed a beat.

Rey nodded. "I don't have a lot on. So thank you, that sounds entertaining."

"We're off now." Harry glanced down at his Rolex. "Drinks with a distant aunt." He turned to Rey. "Why don't we do lunch? I'd love to meet your people at the Swiss end."

"Sounds good to me," my benefactor said.

After they left, Rey turned to me and performed a subtle slant of head toward the door, which Harry was holding open for Alice. "That's your future husband right there."

My eyebrows headed for my hairline. "But he's already taken."

"Mm... I saw how he looked at you."

"Harry's smitten with Alice. They're inseparable. You're imagining things, Rey."

"And you're not interested?" He cocked his head, wearing a faint smile.

"He's gorgeous, and sweet. And..."

"Filthy-fucking-rich. Old money. The best kind."

"But they're engaged."

"She told you?" His look of disappointment confirmed just how invested Rey had become in this marriage idea.

I nodded. "Just then. She's also a friend."

"No one's a friend. Remember that. Just acquaintances."

Our eyes met, his locking onto mine to emphasize that point. For a twenty-two-year-old, he reminded me of an old man.

Then Rey glanced over my shoulder and nodded at someone.

I turned and saw Helmut, one of his many close associates who'd been foisted upon me and whom I refused to fuck again. Our first time was a little rougher than I liked. And by that, I didn't mean passionate, slam-against-a-wall sex. He wanted to do anal, which was not my thing, and I ended up having to bolt before it got nasty.

Rey must have noticed my eye roll. "Play nice."

"I won't go with him, Rey. Remember the deal? Only if I can stomach them?"

"He wants to make amends. He wants to invite you to a party."

"Why don't you go with him?" I frowned. That incident with Helmut had dredged up some dark memories.

Rey shook his head. "Not my scene."

"But it will be mine?" I pressed.

"He's got something I need, Carol."

"Must I?"

He frowned. "Do you like Harry?"

I opened out my hands. "Well, yes. But he's with Alice."

"I can make anything happen. Just give Helmut another go."

"I won't fuck him, Rey."

"He doesn't want that."

When I turned, there stood Helmut with his big, round bald head, his red face brimming with excitement like he hadn't expected to see us.

They were all actors, these scheming men. All about money and power—and nothing was beneath them if they could get what they wanted.

That's where I seemed to play a very important role.

Only... I hoped to keep this period of my life secreted away from the future I had planned for myself. A future that didn't involve fucking randy lords and rich married men.

If I'd wanted to be an escort, I could have set myself up when I ran away from home at sixteen. But meeting Rey that one night and going with him to his exclusive Mayfair home had opened my eyes to new possibilities.

Little did I know that he would become my pimp.

I'd alluded to that fact once. The difference, as he put it, was that I only needed to fuck the occasional rich banker or lord. In return, he supplied me with somewhere nice to live, a credit card, and an Oxford education that enabled me to mingle with the privileged set.

"But won't that sully my reputation?" I asked Rey.

"What happens behind closed doors in this scene remains there. Remember that. They leave the gossip for their bored wives."

Having witnessed the whispers, raised eyebrows, and wicked delight at some juicy scandal or other, I shook my head. "Men gossip just as much."

CHAPTER 2

"Ah, you're here?" Helmut said, as though seeing me was such a surprise.

Helmut dealt in arms, something about which I would have preferred to remain ignorant. But after overhearing the mention of Kalashnikovs, curiosity got the better of me, and I asked Rey about his interest in weaponry. He just fobbed it off, like we were talking about selling marijuana or some soft drug, saying that if Helmut didn't, someone else would. Even as uneasy as that made me, I reminded myself that I just needed to keep climbing that social ladder.

Remaining cool, I sipped my G&T and gave Helmut a civil greeting, as if I'd forgotten about his drunken debauchery.

Rey glanced down at his gold watch. "I best be off. I'm meeting someone at my club."

He whispered something to Helmut, who responded with a reassuring nod. Then Rey leaned in and kissed my cheek. "Remember, I've got big plans for you."

Sucking back a breath, I threw him a resigned half smile. The kind a child might give a parent after being made to eat something unpalatable in return for a reward.

"I believe I owe you an apology," Helmut said in a guttural Germanic accent.

"It took a few visits to a psychologist. But I'm getting there." I flashed a fake smile.

His bloodshot blue eyes held mine. "You did? I mean, it messed with your head that much?" There was a note of surprise in his voice. "I'm truly sorry. I had a bit too much to drink, and I can get a little demanding." He clicked for the barman, ordered a shot of vodka, and then pointed at my glass.

I nodded. "G&T."

"I asked Reynard to arrange this meeting so I could personally apologize."

"I'm fine now. And I was only kidding about the therapy. You really needn't have bothered."

He chuckled at my droll delivery. "You're a special girl, Carol."

I had to fix my stare on my glass to stop my eyes from rolling at his patronizing response.

Helmut placed his large hand over mine. "Can we start again?"

I huffed. "I guess so." I held up a finger. "But this time, we only hang out somewhere public. No hotel rooms."

"That's a promise." He downed a shot, then, wiping his mouth, he pointed at the chilled bottle on the bar. "Leave it there."

The bar person nodded and passed me my drink.

"There's this little gathering tonight." Helmut regarded me. "The invitation stipulates willing partners only."

"Willing?" I frowned.

He fidgeted with his glass. "It's a swingers' party."

"Like partner-swapping?"

"You've heard of those?" He looked shocked, as though I were some delicate flower.

"I'm not completely naïve to the proclivities of certain indolent married couples."

His brow pinched. "You've attended one of these?"

I shook my head. "I'd prefer to sit through endless re-runs of *E.T.*"

He laughed. "I enjoyed that movie." Then he stared at me for a moment. "You've changed from when I met you. You've become more assertive."

I just gave him a subtle smile.

"I've got a nice little blue pill." His eyebrows bounced.

"And you won't touch me?" I stared him straight in the eyes.

His mouth curved down as he pulled an exaggerated sad face. "Am I that repugnant?"

My face remained blank. I wasn't about to sweeten the obvious.

Instead of acting offended, Helmut snorted a laugh. I got the feeling he enjoyed being whipped.

"I'm more of a passive observer. If you know what I mean?"

"You're a voyeur?"

He flinched. "You make it sound sinful."

I shrugged. "Each to their own."

He nodded solemnly, like something else was behind his affliction. "One must come with a willing partner to these events, and what better way to gain entrance than to bring a beautiful woman known for being passionate?"

Although I bristled internally at the insinuation that I opened my legs at the mere pop of a champagne cork, I remained deadpan. "I am passionately ambitious. That's all."

He held my stare and nodded. "And so you are. Good for you."

"I can also do without the patronizing."

He sniffed. "Can't we all."

"I plan to marry well." I toyed with my glass. "And I hate that euphemism."

His eyes narrowed. "What do you mean?"

"'Passionate' is a nice way of saying I'm loose."

He smiled. "I wouldn't put it like that. I'd say you're a hot, beautiful woman who knows the power of what she has." He paused. "So, who's the lucky man?"

"Harry Lovechilde." It just popped out of my mouth. The alcohol had lowered my guard.

"Harry? But he's not that into women, is he?"

My brow contracted. "He's engaged to Alice, a college acquaintance."

"Now I'm confused." He laughed.

"As am I." I looked into his eyes. "What do you mean, he's not into women?"

He shook his head and waved it off. "Oh, it's nothing. Just seen him at the odd gay bar."

"You frequent gay bars?"

"Sometimes." He gave me a sheepish, almost bashful half smile, like a boy caught reading porn magazines.

Harry at gay bars? That left me speechless for a moment. Despite my burning curiosity, I asked, "Why aren't you hanging out with men instead of seducing unwilling females?"

He poured himself another shot and gulped it down. "Do you want the cliché answer? Or the real answer?"

"Let's do real."

"I was raised a strict Catholic. I nearly became a priest."

I expected him to smirk, to reveal he was back to playing with me, but his face didn't move. "So you opted for arms dealing instead."

His face pinched. "You're not meant to know that."

"Anyway, you were saying?"

"Just that I'm suffering from guilty self-denial."

I processed that. "And the cliché answer?"

"The same." He buried a dark chuckle in his glass.

For the first time, I found myself warming to Helmut. In that scene of adolescent grown males, I was quickly discovering that silly games, though amusing at times, obscured those quirks that made us human and relatable.

But I had one more question. "Then why have me come to your room?"

Helmut shrugged. "Too much of this." He tapped the bottle. "And no one knows about my tastes. I like to make out like I'm a hot-blooded hetero on occasions."

"Rey wouldn't judge you," I said. "Goodness knows he's got his kinks."

"Yes, tell me about it. He's never gotten over his stepsister."

My brow creased so intensely it hurt. "Oh?"

"He's never told you about Meghan?"

"No. He never speaks of his life growing up."

"Well, then, all I can tell you..." He paused and gave me a penetrating stare. "This stays here, yes? He is not to know that I told you."

I licked my finger and held it up.

"They got together when she was fourteen and were at it until she disappeared at sixteen. I don't think he's ever gotten over her."

My dinner attempted to rush back up into my throat. I had to take a breath. I knew Rey had a sick alter ego, but as a victim of non-blood-related incest, I nearly choked with a rush of explosive queries.

"Disappeared? You know this how?"

"A close buddy of Rey's. A detective he's thick with who loves a drink or fifty." He chuckled. "And one night, while Rey was flirting with a girl not even old enough to legally drink, the cop leaned in and told me. He swore me to secrecy as he slurred all over me."

All kinds of questions swam around in my head. "She's never been found?"

Helmut shook his head. "I was curious myself after that and went on a bit of a hunt." He shrugged with a sheepish half smirk. "It doesn't harm to have a bit of juice up one's sleeve in this scene."

I acknowledged that advice with a slow nod, well aware of how identifying an influential player's weakness had its uses. It was something I discovered early on, after resorting to blackmail to get a job.

"I even dug up articles relating to her disappearance," he added.

"Was she a Crisp also?"

"No. He's changed his name."

There was so much I didn't know about Rey, and it bothered me.

"What was his parental name?" I persisted.

Helmut poured himself another vodka. "No idea."

Something told me he knew. "So, if I come with you tonight, will you tell me?"

"Mm... Nothing like a bit of stimulating smut to recharge the hippocampus." A shame-faced smile grew. "That governs memory in the brain."

I rolled my eyes as though I already knew that. I didn't, but I preferred pretense over admitting to ignorance. "Then it's a deal. I'll go with you." I held up my finger. "But I won't do anything I don't wish to."

"Of course. We're all gentlemen around here."

"Mm... More like reprobates."

He laughed.

Having diverged from what had piqued my interest in the first place, I returned to the subject of Harry Lovechilde. "So, what makes you think that Harry's gay?"

"Apart from spying him in a dark corner whispering into some pretty boy's ear, I can't say."

I smirked at his sarcasm.

Helmut pursed his lips. "He had a public-school education. You know, boys in close confines. Raging teenage hormones will make one park one's penis where he can." He grimaced. "Sorry if that's a little coarse."

"It takes more than a person's sexual orientation to make me blush." Still, I frowned. "Harry's bisexual, then?"

Did straitlaced Alice know? Maybe she'd leave him. However, it wouldn't worry me if my seriously rich husband liked it both ways.

Helmut regarded me. "I saw Harry and his girl leave as I was pulling up."

"I take it you know him personally?"

"Our little privileged, exclusive world is smaller than you think." He tossed back his vodka in one gulp. "So, what do you think, a bit of a carnal frolic in the suburbs?"

I held his stare. "Rey's real name, and no touching."

"I'm a man of my word." He laid his palm on his heart.

As I finished my drink, all I could think about was Harry's sexual fluency and what I'd heard about Reynard.

Did I want to be affiliated with a pedophile?

And what of his vanished stepsister?

Despite looming questions, I wasn't about to run from the promise of a bright future. I wanted that more than I felt the need to disassociate from someone who paddled in some cesspool of immorality.

And what would Alice think about her future husband's hidden tastes?

What I'd just learned might prove to be the means to separate them. Although not exactly prim, Alice carried idealistic views about true love. She'd made no secret about her aspirations of marrying an adoring husband and being that doting wife and mother one saw in the movies.

Despite my itch to crash her little fantasy by sharing my view on the myth of a happily ever after romance, I would often humor her with some glib comment like "And so you will."

Helmut rose from his barstool. He removed his Amex card from his wallet and gestured to the barman.

After paying, he helped me into my new red faux fur that cost me the equivalent of a month's wage, then he opened the door for me. "After you."

Out I stepped into the crisp, dark night. Revelers charged forth, and I moved aside before they bumped into me. Likewise, for a noisy gang of football fans.

"Mm." Helmut raised his chin. "I like them butch."

I smiled. "Careful."

"I can handle myself, dear."

From sleazy to avuncular, Helmut had grown on me a little.

As we made our way along Oxford Street, I asked, "Why go to this party at all? Since you like men?"

"You haven't met Gregory." He waved at his face and suddenly turned very fluffy. "I went to one of their little shindigs once." His eyes lit up as though he was reflecting on a golden moment in his life. "The man is insatiable. He's gorgeous in every way imaginable."

"Is he gay?"

"Not in an out-there kind of way, but who knows? I mean, Harry has managed to keep his inclinations hidden."

"Is Gregory Harry's age?"

"No. He's in his mid-forties and seriously sexy. Just watching him is enough."

"But wouldn't you feel left out?"

"I've got my boys. Don't worry."

I nodded. "So you're an active homosexual?"

"Shh... keep it down." He placed his hand to the side of his mouth. "Gregory's my obsession, if you like. That's why I want to go. And I'm so pleased that you're coming. I know how open you are about these things."

"I'll take that as a compliment," I responded, unable to keep the flat note from my tone. This reputation for being loose riled me. "But I still don't understand, Helmut. I would be severely frustrated if I were watching someone I couldn't have."

"But that's the allure, don't you see? Wanting something we can't have. It is a major turn on. For me, at least."

I exhaled. "I suppose. But at some point, I'd need the real thing myself."

He chuckled while linking his arm with mine. "Trust me, watching Gregory having his dick sucked feeds my fantasies for months."

Who did I fantasize about?

Harry.

Whenever I touched myself, he had a starring role. Only he struck me as too nice to engage in the kind of wicked games I preferred.

For a truly explosive orgasm, I favored a taboo setting, like a wharf with a stranger who takes me by force. Weird stuff like that.

A psychologist could finance a home in Mallorca on someone like me, who needed such dark, at times twisted fantasies to orgasm. I couldn't understand it myself, but instead of getting hung up, I read books instead.

And now that I'd discovered Harry was bi, I sensed I'd be looking for a new fantasy lover to get me over the edge, which didn't mean I'd dropped my intention to marry him.

I just had to work out how to move Alice on.

I looked at Helmut. "You're only going tonight to watch live sex performed on a man you want to fuck?"

He laughed. "I'd like him to fuck me, actually."

I stopped walking. "I am under no obligation to do anything. Yes?"

"You can sit back and enjoy the show if you like." He turned toward me. "The reason I need you there is that solo males aren't allowed."

He opened a Rolls Royce key tin, and I picked out a pill.

He sent a message to his driver, and within a few minutes, a Bentley arrived to pick us up. As the chauffeur opened the door, I climbed in and breathed in the rich smell of leather. Another reminder of wealth.

Once we were settled, Helmut pressed a button. A fridge opened, and he selected a bottle of Moet. "You like?"

I shrugged. "Why not?"

Thirty minutes later, we arrived at a decorative Victorian mansion.

"How are you feeling?" Helmut asked.

"Nice. The drug's taken effect."

"Yes. It's a good batch." He smiled.

Suddenly, he seemed attractive. Everything was attractive on ecstasy. I also relaxed, knowing he wasn't about to make me perform some lewd act. Friendship I could handle. And it seemed Helmut had become a fountain of information. My kind of friend.

As we stood under the street lamp, Helmut ran his eyes up and down my body. He pointed at my shirt. "Why don't you undo a couple of buttons?"

Who would have thought mammary glands could do so much more than just nourish newborns?

I was just about to question Helmut over Reynard's birth name when a man in a burgundy velvet jacket opened the door. His face lit up on seeing us. He gave Helmut a quick passing welcome before feasting his eyes on me.

"Oh, you came. Splendid." His gaze lingered before doing a quick appraisal of my body. "Please enter."

"This is Carol," Helmut said.

"Caroline," I corrected, holding out my hand.

"Gregory." He leaned in, and his kiss lingered on my cheek. He must have been late forties, seriously handsome like Cary Grant. Tall and dark. And I now understood how he'd become Helmut's object of desire.

"Nice to have you here." Gregory's eyes burned into mine, and I sensed that before long, his lips would be all over my nipples and beyond. Should I let him.

In private, I might, especially with the drug stroking my libido. But I didn't enjoy being watched. Not in a room, at least. Anonymously, however, I rather liked the idea of being seen from a window.

His undressing eyes told me that before long, he'd at least try to touch me. A slight swelling ache flushed me with delicious, tingly warmth, and it wasn't just my jacket I left behind on the hallway stand.

Never say never, my wicked alter ego whispered, taking over, as I pushed out my chest.

Helmut whispered, "See what I mean? Handsome. Yes?"

I stopped. "I can see why you want him. Yes."

He giggled. "I think we'll make good friends, you and I."

He took my hand, and we strode in as a fake couple into a dark pink silk-wallpapered room with enough carved neo-classical detail to hold anyone's attention.

A cauldron of smoke swirled through the air, containing marijuana, cigars, and a cocktail of colognes. In amongst that heady mix was also the unmistakable smell of lust.

There were around a dozen people in the room made up evenly of women and men. They turned, and upon seeing me there, their eyes lit up. I was by far the youngest, and they could probably guess I wasn't Helmut's wife.

Gregory moved about from one person to another, chatting away, and had I not known the nature of that gathering, I would have thought it was just a small, regular party involving excessive smoking, drinking, and drugs.

An orchestra of voices filled the air. The women's giggles shrilled over the men's deeper chuckles, and everyone seemed in party mode. Well oiled, as Rey would have said, after a few hours of drinking. That was when he did his best work, which often involved me hooking up with someone or other he needed to sign on a dotted line.

Duran Duran blared in the background, one couple dancing to "Girls on Film" and waving their arms in the air.

We sat on a bottle-green Chesterfield, sipping champagne, as Helmut leaned in and whispered, "That's the wife."

The woman he indicated might have been in her mid-sixties.

"Oh? And she doesn't mind her husband…"

"Fucking others?" He smirked. "No, it seems. She likes women. Theirs is a special arrangement. Gregory's a dark horse. And built like one too." He giggled.

I watched as the red-haired woman performed her hostess role effortlessly, like a veteran actor who'd performed in the same play over many seasons. She chatted and laughed, and it might have been any normal Saturday night gathering.

Gregory must have sensed my gaze because his eyes landed on mine and lingered, leaving behind a burning sensation on my cheeks.

"I think Gregory's got his sights on you, dear girl. Come on, undo a few buttons. That's a nice silk camisole I can see poking through."

I pushed away his hand. "I'm only here as your fake date. Remember our deal? And I'm expecting Reynard's real name too."

He bit his lip and looked sheepishly at me.

"Oh god, Helmut. You don't know it, do you?" I puffed out a frustrated breath.

"Sorry, sweetie."

"And don't call me that," I said, feeling seriously frustrated despite the euphoria-inducing pill sending waves of warmth through me. Or were Gregory's dark bedroom eyes doing that?

"I am sorry. But we're having fun, aren't we?" He reminded me of a puppy dog, and my lips curled ever-so-slightly.

Before long, the drug and its "let's make love not war" effect began tugging at my will, and the more Gregory's gaze held mine, the weaker my resolve became.

"Even if I was interested in him, his wife's here," I said, as our host continued to undress me with his smoldering gaze.

"As I said, she's into women. I wouldn't worry." Helmut held my stare. "How are you with threesomes?"

"I'd never do that. Got nothing against women who do, mind you. Each to their own."

He laughed. "Something tells me we're in for a fun night."

After that, I mingled and drank champagne, and a warm feeling flushed through me, especially with Greg's dark eyes feasting on my body.

He whispered something to his wife, and she looked over at me and smiled.

Then a striptease commenced.

A sinuous saxophone introduced a seductive Sade tune as our entertainment swayed her hips and lowered her spaghetti straps to reveal a lacy bra.

Helmut returned to my side. "Monique's always the first to start," he whispered. "She loves to show off her new breasts."

Whistles and cheers egged her on, and I sat back, enjoying the show as I might an amateur burlesque performance.

Meanwhile, Gregory kept giving me the eye, and I returned a subtle smile. The drug and the champagne had lowered my inhibitions, and Monique, who was now down to her garter, had warmed me up.

Drugs weren't normally my chosen form of recreation, but they were useful when I had to fuck someone I hardly knew. MDMA lowered my inhibitions and made the orgasms more intense.

Then a key game started, and we moved into a dimly lit room with red lampshades and sofas covered in lush satin and velvet. Paintings of couples performing acts from the Kama Sutra hung on the walls.

"Okay. You know the rules," Gregory announced. "If you don't wish to participate, then feel free to watch and enjoy."

He joined me, wearing a curious frown, and remarked, "I didn't see you drop a key."

"I don't have one."

"Oh, not even to your home?" He smiled, and his already handsome face grew even more so. "No matter. As host, I can choose whom I like."

"I think I might just sit back and enjoy the show."

"You don't strike me as the voyeur type." His finger snuck into the crack of my cleavage, and my nipples ached for his mouth and more.

I wanted his hands crushing me.

But I remained cool, despite this sudden rush of arousal.

Gregory cast his attention away from me, which allowed me to breathe again, not that I was disliking his attention. He rang a bell. "Okay. The rules. No husbands and wives. All new partners."

Gregory then filled my glass and passed me a joint. "Here, this will help."

"I'm not doing this," I said rather weakly, while he continued to fuck me with his hooded eyes.

I was so trapped in this man's allure that the background orgy turned into a blur of tangled bodies heaving away feverishly. It was almost comical, or that could have been the drug making me want to laugh. Marijuana made me laugh at all the wrong moments.

Helmut let out a groan, and when I turned to see what had gotten him hot and bothered, I saw Gregory getting a blow job. He stared me in the eyes as the female guest moved her mouth over his long, thick shaft.

I rose to go to the bathroom, mainly to deal with the liquifying swell between my thighs, when Gregory removed himself from his pleasurer, pulled up his briefs, and made his way to my corner again.

"Oh, how disappointing. I was enjoying that," Helmut said, but then a man near him started to suck another man's dick, and he lost interest in Gregory entirely, following the pair of males to another room.

"Are you enjoying the show?" Gregory asked, joining me on the sofa that Helmut just vacated. "Why don't you remove that pretty shirt?" His voice sounded deep and coaxing.

"I prefer my body parts to remain private." My heart raced, for he smelled so good—an arousing mix of cedar and testosterone.

"This is a big house." One dark brow arched.

"And what about your wife?" I asked.

He slanted his head toward a pink chaise longue where his wife was pleasuring one of the female guests.

"She's pretty happy there, I think."

"Doesn't she get jealous?"

His head jerked back as though I'd asked something silly, like whether his wife liked creamy cakes. "My wife introduced me to this scene. This is all of her making." His hand swept the room, filled with gyrating naked bodies. "I just go along with it. It's fun though." He flashed that sexy grin as his finger again investigated my cleavage. "Especially when someone like you arrives."

I removed his hand, despite wanting so much more. My resolve to remain dressed and untouched was evaporating by the second.

"You don't mind her being with another man?"

He shook his head. "She's into women. As you can see. We're a fluid lot."

"And you like men too?" I don't know why I felt the urge to ask that, although AIDS was something that did concern me.

As though reading my mind, he said, "I've had a recent test since our last get-together. We all do. It's a prerequisite to partaking. And in answer to your question, no. I have lots of gay friends and respect them like brothers, but I'm into pussies. And I would love to taste yours."

"But I haven't been tested." I found it hard to talk without sounding breathless, especially with his suggestive gaze traveling over my body.

"I would risk my life for a night with you."

"Now you're being melodramatic." I rolled my eyes and chuckled, despite my cheeks warming.

"Come on. Let me show you the house."

As I followed him, admiring the décor was the furthest thing from my mind and his too as his arms encircled me.

Drawing me tight against his tall, firm body, Gregory kissed me, his soft, warm lips moving slowly and sensually over mine and teasing my suddenly ravenous libido.

I broke away for air. "I thought this was against the rules."

"I make the rules." He pushed me against the wall, and his mouth crushed mine.

As I surrendered to a haze of need, he removed my blouse and fondled my breasts, moaning as he palmed my spiked nipples.

He gazed at me. "Where the fuck have you come from? You're fucking gorgeous."

When he lowered his briefs, his engorged, erect penis emerged, the veins popping and making the throb between my legs intensify.

"What would you like me to do?" he asked, walking his finger up my thigh.

"I want you inside me," I said breathlessly.

He removed my skirt, then slid down my panties. His lips were on my clit before my next breath, and as I opened up for him, I nearly burst a vein coming all over his lapping tongue.

"My Lord, look at you. So fucking hot." He slapped my bum. "And curvy. You'll make a lot of men happy with this ass."

I pulled away suddenly. It was like he'd thrown ice on a fire. "I'm better than that."

He drew me back into his arms just as quickly. "Needless to say. But you're also irresistibly desirable, and I want to fuck you until you're screaming for me to stop."

"Don't flatter yourself." But despite that sudden cooldown, I was burning for him by this point.

He chuckled and pushed me gently onto the silk-covered bed.

The burning stretch as he thrust into me was so intense the hairs on my arm spiked and my eyes watered. I arched my back, needing every inch to take me to that special place.

"Wet, tight little cunt. My god. You could become my addiction, you beautiful girl."

He held my ass and drove me up and down over his enormous dick. "I want you to come all over my cock."

Before long, my muscles released and did just that, climaxing like never before. An endless mushrooming of color and bliss. I became that flower blooming under the heat of the sun.

Normally, I needed it dark and dirty to come like that, and it seemed this was enough, considering his wife was in the other room.

Within a moment of my own release, his thrusts increased, and his grunts intensified into a guttural growl that filled the room as he came almost violently. He sounded like he was in agony.

We fell back on the bed, and he panted as loudly as if he'd been running a marathon, while I allowed the heat of sex to continue tingling through me.

"You're the best fuck I've had in ages," he finally said. "If ever."

I rolled over to my side to look at him, and he returned a gorgeous smile. Yes. I could quite easily fall for this handsome older man. But I had other plans. And starry-eyed romance was not one of them.

After we enjoyed a piece of cake and some more champagne, I let him take me again and again. Many orgasms later, I'd turned into a sated kitten, and he'd become a very satisfied tomcat who lay with his arms around me in a deep sleep.

Unable to sleep due to sensory overload, I untangled myself from his arms when dawn arrived, careful not to wake him. A quick shower helped me gather my senses, then I dressed and headed off.

It was six in the morning as I headed to the nearest station. I could have hailed a cab, but I felt like walking. The drug still buzzed through me, and it was Sunday, so I didn't need to be anywhere in particular.

As I headed in the direction of the train line in search of the station, Harry Lovechilde entered my thoughts, despite pleasant memories of Gregory fueling my steps.

Something told me it wouldn't be our last encounter.

CHAPTER 3

THE BLEAK STREET IN Hackney where my baby girl now lived reminded me of what my life might have been had I never met Rey.

But then, a year ago, I could never have imagined living in Notting Hill with its charming, gentrified period terraces painted in mid-tone colors. Mine was sky-blue with a bay window that flooded my living room with sunlight.

I stood behind a gnarled tree, symbolic of that rundown area, in the hope of seeing my daughter. I tried my best to remain invisible but had to hide to do so, because wearing a plaid Dior coat, gifted to me by a generous Swiss banker, I looked quite out of place in Hackney.

Oily cooking odors clung in the air, stirring memories of my early years growing up in that awful council home on the outskirts of London. Now my baby, or more accurately the child I gave away, lived in a similar grim street made up of maudlin high-rises.

What if she ended up the same way I did, forced to escape a dirty pig of a man meant to be protecting her? My stomach twisted in a knot just thinking about it.

I'd even knocked on the door one afternoon, but my daughter's new mother threatened to call the agency if I didn't leave. It was not the done thing, she reminded me, which I knew well enough.

I'd signed her away, after all.

Apart from designer coats and lavish dinners, one of the advantages of sleeping with powerful men was the way information fell into their laps as effortlessly as half-naked dancers working in those debauched gentlemen's clubs.

The details of my daughter's address had come at a cost, of course. I had to meet up with that one for a second date. Something I rarely did. There was only one man I'd gladly see again, despite my shunning his recent advances.

Gregory would need to work harder to get me. Or was that just a game I liked to play, a reminder that I wasn't that free and easy after all?

My daughter was now a year old, and while her new mother reassured me she was doing fine, I harbored this uncomfortable yearning to hold her. Maybe even to take her away, especially now that I owned a home in a safe and comfortable area.

But then, how could I rear a child conceived in such a violent manner?

There wasn't a day when I didn't think about her, however, and it was worse at night. Barraged by endless images of her little body attached to mine, and our separation at the cutting of that cord, I'd lie wide awake in the dark, imagining what it would be like to hold her.

Despite my refusal to see her or even touch her at the hospital.

Why hadn't I held her? Fed her? The milk that leaked out of me had gone to waste, and when the nurses asked if I wished to feed her, I went stone-cold, turning away as though they'd asked something unnatural of me.

REY WAITED FOR ME at our usual café, a fine establishment close to Westminster that was frequented by the rich and mighty. Of course.

Like wearing a soft, luxurious fur on a chilly day, I enjoyed mixing with that cohort of nice-smelling, well-spoken men. I'd become an actress who'd grown fond of her role. I enjoyed all the comforts that came with money, something I discovered the moment Reynard Crisp—in his shiny Italian shoes and tailored sports jacket—walked into my life. I'd caught the tube with my last pennies that day, heading to the swankiest bar in Mayfair, where I'd planned to sell myself to the richest man I could attach myself to. I couldn't stomach another day of menial labor, the pay barely covering the rent for my tiny, deplorably damp bedsit. All it took was one drink with this red-headed titan for me to sign my soul away, and in only a matter of days, I found myself mingling with London's elite.

Puffing slightly, I settled into the seat across from him at a table by the window. "Apologies."

Reynard beckoned to the waiter and ordered tea for two before returning his attention to me. "I only just arrived." His brows gathered. "You seem rather rattled."

I nodded slowly and exhaled. Rey knew I'd given my child away. He'd also reminded me that babies were born every second, and it was best to leave single motherhood to those with little else to offer. I took this sober advice with the resignation of someone about to have a tooth extracted.

The waiter delivered a willow-patterned teapot and laid out the matching set in a ballet of crockery. He then brought a tiered plate stand filled with cucumber sandwiches and pastel iced cupcakes.

I poured our tea and chose to abstain from the cakes. My stomach was a bundle of nerves.

"Earlier today, I went to Hackney. That's why I'm late." I traced the blue cup with a freshly painted fingernail.

"You went to visit your baby, you mean?" The alarming intensity in his gaze made me shrink, like a child might in front of an admonishing school principal.

"Can't you do something?" I asked.

"What is it you want, Carol?"

"I want to see her. Hold her." My eyes misted over, and I sucked back the sob that tried to burst from me.

Staring out the window, he sipped his tea, and after a moment of reflection, he said, "We've had this conversation before. You can be a single mother and struggle financially because I won't help. Or you can become a woman of the world. Marry a Harry Lovechilde and raise a brood you can be proud of."

His cool hand landed on mine. "You can't have both, Caroline. Decide which it's to be. I can't help you—and won't —if you go for the former. We made a pact a year ago, and look at you now."

Yes, look at me. I just attended an orgy and have developed a crush on a married man who knows my body better than any other man I've slept with.

After a moment, Rey removed his hand. "Helmut told me you were a smash hit at the Lathams'."

I topped up his cup then mine. "Oh, that degenerate swingers' night."

He chuckled. The only time Rey smiled was when discussing people's bedroom habits. "I'm told you looked to be having fun."

Biting my lip, I chided myself for taking that guard-lowering blue pill. I also thought of Gregory's recent invite onto his houseboat moored on the Thames. Though I'd badly wanted to go, I politely declined.

"Gregory Latham called and asked for your number," Rey added as though reading my thoughts, something he often did. Some days, I wondered if he was supernatural. With that lily-white skin, he might have even slept in a coffin.

"Oh, you gave it to him?" I frowned. I did wonder how he'd gotten my number, assuming it was Helmut.

"He was rather persistent." His mouth twitched into a half smile. "I'm told he's got his talents."

"Is there anything you don't know?" Fire bit my belly. It rankled, the lack of privacy in this world of privilege and entitlement.

"My, you are in a mood." He chuckled.

"Helmut and his fucking happy pills. I am humiliated that the word has spread."

He sniffed. "No one forced you, Carol, so remember that. In any case, Helmut's delivered nicely, and for that, I am very grateful. He likes you."

"No more fucking for my supper."

His brow pinched. "Gutter language does not become you, Caroline."

Caroline had become my name when playing the woman of class, but it was Carol whenever the mask dropped.

Rey was right. I needed to be Caroline.

"Gregory's wife's a serious dyke," Rey said.

"So why are they married then?"

"She's very rich, and only inherits if she toes the line. Her father, a devout Catholic, is still alive. I suppose when he shuffles off this mortal coil, she'll then embrace her sapphic leanings for all to see."

"The wealthier, the more eccentric in this well-heeled cohort."

"Yes. It can be rather entertaining. Wouldn't want it any other way. Leave the boring football natter for the commoners. While they have their little dalliances by keeping streetwalkers in food, our lot prefer to express our peccadillos in five-star luxury. And you must admit, there's never a dull moment." He clicked for the waiter, who happened to be passing. "A single malt and G&T." He gazed at me, and I nodded.

After the day I'd had, a drink was called for. I also took a cucumber sandwich.

"That's better." Rey nodded. "Keep up your strength. There's shopping to do. We have a party to attend tomorrow night. Gregory will be there."

I rolled my eyes, despite warm, fuzzy anticipation flushing through me all of a sudden. "I hear that Harry Lovechilde might be batting for both sides."

"Oh, I know that."

My brow creased. "It's common knowledge?"

He shook his head. "Goodness, no. And it stays here. I suppose Helmut told you?"

"He did." I waited for our drinks to be placed in front of us before asking, "So, do I tell Alice?"

He sipped on his whisky while reflecting on my question. "I'd stay out of it. You don't want to stir the pot where Harry's concerned. Remember, you want him on your side."

Sighing pensively, I had to agree. "Shopping, then?" My mood brightened at the thought of a new gown.

Possessing a good eye for clothes was one of Rey's many talents. He even extracted some joy from shopping, which made me wonder if he, too, had a thing for his own sex. But that theory was quickly quashed after I noticed how he ogled girls barely out of puberty. Another uncomfortable component to this mysterious powerbroker.

Rey nodded. "I must drop into Sackville's for a jacket I've had cut."

We finished our drinks, then he rose and gestured for me to follow.

We walked a few blocks and entered a shop that, with its scrolled signage and green wooden facade, could have existed in Dickens's time.

An older man with a heavy Italian accent laid down his scissors and greeted Reynard as though they were good friends. He then brought out a midnight-blue jacket and had to stand on his tiptoes to measure it against Rey's back. "It will fit perfectly, I'm sure." The man looked pleased.

"That's a lovely jacket," I said, sliding my hand over the smooth velvet.

Rey nodded. "Velvet silk. The fabric of kings."

"My, such high aspirations."

He didn't contradict me, flashing one of his self-satisfied grins instead.

CHAPTER 4

A BUTLER WELCOMED US into the decorative Mayfair dwelling and directed us to a large, noisy salon filled with guests laughing and chatting over each other.

Noticing us there, Harry met my gaze, and his sunny, welcoming smile instantly put me at ease as he strolled over and kissed me on both cheeks before patting Rey on the arm. "Love the jacket."

"Thank you," Rey said. "This is quite a turnout. I was expecting something a little more low-key."

"Well, it's my twenty-first. Got to celebrate somehow."

"Oh, I didn't realize," I said. "I would have brought you a gift."

"No need. Your presence is more than enough."

I met his friendly blue gaze, knowing he meant it. Then I looked around. "Where's Alice?"

"She's here somewhere. I think she's instructing the staff on punch mixing." He laughed. "It was a little too weak."

"Oh, she plans on a big night?" That seemed unusual for Alice, who didn't normally drink. At least, not as much as I did.

But then, I had a high tolerance for alcohol, as Rey often commented. He viewed my ability to maintain a level of coherence while imbibing as a talent, whereas I saw drinking as nothing but an escape.

"We're planning on a big night." Harry chuckled. "Anyway, make yourselves at home. There's lots of everything here tonight."

Going by his arched eyebrow, Harry meant more than just alcohol and food. As that thought passed through me, I noticed Gregory and his wife in one corner.

Despite declining Gregory's invitations, I hadn't stopped thinking about our night of passion. My body fired up at the mere memory of how his body had felt. And as I stole the odd glance, I experienced the same burning desire. He was even taller and sexier than I recalled.

His wife gave me a cool smile. Could she read my attraction to her husband?

Instincts decreed it best to leave complicated marriages alone.

Turning my back, because I couldn't think straight with that piercing stare loaded with innuendo gripping my attention, I took a glass of champagne from the waiter and smiled at Oscar, a friend from college.

His face lit up on seeing me. "Ah, you're here too." Oscar had bulging eyes and was a little too fond of cocaine and nightlife. However, he was also one of those seriously bright individuals who could somehow party his way through a degree.

"So, are you here alone?" he asked.

I shook my head and slanted my head toward Rey.

"Oh, you're still fraternizing with that sly fox." He chuckled. "He's chatting with Lord Pike, I see. Now that's a partnership made in hell."

I cast my attention over to Rey's corner and observed a chubby man with a large cigar dangling from his mouth. "How's that?"

"Lord Pike's into all kinds of underhanded schemes. Rumor has it his old man bludgeoned his way into the House of Lords."

"Didn't they all?"

He responded with a raspy laugh. "My father certainly didn't. God bless his religious soul. But yes, cunning deceit coupled with brutish force will get you far."

Oscar gazed around us. "Oh, there's Hilaria Wilson." He leaned in and whispered, "Story has it that her mother's up for murder."

"That's nothing to be hilarious about," I said, keeping a straight face.

"Yes. Quite ironic. I don't think I've ever seen Hilaria smile. How strange." He frowned as though that thought had only just occurred to him. "Monikers normally maketh the person. Take me. I'm a total Oscar Wilde slave, and my family were never to know that. Now were they?"

I exhaled, thinking of my name, Carol Lamb.

Oscar gave me a knowing look. "Ah... that's right, you're Caroline Lamb. Made famous by her affiliation with the 'mad, bad, and dangerous to know' Lord Byron." He grimaced. "Her words, not mine. I worship him. 'Childe Harold' is a masterpiece."

I'd read about her after someone at college pointed out that my name was the same as that long-suffering girlfriend of the famous poet. Superstitious to a fault, I felt a twinge of regret for not changing my name.

The party went wild after a while, thanks largely to a powerfully fortified punch and copious amounts of cocaine. The rich enjoyed their drugs, and most other pleasurable pursuits, at an industrial scale.

There was dancing, smooching, and screechy laughter everywhere. I wondered at one point whether that opulent home would survive. One vase had already come crashing down while a servant ran to save another, much to everyone's entertainment, for they stopped and applauded.

Harry Lovechilde didn't seem worried as he moved from one group of revelers to another. He'd proved to be an exemplary host, turning every guest into a close friend despite many like myself, I sensed, only ever partaking in small talk.

As I absorbed the beauty of the house's large salon with its sublime sea-green walls covered in golden-framed original art and concave arches housing marble goddesses, I fantasized hosting soirees involving high-art discourses washed down with quality champagne.

I smiled at whoever came my way, and I listened to them babbling all kinds of silly nonsense about someone's eccentric aunt who only employed staff named Mary or John or a paranoid lord convinced a wolfman roamed his property on full moons. Weird little stories that filled the room with laughter.

The wealthier the partygoer, the more juvenile, with their childish diminutives and "Mummy and Daddy" twaddle. I found many rather inbred, a fact that Rey alluded to occasionally. His eyes shone with derision as we listened to some story about Bertie or whomever having his monthly allowance cut for feeding magic mushrooms to the ducks on their estate.

After a while, the champagne went to my head, and I needed some space to collect myself. I hadn't caught up with Alice, and in my tipsy state, I even entertained the wicked idea of breaking the news to her about Harry's inclinations toward his own sex. Something he hid well enough, given those occasional lingering glances. Or was that me staring too often?

Debonair and Hollywood-handsome, Harry made it impossible not to stare.

Alice seemed to avoid me, which was unusual, given how she'd taken me into her confidence. Had she noticed me flirting with Harry? Was I that transparent?

I stepped outside for some air, since the champagne had made me a little lightheaded.

"Ah, there you are," I heard someone say behind me.

When I turned, Gregory, looking all cocky and irresistibly gorgeous, splayed his hands. "Why are you avoiding me? I've called you so often with barely a reply."

Under the garden lamplight, he looked his age, which did little to assuage the desire he aroused in me.

"I've been busy." I cast my attention to the thick trunk of the willow, lit up by a colored light.

He touched my hand, and tingles traveled to my nipples. "I can't stop thinking about you, Caroline. I've been with a lot of women, but none have taken up residence in my dick."

I rolled my eyes even though my body didn't seem to mind, judging from the spark firing up in my panties. His dick had taken possession of my fantasies, too, but he would never know that.

I couldn't allow myself to fall for a married man like Gregory. I knew how people gossiped, and just being at that orgy had potentially savaged my reputation.

"What do I have to do?" he asked, looking desperate.

"Um... not be married." I forced a smile.

"Let's see where this goes. I'll wash the dishes."

I laughed. "Why would you say that?"

"I'll leave her. It's a sham marriage. I'm just the bait. I draw women for her."

I shook my head. How did I allow myself into such a salacious triangle? "I would never do that. I'm not attracted to women. Not that I have anything against people into their own sex. Each to their own. But I'm probably a little too conservative to experiment."

His mouth curled at one end. "I wouldn't describe you as conservative, just young and deliciously responsive."

I refrained from commenting, mainly because he made my heart race.

"I felt you." He touched my hand. "You were charged. Highly erotic. We matched. In every way."

Yes. I came like never before.

I wasn't about to admit that. Especially with him so close.

"You would leave your wife for another night with me?" I asked.

"Well, I'd never be able to stop at one night." He gave me a boyish grin.

I wanted to slap him for weakening not only my knees but also my resolve to keep myself clean for that rich, powerful man I'd set my sights on marrying, despite him not having a name or face. Yet.

I thought of Rey promising to deliver me Harry Lovechilde.

But how?

Gregory led me by the hand to a hidden part of the garden, where, without even a bit of resistance, I fell into his arms. Our lips crushed together in a passionate kiss.

Tongues tangled as his body pressed against mine, the bulge against my stomach promising the release my body suddenly craved.

If I let myself, I could become addicted to this man. Drugs I could reject easily enough, but declining sex with a man like Gregory required the strength of Hercules.

Helpless to stop the fire his passion ignited, I surrendered to his hungry gropes as he smothered my breasts. He breathed heavily and almost grunted as he fondled me before turning me around. I poked out my bum so it rubbed against his cock.

He leaned in against me, and his rough breath tickled my ear. "You're a hot fucking temptress."

At that moment, I ached for raw primal sex like someone dying of thirst might water.

His hand moved up my stockinged leg, one finger hooking under my panties. "Your cunt is perfect."

As he stroked my clit, I gyrated against his dick, which was so hard and throbbing that my breath hitched.

He entered me in one deep thrust, and I had to bite my lip to avoid crying out. This man had the biggest dick I'd ever fucked. As he thrust in and out, I gave way to painful pleasure so intense that my heart nearly leaped from my chest. The danger of being discovered intensified the sensation, adding even more fuel to an already blazing fire.

He bit into my neck, and his groans dampened my ear.

"You're my new fucking addiction." His thrusts became frenzied, taking me over the edge. "Cream all over my cock like you did the other night."

His dirty little comments sparked all kinds of electrical impulses as the intense friction of his penetration set off a fiery release. Muscles spasmed, and a burst of euphoria surged through me.

Gregory then fell against me, breathing like a man who'd run his quickest mile. He kissed my neck and turned me around, and we kissed passionately.

After that, I knew I couldn't deny myself Gregory.

We would just have to keep it a secret. One fucked men like Gregory, but never married them. I sensed we would burn each other out.

I also refused to be swept into some tawdry wife-swapping scene as a remedy for suburban ennui. For over and above everything, Gregory didn't possess real wealth, and that would never do.

"Not a word," I said.

He held my eyes, and a slow, sexy smile grew. "Whatever you want. I'm your slave from this point on."

I rolled my eyes. "Okay. You've had me. So best you flitter off." I smoothed down my shoulder-length wave.

"I want you for an entire weekend. On my houseboat. Yes?"

A weekend of unbridled, endless orgasms with a well-endowed male? I could allow myself that little indulgence, I thought. "Let me think about it."

"Don't play hard to get, Caroline. It will only make me play harder."

"Is that a threat?" I had to ask, despite my body heating again. The allusion to taking me by force aroused rather than troubled me.

He was about to respond when we heard someone coming, and I inclined my head for him to leave first.

I waited five minutes before returning inside myself.

Just as I mounted the stairs to the entrance, Rey met me at the door and gestured for me to accompany him. I followed him to a mosaic courtyard by the side of the mansion.

He lit a cigarette first before speaking. "I noticed Gregory follow you out."

I shrugged. "We just talked."

"I'm told he's a rake. Always seeking to park his dick wherever he can."

"Isn't that most men?" I smiled.

"Oh, come on, Carol—don't play coy. You've also got a little mark on your gown."

I looked down, and sure enough, there was a stain.

"Go and clean yourself up. That's not meant to happen here."

His rough tone made my heart freeze.

I couldn't even find the right response and instead looked down at my shoes. I acknowledged my moment of weakness with a nod before sneaking off to the powder room.

When I returned, I found Rey waiting. I pointed at the mark. "Oops, spilled a bit of champagne."

His mouth barely moved.

Hoping to soothe his dark mood, I added, "I'm sorry. It was careless of me."

"Mm..." He lit a cigar. "Now go and talk to Harry. Shift him. He likes you. I can tell."

"And Alice?" I asked.

He shrugged. "She's not a patch on you, dear girl. Use it to your advantage. If she acts pettish over your flirting with Harry, all the better. That's something most males hate about women."

"Not just men." I pulled a mock smile.

Deflecting my comment, he cocked his head toward the house. "Go. Create a wedge between them."

Parties were meant for fun, not tension, I thought as I released a tight breath.

I left Rey and helped myself to another glistening glass of champagne from a silver tray. I would have preferred to play the role of Cinderella rather than the evil stepsister.

Coming to my rescue, Harry found me, which was nice and made my task of channeling the coquette easier.

"I hear you're killing it at Balliol," he said. "You're also breaking a few hearts." He slanted his handsome head, his blue eyes shining with a hint of mischief.

"Well, I'm not sure about that. But I love being there. It's such an honor. I want to make the most of every moment."

"A commendable sentiment. Most of my lot party their way through their degrees."

"I've noticed. How do they pass?"

He leaned in close. "It pays to be rich. In more ways than one."

I frowned. "You mean they buy their scores?"

"Money is exchanged, but not in that way. Suffice it to say, some of the poorer alumni engage in entrepreneurial activities like composing essays and the like."

"You're joking."

He wore the kind of smile a father would give a child who'd yet to experience the world in all its shades of cunning. "Anyway, you didn't hear it from me."

I absorbed that. "And what of your degree? If you don't mind me asking."

"I'm studying business. Which is the academic equivalent to finger painting for those who can't paint."

I laughed at his self-deprecation. "We are talking Oxford here. A high score is still required to be accepted."

"Let's just say that mathematics was something I've always found easy. So sure, it wasn't difficult to get the grades. And you know, I do like being there. Having fallen into the allure of hedge fund management, I've made some valuable contacts."

"Now you're talking in riddles." I sniffed. "Is that a fund to ensure hedges are well pruned?"

His contagious belly laugh swept me along, and I giggled.

It was while I shared this moment of amusement with her husband-to-be that Alice joined us.

"What's got you two all cozy?" she asked, swaying a little. She must have been hitting the punch hard.

"Just that Caroline was making a joke about hedge funds." He cast me another warm smile, which I returned, despite Alice looking on.

I then excused myself, only to find Alice following me.

CHAPTER 5

"A WORD," ALICE SAID, taking me by the arm—and not in a gentle manner.

Bristling at the way she handled me, I shrugged her off. Luckily, we were alone in the hallway, and wishing to avoid a scene, I cocked my head toward the door. "Why don't we step outside and discuss what's got you so worked up?"

She lifted her chin and pointed at the door.

Once we were outside, I asked, "You have a problem?"

She wobbled slightly, and I helped steady her by holding her arms. "I see that your determination for a stronger punch worked," I quipped, reverting to a lighter tone to defuse the situation.

She pushed me away. "Don't fucking touch me, whore."

My eyes widened. Was this the same sweet Alice who'd been so accommodating during those awkward first days at Balliol?

I took a deep breath to stymie my rising anger. "Don't call me that."

The last thing I needed was a cat fight. I couldn't afford to belittle myself by scratching and clawing with her like two overwrought teenagers fighting over a boy.

"I heard about you at that swingers' party you attended with Helmut and how you let a married man fuck you. And now you're trying to seduce Harry. I know your game. It's disgusting. You're the devil's sister."

I sucked back a breath, feeling like someone had just stabbed me in the gut.

Fucking Helmut.

"Does Harry know?" I didn't know why I asked that, because all I could think about was everyone knowing I'd attended that debauched party.

"He does. He thought it was kind of kinky, but it's fucking disgusting."

"They were all consenting adults," I said. "And besides, I did nothing. That's just a vicious rumor. Helmut's the one who deceived me. I thought I was just going to a party. I was led there under false pretenses."

Words collided in my brain as I tried to assemble more explanations to wipe clean my sullied reputation. All the while, a part of me just wanted to run away from these horrid people whose only dark moments in life were being snubbed by someone of influence or being unable to find the right size in a must-have outfit.

Alice scoffed at my explanations, and instead of continuing to plead innocence, I went rigid with contempt. Pathetic, immature girl. "Besides," I snapped, "I'm old enough to do as I please."

"Does that also include fucking my fiancé?"

"Alice, for goodness' sakes, get a grip. We were only just chatting. There was nothing untoward. I would never do that to you. You've been a friend to me."

I touched her arm, and she shoved my hand away as though it was broken glass. "Not anymore. You disgust me."

Despite Rey's warning not to reveal Harry's secret, I just snapped. "Then how are you going to handle being married to a man who likes other men?"

"Well, of course, Harry likes men. I mean..." Her brow creased. "In the same way I like women."

"So you're bisexual?" I asked.

Her face crumpled in shock and disgust, as though I'd offered her a plate of worms. This woman was far too puritanical for that hedonistic scene where pleasure and excess were as commonplace as gaining a college degree.

I stared into her eyes. "Harry is also attracted to men."

Although we were dimly lit under a Victorian lamp on the cobbled path where we stood, I noticed the blood leave her face.

"What?" Alice shook her head. "No. You're just starting these viscous rumors because you want him. I've seen how you look at him."

"He's been spotted on more than one occasion frequenting gay bars."

She knitted her fingers. "Maybe he likes the music. I don't know. He loves me. He told me he does."

"And you're having a fulfilling sex life?"

"Although it's none of your business, I'm a virgin. I'm saving myself for him."

I nearly laughed at that antiquated concept. But I also had to remind myself of that portrait of Jesus I'd seen in Alice's room and the Bible that sat by her bed. I hadn't met anyone religious before her, raised as I was by a family who only stepped into churches for funerals or weddings.

"Then you should know that Harry likes men. Speak to Helmut. He'll confirm that."

"A minute ago, according to you, Helmut fabricated that you whored yourself, and now you're telling me that he told you Harry was homosexual?"

"Well, bisexual, I'd hazard to guess."

"You'd hazard to guess? You're just making it all up because you want him. You're nothing but a cheating slut."

She slapped my face and reached to pull my hair when I pushed her away. From there, everything went into a hazy, slow-motion blur. Time no longer registered.

She stumbled back, falling hard on the pavement. The crack I heard seemed to muffle my gasp as I froze on the spot.

A pool of blood pouring over a bed of white flowers, like watercolor on wet paper, snapped me out of my daze. My heart reached my throat, and panic filled every cell of my body.

I bent down and tried to revive Alice, but she was unconscious.

A shadow darkened the path, and I turned to find Rey standing over me like a phantom.

"She stumbled back," I gasped. "I just pushed her away because she was pulling my hair and hitting me."

"Shh..." He placed a finger over his mouth. "Go back inside. Don't mention a word."

"But she might be dead." My voice choked against a flood of anguish.

"Go back inside. I'll handle this. Alone. Again, not a word."

A stuttering breath left my chest. "I can't go back in there."

"You have to." His eyes were wide and imploring, as if my life depended on me going back to the party. "If someone asks where you've been, tell them you were in the powder room. Okay? Go there first. Fix yourself up, and remember, act like nothing happened."

"But what about Alice?" I pointed at the inert body lying on a bed of bloodied flowers. Had the situation not been so serious, it might have conveyed something profound, like a work of art proclaiming lost innocence.

He tilted his head sharply. "Go."

CHAPTER 6

A WEEK AFTER THE party, I sat at a police station being questioned by a detective, clawing at my sweaty palms. Taking a deep breath, I stuck to my police statement and said again, like an actor going over her lines, "After noticing that Alice was agitated, I tried to calm her down and convince her that everything would be fine."

The detective stared me in the face for a prolonged period, and I looked him in the eyes, keeping my expression as blank as I could despite an endless battle of nerves.

"Can you please elaborate on what was causing her agitation?"

"Alice was worried about her studies and how she'd fallen behind, that she'd fail to meet her religious family's expectations if she switched degrees. She wasn't enjoying her theological studies."

"So you think she might have tried to harm herself?"

"I don't know, to be honest. I don't think she could have done that. But I have no idea where she went after I spoke to her."

"Someone at the party noticed her raising her voice at you before she disappeared."

That threw me. I'd thought we were alone in the hallway.

I shrugged. "It was really nothing."

"Tell me anyway," the detective said.

I took a breath and crossed my hands, observing how his eagle eyes followed my every gesture. "Alice had been drinking." I put on a shy smile. "She thought I was flirting with her fiancé."

"That would be Henry Lovechilde?"

I nodded.

He closed his notebook and turned off his recorder.

"You're close with Reynard Crisp, I believe."

My heart shifted slightly. "Um... yes."

"That's all. You're free to go. But if you're planning on travelling far, you must tell us."

"Am I a suspect?"

"Everyone from that party's a suspect, Miss..." He looked down at his notes again. "Lamb."

It ended there. The police didn't question me again, and I was relieved, despite still wondering why the detective had mentioned Reynard.

"Did you stick to the story?" Rey asked as he sat in my Notting Hill living room, which was in sad want of knickknacks, paintings, and all those personal touches that made a home warm and inviting.

I hadn't been sleeping well, so going shopping for home décor was the farthest thing from my mind. When I did manage to sleep, I saw Alice glaring at me, pointing into my face, screaming all kinds of gut-wrenching abuse.

"What did you do with her?" I'd lost count of how many times I'd asked. Each time, Rey sidestepped the question.

Alice's parents had contacted me multiple times after someone had told them I was the last to see her that night. I even had to ask the police to intervene, worried they'd continue to hassle me.

"Everyone thinks I had something to do with it." I walked the length of the room and looked out the windows onto a street busy with people who, going by their relaxed demeanor, weren't being haunted by a ghost.

"Stick to your story, Caroline. They have nothing on you."

"So, are you going to tell me? I'm losing my mind." In contrast to his nonchalance, I continued to pace about, wringing my hands.

He sipped the whisky I'd poured him and grimaced. "You really need to upgrade your liquor."

"Oh, for fuck's sake, Rey."

He went from blank to disdain in the blink of an eye. "Lower your voice."

I fell onto the couch and buried my face in my hands.

"Needless to say, I cleaned up your mess." He took another sip of liquor, lit a cigarette, and leaned back like a man without a worry in the world. "Now you owe me something."

I dropped my hands and locked eyes with him. "What do I owe you?"

"First, you marry Harry Lovechilde, and then we'll discuss it."

I pushed aside the deluge of questions surrounding my debt to him and asked, "How am I to do that? It's up to him, isn't it? And when I saw him that one time recently, he was shattered over Alice's mysterious disappearance."

Rey nodded, appearing lost in thought. "Hang out at his favorite bars and be there for him. Hold his hand. Seduce him."

"He may not even be into women in that way. After all, he hadn't consummated his relationship with Alice."

"I know he's a family man. He admitted that much to me one night. He needs an heir. That's how these dynasties work. They marry, have a family, and play on the side."

I pursed my lips. "Is anyone good in your world?"

He smirked. "Remove those rose-colored glasses, Carol."

I began to pace again, then turned to him. "So what if he doesn't want me?"

"He will. Most men want you. You're beautiful. Shapely in the way most men like their women." He paused. "You speak well and can hold your own in an intelligent conversation. Those are essential qualities for men like Harry. Old money affiliates with their own kind."

"But I'm not."

"As of now, you are, dear girl. Your upper-class parents died in a car accident, and a wealthy grandmother brought you up."

My eyebrows raised. "What if they ask about my parents' backgrounds? My grandmother?"

"I'm putting together a fetching narrative." A self-satisfied grin formed. "One that is foolproof and untraceable."

"You've got it all figured out." I shook my head. "Is Alice untraceable?"

He nodded. "Nothing to worry your pretty head over."

"And what if Harry refuses me?"

"He won't."

"How can you be so sure?"

"I've seen how he looks at you. Engage him in interesting conversation. He's not a fan of gossip."

"Mm... Nor am I," I murmured.

He smiled at my world-weary tone. "Dazzle him with your clever tongue and offer succor in his time of grieving. That's the best aphrodisiac."

I was only half listening by now, because all I could think of was Alice and how she'd vanished without a trace.

I'd killed her.

Accident though it was, I still killed her. Pure and simple.

And here was this man, who by the minute continued metamorphosing from an enigmatic, velvet-tongued titan into a cunning schemer who might have been the devil himself.

And I was about to sign on the dotted line to seal my deal with this devil. I had no other choice.

He rose. "Succor him."

My brow pinched. I'd been a mile away. "Suck him off?"

"Oh, Carol. Now you're showing your ignorance." His derisive chuckle made me want to throw something at this man I'd found myself chained to. "Give him support."

"I know what 'succor' means," I snapped. "I thought you said something else. That's all."

"Now you're being petulant." His patronizing glare faded. "I'm meeting Harry tomorrow to introduce him to a hedge fund manager. Why don't you come along?"

I walked him to the door. "Give me the details. I'll be there."

He leaned in and kissed my cheek. "You'll do well, Caroline." He lifted my chin. "You weren't responsible. She was attacking you. Remember?"

"Yes. But I don't know why we couldn't report it."

"Because you would not be standing here. And you'd soon find yourself locked up for manslaughter, at best. Murder, at worst."

A stuttered breath left my dry, bitter-tasting mouth. "Could they have saved her?" I'd already asked him that question. It stalked my sanity.

The slight shake of his head in response was all I needed this time, and that's when I finally shook off the dark cloud engulfing me.

I squared my shoulders and lifted my ribcage, hearing a slight crack in my spine after hunching for a fortnight. Reynard was right. It was just pure bad luck, and I had no other option but to move on.

"Then let's never speak of this again," I said. "Only... I can't control the police and their badgering."

"That will stop. They have nothing on you. It's circumstantial. That's never enough."

That day, as I watched Reynard walk away, I killed Carol Lamb forever.

From that moment on, I became Caroline, the society woman, who would be known for excelling at college, marrying well, and raising beautiful, intelligent children.

Chapter 7

Rey was right about one thing: Harry had eyes for me. He seemed to single me out whenever we ran into each other, which wasn't a coincidence, since I made sure I moved in his circles.

On those occasions, Harry would buy me drinks and confide in me. I became that sympathetic friend listening to a man who'd lost the love of his life. Or so he described Alice, making me feel both guilt ridden and a little jealous, though I had no right to the latter.

I'd grown seriously attached to Harry, who wasn't just handsome but warm and receptive. The more time we spent together, the more I wanted to be in his life.

Then, one night, around two months after that fateful party, he invited me back to Mayfair. In his jaw-dropping bedroom, which could have been an art gallery, we became more than just good friends.

Harry wasn't the god in bed that Gregory was. No one could compare to Gregory in that regard. But Harry still enjoyed my body, and I gave him everything.

By that, I mean everything. I distanced myself from Gregory, despite missing the excellent sex.

We often ran into each other at parties, and the temptation to allow him to lead me somewhere dark and private was so great, I had to muster the strength of Hercules not to surrender. One night, he even almost forced me, which was so hot that I took it out later on my new love. Only Harry lacked the sort of dark desires that I craved.

I begged my older former lover to leave me alone. He almost caused a scene at one of our many gatherings, and Rey had to step in. After having a word with Gregory, Rey reminded me not to sabotage my relationship with Harry and to keep the endgame in sight. Then I could allow myself all the pleasures I wanted.

By the end of that same year, I turned twenty-one. I also received a perfect score for an essay on the highly controversial rise to power of Elizabeth, daughter of Henry VIII and Anne Boleyn. Despite all opposing forces, Queen Elizabeth I became one of the most successful monarchs in the history of England.

I poured my heart and soul into that essay, because it highlighted that success and brilliance weren't always demonstrated by those brought up on love and good nurturing, but rather the opposite.

Perhaps there was a little of me in that story.

Whichever way, writing that essay fueled my ambition to become something more than just a woman who liked to move amongst powerful men.

Harry met me at our regular Oxford pub where most of the Balliol alumni hung out. He reached for me and kissed me on the lips, his eyes on mine, full of love, and my heart bloomed like a summer rose.

I loved Harry, not in that lustful, passionate way I experienced with Gregory, but deeply. Tenderly.

"A perfect score." He whistled, looking genuinely pleased for me. "I've never known anyone to be so devoted to their studies. You're an inspiration. Well done, Caroline."

I smiled, my soul singing. Having a close friend who genuinely believed in me made me want to shine for him.

"A G and T?" he asked.

I shook my head slowly.

His eyebrows rose in surprise.

"What, am I that much of a dipsomaniac?" I laughed.

"No. But I haven't known you to say no to the odd drink."

A smile grew on my face as I played with my long red fingernails. "I've got news."

He slanted his head, looking curious.

I took a breath. "I'm with child."

His eyes widened, and my heart raced in anticipation of how he might respond.

I'd only discovered a day earlier, after persistent nausea and a missed period led me to a doctor, who quickly informed me I was pregnant. It should have worried me, but it didn't. Even if Harry didn't wish to be involved, I would find a way this time.

"It's mine?" he asked.

I nodded. "I have only been with you."

He remained wide-eyed and seemingly lost for words.

"You don't have to do or say anything. But I am keeping the child."

As if lost in thought, he just kept staring at me. Then, after a long silence, he shook his head. "I would never walk away from you. Not in that condition, at least."

"Harry, I don't want you to feel obligated. I know you're young and still setting your future."

"I'm filthy rich, Caroline. If I wanted to, I could survive many life-times and bring up a large family while living in luxury. I'm not too young."

He smiled and my heart leapt for joy, sensing what would follow.

To quote Charlotte Bronte... "Reader, I married him!"

We waited until our child, Declan, was born, then we married at Merivale, Harry's family home, and now mine. Smitten with their first-ever grandchild, my new in-laws welcomed me into the family with open arms.

The moment I laid eyes on Merivale, I was enamored. Classic treasures mingled with modern pieces. Gilded frames hung on brightly colored walls, while fine collectibles wove a rich tapestry of opulence. At first, I didn't know where to look. The library, with its wall-to-wall dark-wood shelves filled with enough knowledge to empower all of society, became one of my favorite rooms.

The Lovechildes had called Merivale home for three hundred years, and their presence could be felt through the many family portraits. At night, their eyes seemed to follow me. But I was far from spooked. I relished that historical setting as someone who'd been starved of culture might a visit to the Tate.

During the wedding festivities, which lasted a whole weekend, Rey asked if we could take a walk around the sprawling grounds—a botanists' paradise where, by evening, an uplifting earthy fragrance acted like a happy pill.

Although I read something in his eyes, like a scheme brewing, I welcomed a break from the nosy guests. Lying about my past was exhausting, and the more champagne I drank, the more likely I was to stumble on some key detail. One could only keep up a façade for so long.

Apparently, it was customary at Merivale to celebrate for at least two days, sometimes even a week, for large events like weddings or birthdays. The former castle, refurbished in the 1800s with a blend of Gothic Revival and Italian style, effortlessly transformed into a luxury hotel. And the Lovechildes knew everyone worth knowing, it seemed.

Tiring as it was, having to keep up my pretense was a small trade-off for living this dream. Each day, my heart pumped with anticipation thanks to this Cinderella fantasy I'd fallen into.

I also loved being a mother. When I cradled Declan close, I sometimes felt a surge of love so tender and overwhelming that tears would sneak into my eyes. When no one was watching, of course. Raw emotion was a definite no-no for Caroline Lovechilde.

As the sun fell on Merivale that night, a fountain with a bronze statue of Mercury glistened in the golden light. Another beguiling favorite in that endless treasure trove of wonders.

Rey and I strolled to the hedged labyrinth.

"What a splendid sight." He paused and looked ahead, pointing at the silvery sea gleaming in the twilight.

"The view from upstairs is rather special," I said.

"You did it. I'm proud of you."

I paused. "You sound like my father."

"I am something like that, I think." His mouth twitched into his customary smirk. "I own you."

My brows collided. "That's a little stifling, wouldn't you say?"

"We have a deal. Don't we?" He tilted his head.

"Yes. But I'm not sure exactly what that deal entails."

He pointed to a green, rolling hill. "I want that land."

I almost laughed. "And how will I do that?"

"You'll find a way. I'm a patient man. I can wait. But one day, that land will be mine. That's the deal."

I was about to walk away when Rey grabbed my hand. "Remember, Caroline. I own you."

We locked eyes, then I left him behind as I went back to join the guests.

Yes, my star had risen. But that ascent came at a cost.

ONE MONTH INTO MY marriage, I cheated.

It wasn't something I was proud of, but I was helpless to do otherwise.

I was alone in London when someone patted my shoulder. I turned and there was Gregory, and my body, starved of passionate sex, did the deciding.

Without even uttering a word, I followed him. We jumped into his car, we drove somewhere quiet, and there, he fucked me raw in the backseat.

Harry was also having his time in London. I knew what it was about. He'd assured me he was being careful and wearing protection.

Harry knew I knew about his occasional dalliances. Earlier in our relationship, I confessed to being aware of his predilection for his own sex. "As long as you're clean about it, I don't mind," I'd said.

As it was, Harry and I hardly made love, but any time we did, I seemed to conceive. Gregory had had a vasectomy, so that allayed any possible confusion as our affair continued.

"I'm not leaving Harry," I told him one night while lying in a discreet London hotel bed.

"I can't wait another month like this past month."

"You're going to have to. I'm pregnant."

He shook his head. "I'll go crazy without you. I love you."

"Oh, Greg, it's lust. We're just a good fit."

"There's no denying that. But what about you? You're just as needy for this. For us."

I nodded. He was right. I had a big appetite when it came to sex.

In the end, it went badly between us.

Gregory arrived at Merivale, drunk and banging at the door, threatening to cause a scene if I didn't speak to him. By this stage, I'd had enough, and heavily pregnant, I sent him off. But it wasn't until my third child was born that our affair ended properly.

Five years later, I began a clandestine relationship with Will, Harry's hedge fund manager. Will, handsome and ten years younger, was at Merivale often, even while Harry was away in London. He was no Gregory, but he was good in bed and possessed the type of virility that could keep me happy for years.

I had it all... but for that ball and chain that was Reynard Crisp.

CHAPTER 8

PRESENT DAY
VOLUBLE AND ANIMATED AS EVER, the family spoke over each other as we gathered together in the sunroom—or the yellow room, as we liked to call it—overlooking the pool.

Declan and Theadora sat on the floral sofa I'd just had upholstered, holding hands like they'd only just met. Eight years into their marriage, they were still very much in love, it seemed.

I'd never held anyone's hand in public, only Cary's, but that was his doing. As a self-proclaimed romantic, he initiated all those delicate gestures.

Theadora had turned out to be a surprising creature. My resentment toward her had diluted over the years. She wasn't easy to dislike, given how she'd taken to her role as a Lovechilde as effortlessly as the graceful Princess Kate who, despite her lack of blue blood, had been a refreshing addition to the royal family.

Cary stood close. "It's noisy."

To me, it was more like music. I smiled at my healthy, energetic grandchildren.

Mirabel entered and twined her arms around Ethan, whose face lit up every time they were together. If I'd hated Theadora in the beginning, then the bohemian Mirabel had made me crash to an all-time low. I'd never been one for that earth-mother mentality. After all, modern science was there to be utilized. Botox, collagen fillers, high heels, and laser procedures were all invented for us to make the most of our assets, I'd always maintained.

"Joni Mitchell's as bubbly as ever," Cary whispered.

I chuckled. "And bright. Orange and green. Oh, spare me."

He laughed and squeezed my hand. We often joked about the dress sense of my daughters-in-laws: Theadora in her red, body-hugging choices and Mirabel with her boho hand-me-downs.

It didn't matter in the end, because they'd both delivered beautiful offspring.

"You've got the entire brood here today, I see," Cary said when Savanah arrived, her husband close behind. Carson pushed their double pram, wearing the cheery demeanor of a new father with sleep-deprived eyes to match.

"Ah... another pair to add to hoi polloi."

"They're hardly commoners." My brows gathered. "Did I just note a hint of cynicism?"

"I'm not a big fan of newborns. You know that." He kissed my cheek and then headed outside to the pool area where Julian tossed a ball to Bertie, my cherished corgi.

Cary remained a mystery in many ways, given my growing questions about his past. As someone who'd spent her life living a lie, I couldn't cast him away, however. That would never do. I was far too besotted. Nevertheless, curiosity had gotten the better of me because the longer we stayed together, the more I wanted to know about this man who'd stolen my heart.

I never thought I'd fall this hard. It wasn't just lust, either. He had me in the constant thrall of desire, but my feelings went much deeper. Indefinably so, for someone like me who'd never really known the meaning of passionate love. Suffice it to say, Cary was the only man I'd ever known who could set my pulse racing just from a sweet smile.

Savanah hugged me.

"How was Antibes?" I asked her.

"Wonderful. I think I might have had ten minutes' sleep."

I smiled. "For someone rest-deprived, you're blossoming."

"I'm so happy, Mummy." Her bliss acted as a contagion. I couldn't carry any dark thoughts with her and her beautiful pair of babies smiling back at me.

The day she delivered a boy and a girl into the world, no one was more surprised than me. After two heart-breaking miscarriages, Savanah had finally become the mother she'd dreamt of being. Dependable, strong, and loving, Carson proved the perfect partner, having brought my daughter back from the brink of self-destruction to her current state.

Manon came waddling in. For a small-framed woman, she was carrying a heavy load.

"Ah, there's Mannie. My god, she's about to pop any minute," Savanah said.

As we looked on, Drake followed her in.

"Mannie tells me that Drake's just scored a role in London as head of intel security for MI5."

"That's classified information, isn't it?" Cary asked, joining us and kissing Savanah on the cheek.

"Well, apparently not. I mean, he's not going around in a trench coat." She giggled.

Carson looked mystified. "Trench coat?"

My daughter laughed. "Not that kind of trench coat. You and your dirty mind."

He placed his arm around her and drew her close, kissing her hair.

Theadora tinkled her glass for our attention. "Cian's about to start."

"That's right," Cary said in his dry manner. "We're to be graced by a concert."

I couldn't tell if he was being sardonic or not. Whichever way, I loved him, and I loved music. Especially piano. That was one thing I got from my foster mother. As a keen player herself, she'd taught me scales and pop songs, which I swapped for classical music at high school.

We filed into the ballroom, where a brand-new Steinway sat proudly in the corner, shining in the afternoon light like a glossy black stallion.

My handsome grandson, Cian, now seven, took a seat and performed a song by Debussy, my favorite composer. My attention shifted from this angel on a stool lowered so his little feet could reach the pedals to out the window at the blue sky. Just as his little fingers ran up to the crescendo, birds soared past, and the synchronicity between creativity and nature made my soul sigh.

Even the babies remained quiet, which I found rather moving.

Meanwhile, wearing an unshifting smile, Ethan filmed his virtuosic son, whom I imagined, one day, on the world stage. The thought filled me with pride and joy.

Taking after her wild-spirited mother, Rosie, his younger sister, leaped and whirled about. One's heart would have had to be made of stone not to be entertained by my beautiful granddaughter's sylph-like movements.

"You've got your own little Isadora Duncan," Cary whispered.

Instead of embarrassment, I felt a warmth swelling in my chest. "I prefer my grandchildren bursting with creative expression rather than peering down at their phones."

"Give them time." Cary's half smile made me wince. He was right. Their pure little hearts wouldn't always remain that way. But I brushed that thought aside, despite my future mission to deter them from the dumbing-down influence of social media.

At least Cian and Julian attended the best school money could buy, as would all my grandchildren. It had been a bit of a battle with Theadora at first, who believed that a state-school education would keep her children real.

Finishing in a perfect flourish, Cian stood up, wearing a shy smile at our rapturous applause. He looked over at his mother and Theadora as they huddled around him to show their appreciation.

Ethan had tears in his eyes. Fatherhood had turned him into a sop, but I could no longer lambast him for choosing a hippie over someone of his own class, especially since my extremely talented grandson was the product of such a union.

That boy would do the Lovechilde name proud. Of that, I was certain.

The dream I once held for my offspring had now shifted to my grandchildren. Nothing would please me more than to see them genuflect before the King in receipt of a knight- or damehood.

As Rosie glided before us, I turned to Ethan. "I see her ballet classes are taking shape."

He smiled, every bit the proud father. Aged four, Rosie was a beauty with large green eyes and that shock of thick red hair. While Cian was a physical carbon copy of Ethan, Rosie was her mother.

"She's beautiful. They put on performances all the time. It's heart-melting."

I smiled at my now-sentimental son. Whatever happened to the playboy who favored sports cars and bimbos over books and cozy conversations?

Oh, we'd all changed. Even Declan, who once upon a time dreamed of being a fighter pilot. With much too many a sleepless night for me, he'd fulfilled that dream, but later he'd swapped a cockpit for a farm.

His organic farm and flourishing market for local crafts and all things organic had become so popular among locals and tourists that he'd just signed a contract for a worldwide franchise, delivering even more money into the Lovechilde coffers.

Janet arrived to announce that afternoon tea had been served, and we all made our way to the back area.

"That was fantastic," I said to Cian, giving him a kiss on the cheek. He looked up at me with those familiar, big dark eyes. He was the spitting image of Ethan, but that's where the comparison ended, because his quiet, respectful, and studious manner was a wonder to behold.

Rosie, his little sister, was quite the opposite as she hugged onto her father's leg. He lifted her and whizzed her around. In her flowing tulle dress, she reminded me of an Arthur Rackham fairy.

Julian, the athlete of the family, kicked a football around as his cute younger sister clutched her teddy bear and chased the ball.

As I watched them with great amusement, Janet came over to announce a visitor.

"It's Sunday. Send them away."

Her brow puckered. "It's Mr. Crisp."

I puffed out a sigh, and Cary, who missed little, gave me one of his sympathetic smiles.

"Okay, show him to the library," I said. "I'll be there in a moment."

I went over to Declan.

"Darling, can I have a word?"

He let go of his wife's waist, which he'd been clinging to all day, and followed me outside.

"What's up?"

I bit my lip. "I've got a problem."

CHAPTER 9

Cary

IF I WEREN'T SO drawn to Caroline Lovechilde, I wouldn't have stayed, given the restlessness that always prompted me to indulge my inner T. E. Lawrence and visit the Middle East. Source inspiration for that story that refused to write itself.

I hadn't planned for a life of domestic bliss centered around a cluster of newborns and noisy, albeit cute, kids. That was never on my to-do list. A vasectomy had seen to that.

So how did I get myself involved with a family of toddlers and adolescents? I preferred conversations that didn't involve talking ducks, teddy bears, and silly but amusing pranks.

The magnum opus I'd set myself the impossible task of creating sat dormant. Nothing but blank pages. Most days, I either read, drifted around that impossibly beautiful estate, or fucked Caroline's brains out.

The woman was insatiable. Despite having lost count of the liaisons I'd had over my forty-year sexual history, I'd met no one like her.

And she liked it rough too. That was a little strange, but also very arousing. I'd never been one to push a woman against a wall and fuck her hard from behind, but Caroline came like a rocket the harder I played. And so did I.

As her layers peeled away during our time together, I caught hints of a woman with a past she'd rather keep hidden, yet on occasions her mask would slip and I'd catch a real glimpse of her damaged self.

Sex, especially mind-blowing sex like the kind we shared, made us raw and thus exposed vulnerabilities. It certainly had for me, for I wasn't sure how long I could keep up this charade I'd been performing for over thirty years.

Some days, I really thought I was Carrington Lovelace. Other days, I'd regret that name. But then, how was I to know I'd fall madly in love with Caroline Lovechilde?

Love?

Was I really in love?

Despite being the most intense woman I'd ever known, Caroline brought a sense of wholeness into my life, as though she'd miraculously unlocked the best version of me. I could finally be the man I always thought I could be, given the right circumstances.

Not having to worry about money helped. But that wasn't the reason I was there.

She was my soulmate.

Some days, I wanted to tell her.

Tell her everything.

But how could I?

Caroline was a snob. I should have loathed that about her, but she redeemed herself often enough. I'd seen that substantial check she'd tried to hide, made out to a women's shelter.

Her blemishes, despite being cringeworthy at times—like her bigotry toward the common classes and adulation for the royal family—only added to her charm. Like that potentially ruinous streak on a work of art that surprises by turning the painting into something unique and priceless.

Beautiful, intolerant, erotic, intimidatingly bright, and flawed was how I would have described her. And the longer I remained by her side, the deeper I fell.

Then I slipped up.

We'd been enjoying the sunshine when she mentioned something about the hallways of Oxford, and I forgot my lines. You see, I'd never even stepped onto the grounds of that celebrated college, let alone studied there as I'd told her.

Caroline, who rarely missed a thing, had creased her brow slightly and continued to read her magazine.

Like my name, I regretted that narrative too. Nothing but shabby research, enough to make a seasoned writer hang their head in shame.

Then Caroline spoke, bringing me back to the present. "I hope this isn't too rambunctious for you."

I smiled. "The piano recital was worth it. You've got a prodigy in the making with Cian."

She gave me a dismissive smile like one might at an exaggeration. Despite her many foibles, hubris wasn't one of them.

"So what did Reynard want, if you don't mind me asking?"

We were still rather formal with each other on occasions, especially around matters relating to Reynard Crisp.

Her lips formed a tight line. She would not let me in. Again.

I held nothing but contempt for that loathsome creature whom I sensed had something over her—the details of which she refused to share.

Yes, there were plenty of hidden skeletons in Caroline's cupboard.

I couldn't talk, however, because when it came to skeletons, mine rattled around too. I just hoped they'd remain hidden, only the closer we became, the more that secret little closet of mine slowly creaked open.

"Was he here about the police investigation regarding that woman's remains?" I asked.

I was scant on details, but from what I'd gathered, the remains belonged to a girl who'd disappeared after a party at her deceased husband's London home.

"Yes."

I held her hand. "You know you can talk to me, don't you?"

Her eyes held mine for one of those prolonged, enigmatic gazes.

"London. Tomorrow. Same place?" I asked, knowing that something salacious might lift her spirits.

"Yes." Her face brightened a little.

She rose and went to Declan. Caroline only ever shared her problems with her eldest son, whose attitude toward me was a little strained, to put it mildly. He had good cause to be suspicious.

After a brief comment to her son, Caroline turned back to me and crooked her finger.

I forgot what I was thinking and lifted myself off the couch to follow her out of that crowded family room, ogling her curvy ass.

Wild horses couldn't drag me away from her, especially when her inner vixen made a show.

Chapter 10

Caroline

"You're now a great-grandmother, it would seem." Savanah sat on the sofa in my office-come-library with her newborn, Lilly, suckling her nipple.

"That makes me sound old."

"You just started young, Mummy."

I thought about myself as that confused seventeen-year-old giving birth to Bethany, who, despite everything, had delivered unto me a bright and increasingly indispensable granddaughter. Manon, with her take-no-nonsense approach, was more like me than any of my children, especially since she'd shed that mean-streets upbringing. Not only did we share the same features, but Manon possessed an eye for detail and was driven to become something more than just a wife and a mother.

Manon was now running Merivale almost single-handedly and doing a fine job at it. Something I discovered upon my return from Como. I'd only meant for my holiday with Cary to be one week, but I'd fallen in love, not just with the man that little more, but also with his delightful villa. The honey-bricked house, despite having only three bedrooms and two bathrooms, sat right on that enchanting lake.

I hadn't wanted to leave. A first for me. I'd always been so attached to Merivale. Even my trips abroad or to London made me homesick. Como, however, was entirely different. Waking up in Cary's arms to sunshine, warmth, and delicious Italian cuisine was like a dream come true.

"Are Manon and Drake to marry?" I asked.

Savanah nodded. "Mannie mentioned she would wait until her body had returned to shape for the photos."

"And the child?"

"A girl. Evangeline."

"Lovely name." I meditated on that for a moment. "Evangeline Winter."

"Manon's thinking of Lovechilde-Winter. She wants our name in there somehow."

I nodded slowly. "That means Bethany will come swinging by, I suppose."

"Yes, big sis will use the birth of her grandchild as good reason to pounce upon us." Savanah rolled her eyes. "She's got herself involved with a rock star."

My recently injected brow struggled to frown. "Really?"

"Carson's agency did the security for the band, and there was Bethany, hanging around in the green room. The rock star's twenty-five, I'm told."

"Are they successful?"

"Very. They're called Wild Side. I uploaded their latest song, and it's catchy. Even Carson likes it, which is saying something, given his living-in-the-sixties tastes." She chuckled. "The concert was a sell-out. So he's obviously rich."

Bethany with a rock star? That took me aback, given her history with older men. "But she's nearly forty."

"She's had a lot of work done, Mummy. She looks like Kim Kardashian without the big bum."

Having had work to firm up my sagging breasts plus a chin tuck, I wasn't about to criticize my first-born for warding off the ravages of gravity.

I nodded pensively. "If it keeps her out of trouble, all the better."

Savanah smiled. "Never a dull moment with Beth."

Drake knocked at the entrance.

"Come in," I said.

Savanah placed her beautiful, drowsy baby into the bassinet and got up to hug him. "Congrats."

"I've just come from the hospital." He smiled brightly.

Drake had kept his mathematical abilities hidden from us in the beginning. Not that I held that against him. I viewed vanity as an ugly human trait. It did, however, come as a complete shock when he announced he'd not only gotten a college degree but had also become an expert in cyber security.

At twenty-five, that was some achievement. I had to ask him how he managed that, and he sheepishly owned up to hacking computers during his misspent youth.

Now very much a changed person, he was the right choice for my granddaughter. He would always stand by Manon. Of that, I was more than certain. And strong, dependable individuals were what our family needed to remain a tight, successful, and powerful unit.

"Evie is beautiful." Drake looked like he might cry.

"Oh, you've shortened her name already?" I preferred the name Evangeline.

He shrugged. "She looks like an Evie to me. Big girl."

"What was her weight?"

"Close to nine pounds." He glowed, a proud father.

"Well, congrats again." Savanah kissed him on the cheek and then turned to me. "I best mosey off. Ta-ta."

I waited until Savanah and the baby were gone before speaking. "Thanks for coming here at such a time. And from London."

"That's okay." He smiled faintly.

"I know what I'm about to ask will involve some risk."

He stared at me without blinking.

"Basically," I continued, "I need a file from Scotland Yard. Can you get in there?"

"That's big." He exhaled. "I mean, I have access, but it's a punishable crime."

I nodded pensively. My regrettable past was about to put my family at risk.

Can I do this?

I have to. What else have I?

He scratched his neck. "Let me see what I can do."

"If it's too risky, then abort." I passed him a sheet. "There are the details. Please destroy them once you've committed the name and date to memory."

He stared down at the handwritten note I'd given him with Alice Ponting's name and the year she went missing.

"I need a forensic report," I said.

"Um... I might have a better idea. A safer one. I have this friend..." He paused and thought for a moment. "It might work better if I try this outside of the agency." He returned a restrained smile. "I love my job."

"That's understandable." I tapped a gold fountain pen on the leather-topped desk.

"This friend is better than me with getting into systems."

I nodded. "Tell him to name his price."

"That might do it. Billy's saving on a deposit for an apartment."

That name rang a bell. "Oh, is that the red-headed boy from Reboot?"

He nodded slowly.

"Then, for the right information, I'm happy to pay for that apartment." Given that unfortunate incident when I accused Billy of stealing a ruby necklace, I felt I owed him that, at least.

Drake's eyebrows arched. "You might be looking at four hundred thousand pounds or so, Mrs. Lovechilde."

"Caroline." I stood and smoothed down my skirt. "Let me know if he's amenable to the task."

He nodded. "I'm seeing him tonight in London for a drink. I'll speak to him and will let you know."

Off he went, and in came Cary, the love of my life and the reason for my recent bout of insomnia, which had nothing to do with our very active sex life.

"I thought I'd take Bertie for a walk up to the cliffs. Interested?" He wore that sexy smile that made it impossible to deny the man anything.

"I'd like that. Just give me a moment to change into sensible shoes."

"Of course." He strolled over to the library and selected a book, almost without looking, as though he'd memorized the vast collection of titles housed in those floor-to-ceiling shelves.

Wearing fitted cream slacks and a green polo that hugged shoulders taut and strong from a lifetime of swimming, he epitomized the kind of masculinity that drove all women, even those half his age, crazy with desire. I was no exception.

Having returned to the library, I lingered in the doorway, absorbing his beauty. I wondered about him. There were too many inconsistencies in his backstory that I could no longer ignore.

But if I poked around in Cary's past, what would I find?

The thought of not being with him terrified me. I was so in love with him that I'd started to sympathize with women who fell in love with dark characters.

I could never suspect Cary of evil, however. Surely not. Or was I so dazzled by his masculine charms that I'd been blinded?

The book he held had him engrossed. Now, that sent a sizzle of heat through me. A man with a book, looking totally lost to the world.

Knowing what lay beneath those fitted slacks helped.

The man was a stallion.

My stallion.

He must have sensed me staring, for he looked up just before Bertie scampered into the room and jumped all over Cary, licking his hand. I loved my dog, but hated his slobbering tongue on me. The clever dog had learned this well enough and now chose Cary to pounce all over instead.

Once we were on the grounds, I looked above at drifting variegated gray clouds swallowed by fast-moving black ones. "Rain?"

He nodded. "We'll make it a quick walk."

I paused and turned to face him with a smile. "I could have a better idea."

He pushed his body against mine and kissed my neck. "You're a minx. A very sexy one."

I laughed as I pulled back from his arms.

A quizzing frown grew on his perfectly proportioned forehead. "Why the dark side of town?"

Jarring as that sudden change of subject was, I chose silence.

CHAPTER 11

Cary

CAROLINE GESTURED FOR US to continue the ascent to that breathtaking view I'd grown so attached to that I'd stopped missing Como. Standing on the edge of the cliff, overlooking a restless, cruel sea, pumped inspiration through my veins.

"Why that East London hotel?" I asked.

"We all have our little peccadilloes." She kept looking ahead.

My lips tasted of salt, and spray dampened my face as the sea thrashed against the cliff face.

"So being forced is a fantasy?" I persisted.

"You seem to enjoy our little game."

I couldn't deny that, despite feeling a little disturbed by it. "This is the first time I've been asked to play rough."

With the wind in her hair and those almost-black eyes, this woman had me. All of me.

But engaged to be married?

How could I have allowed myself to be talked into that?

At least Caroline wasn't pushy. The fact she hadn't asked to set a date was rather surprising. I wasn't about to point that out.

"Are threesomes your thing?" I had to ask.

"No. I'm too possessive for that." She returned her gaze to the roaring ocean.

I took her by the waist and swung her into my arms, taking to her soft, full lips like a man stealing a kiss from an out-of-reach woman he'd been craving for a long time. "Let's go back."

"Mm... You seem a little hungry." She gazed into my eyes and smiled.

"I'm always that around you. Even the other night, despite being confronted." We began to move off, but I paused. "Will you ever tell me why?"

"Oh, Cary, please allow me some secrets."

A silent sigh, more resignation than frustration, exited my mouth. I couldn't deny her that, given my own history.

THE FOLLOWING DAY, I was in London doing some shopping—an activity that had become a habit since Caroline, while kissing me passionately one night, slipped a credit card into my hand.

As that card sat on my palm, I looked down at it, rather speechless, for I knew what it meant: I was about to become a kept man.

"Caroline, I'm not here because of your money."

At first, maybe. But that had quickly faded once my feelings for this beautiful, complicated woman deepened.

By that stage, she knew me well, because she unzipped her dress and stepped out of it, standing before me in a silk slip with her full breasts spilling out. I became tongue-tied as blood rushed from my brain, and all I could do was take her and her money.

It didn't take long before I got into the habit of visiting my favorite antiquarian bookshop or the charming Italian tailor close by who understood my body like a fine sculptor might.

Clutching a first edition of Brave New World, I hailed a taxi and tucked the book away in my leather satchel.

Ten minutes later, we arrived at my destination: the seedy part of town.

The driver gave me an odd look. In my bespoke sports jacket and expensive leather shoes, I probably looked out of place.

"Is this right, mate?" he asked. "It's a little dangerous around here."

I gave him a fifty. "Keep the change."

He soon dropped the paternal role, his face lighting up. I'd made it my mission to support the underpaid, because I hadn't forgotten from where I came.

Tramping along the uneven, shadowy cobbled lane was like time-traveling. It had probably been a haunt of Conan Doyle and Jack the Ripper. Not much had changed in its long history, for, hidden in dark corners, pimps and dealers rubbed their hands in the cold.

I entered a dim, musty pub I imagined had seen its share of humanity in all shades of darkness. And as I stood at the bar to order, I read a stained placard boasting that Dickens had drunk there, which somewhat sweetened my visit. If this hovel was good enough for the celebrated writer, then it was fine for me. Before I met Caroline and her exclusive clubs with their astounding mosaics and frescoed ceilings, I was more at home in a pub that served society's fallen rather than the bleached elite.

After I ordered a pint, a blonde wearing dark glasses and a leopard-skin coat sat on a stool next to me and ordered a gin.

I nodded a greeting.

Her red-painted lips curled slightly in return.

"Quiet night?" I asked.

"For you or me?"

"I'm just here for a drink and the atmosphere." I looked around. The place was dotted with lonely, wordless souls. Even the music had a warped sense of not belonging, like it had been turned on in the fifties and left to run.

She clicked her fingers for another hit of gin, and after she downed her shot in one gulp, she gestured for me to follow. As we walked along that grim setting, streetwalkers of all shapes, sizes, and genders stepped out of the shadows.

The night had just arrived, and cars crawled along as nocturnal creatures put on their show.

We arrived at a crumbling hotel that probably had enough DNA spread around to keep several forensic teams busy. While the façade of the establishment might have made developers salivate over the prospect of repurposed apartments, the interior bore the sad neglect of a cheap eighties' makeover.

I followed the woman down the hallway, and despite the elevator, she walked up the stairs. Her heels echoed loudly on the floorboards as we arrived on the second floor.

She opened a door, and we entered a room that smelt of decay and perfume.

"So, this is your place?" I asked.

"Sometimes." A neon light from across the road flashed in the room, making it easy to navigate.

I went to turn on the lamp when she stopped me. "Oh?" I asked. "We're to be in the dark?"

"There's enough light."

She took off her dark glasses, but I still couldn't really see her eyes.

I went to remove her jacket when she slapped my hand.

"Don't," she snapped.

"Um... I thought you invited me here to fuck."

"I might have just wanted the company." She picked up a bottle of gin.

"At least take off the coat. Let me look at you."

"I'm not sure if you're my type," she said in a thick cockney accent.

The pulsating red-and-yellow neon sign from outside tinged her face with a warm red glow before the hardness of yellow showered her heavily made-up face.

She didn't move as my lips connected to the nape of her neck, the taste of perfume bouncing off my tongue.

I removed her jacket, and it fell to the ground. She was dressed in a tight mini and a low-cut, fitted blouse, and as I went to fondle her breasts, she slapped me.

"Don't touch."

I nearly laughed but kept my cool.

In response, I ran my hands up her legs and groped her ass instead. She had my type of curves. Enough flesh to rub against. I wasn't a fan of skinny women. The gym had reshaped their figures. I preferred soft, full curves, and this woman had plenty.

I wanted to be inside her, to ride her hard.

I ran my finger over the crotch of her panties and discovered it soaking wet. She had the same idea, it appeared.

Or so I thought. Turning to face me, she pushed me away. "No."

"You're making me fucking hot for you."

She shrugged. "That's your problem."

"That's not what I'm feeling." I touched her lace panties again.

"How do you know you're my first?" She smirked.

I removed some crumpled notes from my pocket and tossed them on the table. "Then just let me rub against those big tits."

Her head tilted, and the flashing light on her face showed me a woman riddled with contradiction.

"You want this." I pushed her against the wall and kissed her roughly. Her wide mouth allowed my tongue in before she pushed me away.

Getting these little tastes proved a torturous form of foreplay, but it was thrilling, especially after copping a feel of her drenched panties.

"Who else have you fucked tonight?" I asked, rubbing my body against hers.

"None of your fucking business." She shrugged out of my hold.

"Then why are you here?"

"Make up your own story."

I threw down more crumpled notes.

Wiggling her fingers, she gestured for more.

Hankering to see her naked all over, I gave her everything I had.

She popped the notes in her handbag. "Why aren't you in the suburbs fucking your wife?"

"I don't live in the suburbs. And I don't have a wife."

A lie. But this was a game. I was no longer a man trying to rewrite his life, but someone anonymous.

"I don't even know your name."

"What name would you like?" She wore a provocative grin that only added to her carnal appeal. She dripped with sex. Smelled of it. And I needed a taste.

"Druscilla."

She laughed. Although it was more of a dark chuckle, this was the closest to lightness she'd gotten. "It's ugly."

"What about Suadela?"

"Complicated."

"Like you," I said. "She's a mythological Roman seductress." I took her hand and drew her close. "Enough talk." I tugged her skirt until it ended up at her feet.

As her heavily kohled eyes held mine, she allowed me to remove her top. Her large, naked breasts tumbled out, and my pants tightened.

I bit at her nipples gently and teased them. Clutching her ass, I knelt so that her pussy touched my mouth. She tried to pull away, but this time, I held tight and ravaged her.

Her musky, dark scent did things to me that sent an aching need down to my cock. I needed to feel all of her.

Her angst. Her mystery. Her hunger.

Her convulsing body soon unleashed an addictive flavor all over my tongue. She leaned against me, and I felt her racing heart beat against my body, then she removed herself from my hold and stood before the window, gloriously naked for all to see.

This was her thing, I sensed. For me, voyeurism only added to this erotic adventure.

I removed my trousers and lowered my briefs, my penis throbbing with anticipation as bodily lubrication dripped from the head. I rubbed my cock against her warm ass while running my hands over her tits. She softened slightly, her breath stuttering as I fingered her.

Her wet, warm pussy felt ready and willing, and her head fell back. But then her body went rigid, and she pushed me away.

"What's the problem?"

Her eyes were on my dick as I held it in readiness, teasing me as she ran her tongue over her lips. Then she poured herself a drink before returning her attention to my hard dick.

This was a game.

Her game. Not mine anymore.

I walked over to this woman of little words and put her glass down. Then I grabbed her roughly.

And she finally smiled.

Yes. I knew what she wanted.

It wasn't my thing. I was a pacifist. Hated anything vaguely violent, especially around women, but she made me crazy for her.

I pushed her against the wall by the window so anyone from the street could see us. Although she struggled, I held her there with her arms up high against the window.

She poked her ass back and pushed it against my cock as a reminder this was all just playacting, because she wanted it too.

I pushed my knee between her thighs to spread her out and leaned in close. "You like this, don't you?"

She whimpered. The first sign of surrender.

I entered her in one sharp thrust. The friction and tension acted like a tight piece of elastic around my dick. I slid into her, going deep, and she moaned as she took all eight inches of my thickened cock.

Her moans intensified as I pumped into her. Euphoria threatened to burst one of my veins with each thrust.

I built and built with her against the window, writhing and moaning. Whether she was in pain or pleasure, I could never tell.

Under the spell of deep, dangerous pleasure, together we danced in time with each other. The fit perfect. Her breathing heavy, like mine.

As she cried out, her muscles spasmed.

"Yes," I gasped. "Come all over my cock." I kept pounding until I orgasmed like thunder, an endless stream, as I grunted. Our bodies stuck together.

A cocktail of tension and want swam inside her.

I released her arms, and she nearly sank to the floor. Then she turned and slapped me.

"You didn't like that?" I wasn't sure whether to be alarmed or amused. More the latter because I couldn't help but laugh.

"What do you think?" Her lips curled ever-so-slightly. And on that enigmatic note, she picked up her clothes and headed to the bathroom.

CHAPTER 12

Caroline

"SHE'S BEAUTIFUL," I SAID, rocking Manon's newborn in my arms. My many grandchildren had brought joy into my world.

I touched Evangeline's little nose and breathed her in like I would a rose.

Manon took her daughter from my arms so she could feed her. It was a lovely, warm, sunny morning, and the women of our family joined me, sitting outside by the pool, where Julian swam with vigorous strokes.

"At this stage, he'll become an Olympic swimmer," Savanah said with a chuckle.

"He's even asking Declan if he can go to London for the under-thirteen trials." For some reason, Theadora looked at me. "He's still too young. Don't you think?"

I took a moment to respond. "I'm not sure. Maybe Cary's the best person to ask, since he's the swimmer amongst us."

"I will." She turned to Manon, who was breastfeeding. "So, when's the wedding?"

Manon wiped her daughter's mouth and placed her back in her basket. "We haven't really set a date."

"You will marry, won't you?" I asked.

"I think so."

Savanah studied her niece. "Is there doubt?"

"Oh god, no. We're in love."

I smiled at my granddaughter. Her infectious optimism always buoyed me, which was what I needed right then. Although I, too, was so madly in love that I was no longer certain about anything.

Declan arrived along with Charlotte, who was charming in her pink tutu. He kissed Theadora, who looked adoringly at their little girl before giving her a hug.

"You've just come from ballet classes?" I asked.

"She shone." Declan smiled with pride. "I even watched the last dance." He directed a loving glance at his daughter, who was the spitting image of Theadora. "A natural. Takes after her mother."

"Oh, I don't know, Dec, you're a pretty good dancer," Savanah said.

He chuckled. "Now you're just being nice."

"How did the negotiations go with the franchise?" I asked.

Declan was about to respond when Ethan came bouncing in, carrying a box of fairy cakes dressed with pink icing.

"This calls for tea," I said.

Janet, who was within earshot in the common room, filling vases with fresh flowers, looked over at me and nodded. "I'll have Tracy arrange that now."

After the tea was served and the children, having had their hit of sugar, ran around with abandon and chased the dogs, I returned my attention to Declan.

A question about his recent windfall was about to leave my lips when Cary arrived, looking ruggedly handsome after his walk. With his wind-tousled peppery hair and flushed handsome face, he made my knees weak. Even after a year together, I still swooned.

Would I ever stop lusting after him? It was like I'd turned into a teenager. However, unanswered questions about his life bothered me. Something I was keeping to myself.

Ethan turned to Declan. "You signed the contract yesterday, I believe."

Declan rubbed his neck and looked at Theadora before answering. "Yep. Sure did."

"A cool two billion pounds." Ethan whistled. "Who would have thought?"

Declan nodded reflectively. "It has come as a surprise."

"They're to run the exact farming model and crafty, organic markets in Provence and other tourist hotspots in France, Switzerland, and Germany, to start with," Theadora said, wearing the proud smile of a wife whose husband was about to conquer the world.

While we processed that rather astounding outcome to a project I'd once deemed frivolous and a waste of my son's resources, nine-year-old Julian returned and jumped into the pool to show his father and Cary his progress.

"Time me," Julian said to Cary, who'd become the boy's swimming coach.

Cary pulled out his phone and signaled for Julian to start.

When Julian finished his four laps, he pushed himself up on the ledge of the pool. His blue eyes, just like his father's and my late husband's, brimmed with expectation as he looked up at Cary.

"That's a record," Cary declared with enthusiasm, as though he'd broken it himself. "Thirty seconds. That's a ten-second improvement."

Julian rubbed his hair with a towel and grabbed a fairy cake, wearing a wide, satisfied smile.

Cary patted his shoulder. "At this rate, you could enter the under-thirteen nationals."

Julian looked keenly at his father and mother, blatantly seeking their permission.

Declan shrugged. "Sure, why not?"

Theadora didn't look so pleased.

"You're not so happy about that?" I had to ask.

Declan placed his arm around his wife. "She wants all our children to pursue the arts."

Cary nodded but said, "You can't force creativity. You're either born with it or not. Sport still thrills and entertains."

"But it's a momentary thing," Theadora argued.

"It's temporal like dance, I suppose," Cary admitted. "But without desire as the major driver, art cannot be."

He looked at me for some reason, which made me wonder if he meant something else.

Julian stared up at him wide-eyed, hanging off his instructor's words as though it meant everything to have Cary's support.

"Wise words," Declan said, kissing Theadora yet again. I'd lost count. Their public display of affection, as with Ethan and Mirabel's amorous exchanges, was something quite out of the ordinary to my mind.

While my inner cynic, somewhat tempered by age, might have once baulked at such sugary exchanges, I found solace in knowing that they were all in love and thriving.

The grandchildren, much to my delight, had also taken to Cary, despite him being a little awkward around them at first. He'd even read them books by C. S. Lewis and Enid Blyton in the library. With that deep, sonorous voice, he always engrossed them and me, too, since I'd missed out on those timeless stories growing up.

Carson arrived and hugged Savanah then went to the twins. He lifted them both from their cribs and cradled them lovingly in his muscular arms.

They'd chosen to remain at Merivale, which heartened me. The estate was large enough to house everyone while still maintaining a level of privacy. That was the beauty of double-brick walls.

I would have loved Declan and Ethan there, too, but they seemed happy living in their cottages, as I often referred to their homes, despite their protests to the contrary. But then, every dwelling looked small compared to the majesty of Merivale.

Despite Carson's burgeoning security agency often taking him to London, Savanah insisted they live at Merivale. Manon also wanted to stay on. I sensed Drake was still a little hesitant, but Manon held her ground. Merivale had her heart, and she vowed to stay until her last breath.

I turned to Declan. "Can we talk somewhere?"

He gave me one of those What is it now? looks. We'd had a lot to deal with over the past few years, so I couldn't blame that cautious response.

I went over to Cary and whispered, "Half an hour?"

He almost winked at me, which made me recoil and smile at the same time.

Declan stepped into the library.

"Close the door," I instructed.

"You've had it fixed." He shut the door. "At last."

I nodded, exhaling.

"So, what's up?" he asked.

"I think I owe you an apology."

"Oh?"

"Well, I wasn't exactly supportive of the organic farm."

"That's okay, Mum. As a father now myself, I get that concept of familial expectations. And you had yours. Anyway, we've all found our calling, it would seem." He held my gaze for a moment. "You seem happy with Cary. We've noticed a change in you."

"As you once said, love changes us."

Declan nodded. "So, when's the wedding?"

"Not sure. Cary keeps sidestepping it." I gave him a weak smile. "Not that I'm hounding him."

"But he's devoted to you." He frowned. "And we all like him."

"That's encouraging, I suppose." I sighed. "You'd think he'd want to become a part of all this. Make it official."

"What about a prenup? He is living here."

I crossed my hands and shook my head. His look of surprise acted as a reminder that I'd taken my eyes off the road.

"The solicitor wants me to," I said.

"Speaking of lawyers, tell me about the police investigation."

The chill in the air from talk of vague marriage plans turned icy.

I took a deep breath. "There's not much to tell. I've given them everything I know."

"Clearly that detective had something to do with it. The cigar stub found at the burial site proved that. And what of Crisp?"

"He's distanced himself from us, darling." At the mention of my nemesis, a cold streak down my spine made me shift in my seat. I expected Reynard to burst into my life at any moment and make demands.

"Can't say I'm unhappy about that."

"At least Elysium is welcoming a better class of guest since Rey's Russian cohort stopped arriving," I said.

"I've heard Manon and Savanah have taken over the running."

I nodded. "Manon is proving to be a powerhouse."

"She not only looks like you—she takes after you."

I studied him before responding. "She's evolving." Fiddling with my pen, I searched for the right words. "I called you here to discuss a delicate matter that must remain between us."

I wasn't about to fill in the blanks and point out Theadora's unfortunate penchant for gossip.

Reading me well, Declan wore a rueful smile. "My wife can keep some secrets. She's just not an expert like you."

Touché.

I knitted my fingers. "It's about Cary."

His eyebrows drew in slightly.

"I believe you and your brother had him checked out once. Yes?"

He rubbed his neck. "Well, yes. After we spotted him in the car with that woman."

"Lilly, his late wife."

"Right. Yes." He took a breath. "We didn't dig that deep. As I recall, his background wasn't easy to trace. I think we got a little distracted and left it."

"Left what?" I pressed.

"No one had heard of him at Eton. That's as far as we got." His brow creased. "Why?"

"He slipped up over Oxford."

"Well, it might not be much. He seems like a good person. Julian loves him."

I smiled. "It's nice to hear you say that. I think it would mean a lot to Cary to know that."

"We've all been very welcoming. He can't be that insecure, surely."

I nodded slowly and breathed out the tension in my chest.

Shifting away from the subject of Cary, I added, "I'm proud of you." I chose my words carefully. "I wasn't exactly welcoming of Theadora all those years ago, but she's become an excellent asset to the family."

He rose. "You make her sound like a commodity."

"Yes. You're right. Apologies." I smiled. "She has a regal bearing. Fits in well with our lot."

His frown faded. "I'll take that as a compliment." As he stood at the door, I could see in him that young boy who always won at cricket and made his father proud. "Maybe you should say that to her sometime."

"I think she understands it by now. We share in our passion for classical music."

"There's also Mirabel. She's rather frightened of you." He chuckled.

"Really? I am doing my best. You know me—I'm used to our lot."

"That's the point, Mother. She is our lot."

I nodded. He was right. I needed to smile more at my daughter-in-law, despite my profound dislike of sandalwood.

After Declan left, I walked to the window. The ocean lay still, a glittering mirror of the sky. Unsettled thoughts drifted away as I thought of Cary waiting upstairs, and after undoing a couple of buttons on my shirt, I went to join him.

CHAPTER 13

Cary

"I'M SORRY. YOUR CREDIT card has been declined," the shop assistant said.

Feeling like a first-class idiot, I peered down at the first edition of Sons and Lovers. "Oh, my apologies," I said, before leaving the antiquarian bookshop with a head full of questions.

On my phone, I scrolled to my banking app, where I discovered my credit card had reached its limit.

I could only shake my head in disbelief. I'd spent fifty thousand pounds in a month. On what, exactly?

I was hopeless with money, and that book that I'd been writing for thirty years remained a work in progress. It was getting rather embarrassing at those social events Caroline loved to either host or frequent. Being asked how my historical novel on Charles II was coming along was like being asked why my first marriage didn't work out. Maybe not as personal as why I escaped Elise, but equally as unsettling.

I couldn't keep coming up with the sad excuse of writer's block or blame Merivale's library and its treasure trove of distractions. An original edition offered more allure, it seemed. Even the charming sixties typewriter Caroline had gifted to me failed to rouse my drive.

I called the solicitor involved in the sale of the Como villa. I couldn't keep asking Caroline for money.

"I've got good news and bad," he said in his heavy Italian accent.

"Give me the bad first." I leaned against the black walled façade of the bookstore.

"The property has many caveats."

"There are debts to cover?"

"Yes. The debts are substantial, signore."

"Right. So, how much are we talking here?"

I could have done this on my last visit to Como, but with Caroline there, the only thing on my mind was sex, food, and her.

Also, money, like my past, wasn't a subject I liked to discuss.

"After everything is settled, and with the generous offer being made, you're looking at ten thousand euros."

My heart sank. "Oh, I see." I'd been expecting at least half a million. I knew Lilly had some debts, but she hadn't exactly involved me in that side of her life.

"I will inform you once the settlement is complete. I will deposit the money into the Markus Reiner account I have here, yes?"

"Yep. That's the one."

I ended the call.

Why hadn't I set up another account?

I jumped in my car and headed for Whitechapel.

Caroline would lift my credit limit at the blink of an eye, but that didn't sit well with me.

I loved her more than I could have imagined, which was a surprising outcome. In my history with women, it was always about sex, and, yes, I admit, the wealthier the better.

After Elise and her charming-free-spirit act swept me off my very immature feet, I'd lived a life of indigence, subsisting on crumbs, and I also had to contend with her extreme, at times violent, moods.

I'd run away and constructed this new version of myself—determined to avoid those waifs who needed saving. Soon, however, it became me who needed saving.

I was about to drive off when a call came from the woman who still made my heart skip a beat. "Caroline."

"Change of plans. Can we meet at Mayfair? I'm there now."

"I'm just on Oxford Street, leaving now. Is there anything I can get you?"

"No."

The phone went cold, much like her tone. My spine stiffened, and I sucked back a breath.

Thirty minutes later, after being caught up in a traffic jam that would have had a Buddhist monk shouting obscenities, I arrived at her charming, palatial Mayfair home, which boasted a splendid view of Grosvenor Square.

A new face opened the door.

"Hello, I'm Cary, here to see Caroline."

"Yes, sir, she's expecting you."

I passed through the door and, upon entering the salon, found her on the phone.

"Okay. If you must," she said and closed the phone, looking rather dour.

I kissed her on the lips, but that subtle curve to her mouth did little to warm the atmosphere.

She looked up at the new butler. "That will be all, Vance."

"He's new." I sank into an armchair.

"Yes." She remained remote, and I sensed something about to come crashing down.

"Is there something wrong?"

As she gazed at me, the doorbell sounded, and from a distance, I heard a male voice.

Vance arrived to announce the visitor, Reynard Crisp, following him to the door.

Caroline gestured for Crisp to enter.

The tall, haughty man regarded me with a curt nod. We shared a mutual dislike that neither of us tried to hide.

That man spelled trouble, and despite my occasional question regarding their odd pairing, I remained none the wiser. Like Caroline's erotic games, her relationship with that creep resided in the "don't ask" portion of her life.

I rose. "I might just go for a walk, then."

Caroline gave me one of her enigmatic, forced smiles that could either be construed as an apology or something else. The longer I knew her, the more mysterious she became.

However, mystery was proving to be an aphrodisiac, I was discovering, because I wanted her more than ever.

CHAPTER 14

Caroline

REYNARD WATCHED CARY SAUNTER off, wearing one of his sanctimonious smirks. He waited until the door closed before speaking. "He's still around, I see."

"We're engaged."

"I know that. I was at that party." His eyebrow arched, and his face assumed the same how-silly-of-you expression I recalled from when I was nineteen. It brought back memories of him tut-tutting me whenever I acted impulsively.

"That was some time ago," he added. "Is the prenuptial taking that long to draft?"

I stared him down. "What do you want?"

He smiled at my sharp tone. Rey was the only person I knew who took delight in rousing angry responses. "Since we're on this subject of nuptials, you're the first to hear about my upcoming marriage."

"A card invite would have sufficed."

He chuckled at my dry tone and walked over to the decanter, which he held up. When I nodded, he poured whisky into a crystal tumbler and passed me the drink then poured himself one.

He sat. "I'd like the function to be held at Elysium."

I puffed out loudly. "Why?"

"Why what?" he asked, flicking through a Time magazine in a desultory manner.

"Why marry? I thought you were sworn off it."

"Why not? You, of all people, recognize the benefits of having an intimate partner to have and to hold."

"But Natalia? A girl brought up by thugs? No matter how much designer clothing she wears, she can't hide the gutter from whence she came."

His mouth curled almost in delight, like I might have just described a prized horse. "Oh, Carol, not everyone possesses your stylish, regal bearing, despite your own former relationship with the gutter. Remember where you come from before digging in that spiky heel."

"I'm curious. Why her?"

"Because she understands me, and she's good at what she does."

"Won't she want to start a family?"

"Maybe."

My brow pinched.

"I've changed, Caroline. I've somewhat mellowed. And a few nice young children, especially a girl or two, wouldn't be that bad."

I shook my head. "I hope that isn't what it sounds like."

"You have a dark mind, Carol. You're more like me than you would care to admit."

I rose from my seat and headed to the window. "I'm nothing like you."

"So, I'll have Natalia talk to Manon to book Elysium. Yes?" Rey chuckled. "Strange how things pan out. Manon was once my intended, and now she's the one who will oversee the ceremony."

"She'd never agree to event-manage your wedding. Besides, she's a new mother."

"I don't care who manages the event." I turned to answer, but his eyes darkened as he added, "The wedding will take place at Elysium, and the Lovechildes will attend."

"I can't make my children do anything, Rey. You're not exactly their favorite uncle, so to speak."

He stared me straight in the eyes. "I won't take no for an answer, Caroline."

Yes, I knew that well enough. The man could move mountains and throw lightning like some malevolent mythical god. Only Rey was flesh and cold blood.

Resigned to giving him what he demanded, I sighed. "Send us the details, and I'll see what I can do. I'm certain Manon and Drake will decline."

"That won't be a loss. I only want our lot there."

"Manon is one of us. More than you care to think. Remember your roots, Reynard."

"They're long buried, just like yours." He gulped back his drink and poured two more without asking me this time. Like he was preparing me for more bad news. "Which brings us to the issue of those exhumed bones."

I took the glass and sipped like a woman condemned. "That malodorous detective keeps poking around."

Rey didn't respond.

"You were meant to deal with it, so it would never come back to haunt us." My throat constricted as I controlled a battalion of emotions. I wanted to scream at him for making a mess of what could be my doom.

"Yes, well, Jim was a chain-smoker. I suppose he didn't figure that I'd develop that site."

"Why did you?"

Rey shrugged. "The building was condemned. My hand was forced."

"But you must have known this could happen." Until the opening of this investigation, I'd almost laid that gruesome chapter to rest. Except for those nightmares when Alice made a haunting appearance, poking her finger into my face like she had that fateful night.

"The point is this, Caroline—you're the primary suspect."

"No, I'm not. It's your late friend Reilly, who everyone knows was connected to you."

"I can make this all go away." He fluttered his fingers as though we were talking about something light and frivolous.

As I watched Rey fill his glass once more, I had a sudden urge to have him removed from the house, to unchain myself from him forever.

"Well, then, let's hear it," I said.

"I want Elysium and that crumbling estate next to it," he said. "I'm told they can't afford the rent. They're running the farm down. It's not producing."

"I know about that. Declan has expressed interest in working with the farmer to transition into an organic producer." As his bloated request began to sink in, I shook my head. "My family won't sit back and allow it."

"Then Elysium, for now. Sign that over, and I can make this investigation go away."

I bit my lip and, taking a deep breath, finally asked, "Why? You've got all that land behind it."

"But Elysium is prime land. The views are matchless. You know that."

"I know you want to fill it with your drug-dealing riffraff and install a seedy men's club. It sickens me. The proximity to Merivale and the children..."

"We had a deal, Carol, and now I've come to collect."

"Yes," I said bitterly. "My Mephistophelean nightmare."

He chuckled. "Oh, Carol, look where you are." He pointed at the stunning view of Grosvenor Square. "You wouldn't have any of this. You wouldn't have met Cary, whom I can see you're madly in love with."

I rolled my eyes. I couldn't tell what disturbed me more, that my passion for Cary was so obvious or that Reynard was right.

A thought suddenly occurred to me. "Did you have that building brought down on purpose?"

Rey shrugged. "You always see the dark in everything, don't you?"

"When one is dealing with the devil himself, what do you expect?"

"The long answer is that the site needed to come down," he said after a moment. "There's a need for apartments, and I took advantage of an opportunity. That's what we do. We expand our empires. You, of all people, should know that." He cocked his head. "However, I'm not quite sure how you're expanding yours, since you've become somewhat distracted."

"Don't patronize me." My anger had made it to my vocal cords, and I rubbed my nails vigorously. I needed to vent soon, or I would scream in his face.

"But a penniless author who hasn't even been published? Carol, you could do better than that."

"It's none of your business. He's not completely penniless. He owns a charming villa in Como, which has an idyllic view of the lake. The land is worth millions, should he sell. Although I hope he doesn't." I puffed. If only I was on that splendid lake, sipping on an apéritif, instead of staring down Satan himself.

"Hm…" He walked over to an Art Deco statuette of a dancer and stroked it as he might a living woman.

"And the short answer?" I asked, reverting back to the gut-wrenching subject of his building site being cleared.

Distracted, Reynard gave me a questioning frown before a crafty grin smoothed out his wrinkles. "Oh, there is none. It's just unlucky that Alice's bones were discovered."

"But that detective Harding is determined. He's never going to just let this slide, even if I were to agree to your terms."

"Oh, but he will." He looked pleased, as though he'd just checkmated me.

Of course. He knew someone higher up. How could he not? Reynard Crisp was a modern-day Machiavelli when he wasn't playing Mephistopheles.

I sighed. "Let me sleep on it."

"Not too long. You don't want that detective poking around."

"They already have. There's a forensic report, I believe."

"That can go away too."

I shook my head. "When did you become God?"

"That happened while you were scrambling for crumbs, Carol."

Tired of his pompous presence, I rose and said sharply, "I'll see you out, then."

"Oh, and Natalia wants a big wedding."

"We'll be there. My children, however, I doubt."

As I opened the door to the salon, I saw Cary climbing the stairs, and despite my earlier petulance at his unwillingness to discuss marriage, I smiled. He was that beam of sunlight penetrating through dark clouds.

Reynard passed Cary by without so much as an acknowledgement.

Once we were alone, Cary turned to me. "You look a little rattled," he said. "I mean, you seemed that way earlier, too."

I took him by the hand, almost pulling him to me. "Let's go upstairs."

I called Vance and asked him not to disturb us, then followed Cary up to my bedroom. Once there, I turned on some music. This was hardly the time for tender sex.

Cary smiled. "That's rather raucous."

I pointed at his trousers. "Show me."

The man was so endowed that I couldn't get enough of his beautiful penis. He lowered his briefs, half erect already.

Just the mere hint of sex, and Cary fired up.

I removed my top and played with my breasts. I wanted to watch him go hard. Then I moved over to him, and donning my inexperienced-girl act, I purred, "What would you like, sir?"

"I want you to suck my dick." His eyes had gone dark with lust, for although I sensed his hesitation, his dick seemed to love when I acted the innocent, clueless girl. It was a game I once played with Gregory.

I took Cary's hard dick in my mouth. Pretending to be unsure, I used my teeth to garner a hard-edged response.

After what had just taken place with Rey, I needed rough sex.

"Ouch."

I bit my lip. "I'm sorry, sir."

He grabbed my head and pushed it back down to his cock. "Mm... That's better," he moaned as I moved up and down that thick shaft.

"You're getting better at this." He let out a groan, then unclasped my bra and fondled my breasts. "I want to fuck these tits."

He rubbed his dick between my breasts, and the blood-engorged head poked up to my chin.

He then removed my panties and fingered me. "You're fucking drenched. You want my dick inside you?"

"No, sir. It might hurt."

"I'm going to fuck you anyway." Lifting me up, he tipped me over the Louis XIV table and entered me in one hard thrust, continuing to penetrate me deeply as I whimpered and moaned. Pleasure and pain rippled all the way to my toes.

He continued to pound until a euphoric release trembled through me, and Cary climaxed like a man possessed.

CHAPTER 15

Cary

"WHY?" I ASKED, WIPING myself down with a towel.

"Why what?" Caroline rested against a red velvet cushioned bedhead.

"That was rough. Did I hurt you?"

"No. I was highly aroused, as always. You must have felt that?" She arched an eyebrow. "I didn't fake those orgasms." Her lips curved ever so slightly.

Was she being sarcastic?

I just didn't know her that well. Our discussions always revolved around intellectual matters like philosophy, literature, or politics, which I found stimulating. Small talk wasn't one of my fortes, nor was discussing emotions, for that matter.

Caroline was the first woman I'd known who didn't talk about our relationship, which was both refreshing and frustrating at the same time. I wanted to know her on a much deeper level.

"But why the forced-sex thing?" I persisted. "I'm just curious." More than that, our sex play left a lingering aftertaste that I likened to artificial sweetener, and it kept hounding me.

"You're not exactly forcing me, though, are you?" She wore a coy smile that rendered her inscrutable again.

I frowned. "I'm not used to that form of lovemaking, that's all."

"Are you unsatisfied with our sex life?"

I poured a glass of water and offered it to her, then I poured one for myself. Awkward conversations always made my mouth pasty. "No. Quite to the contrary. I would have thought that obvious."

Clad in a towel, I settled onto my favorite armchair by the French doors facing the park. The sculpture of the masked lovers on horseback caught my eye, and when I allowed my mind to wander, that whimsical creation transitioned into Caroline and me, hiding ourselves under masks.

She'd never really talked about her life growing up. I hadn't either, so I had no leverage there.

Was my story worse than hers?

"We're all allowed our dark little secrets, Cary." She patted the bed. "Now come here and kiss me."

I laid with her, took her into my arms, and kissed her as tenderly as I'd ever kissed anyone.

Her lips tasted of sex, and my dick lengthened. Men of my age normally needed the help of a pill to get an erection so soon after fucking. That was my experience.

But I'd met no one like Caroline before.

Everything had changed. I was no longer that man.

I MOVED MY FOCUS from a blank page on my screen to the window. That green room, as it was known, had become my favorite for its meditative view of the sea. It was there that I would spend hours tapping out the odd desultory paragraph before returning my eyes to the sky or the ever-changing body of water, imagining the many journeys it had made.

Caroline entered. "Busy working, I see."

"Not so much. Just doing what I do best." I chuckled. "Staring out the window."

"Yes, the views here are rather distracting, aren't they?"

I studied her and searched her eyes for judgement. Caroline missed little, and she'd noticed how I preferred to either walk or read instead of write.

"You've used up all your credit, I see." She walked over to the sofa and took a seat.

I forgot to breathe for a minute. "Yes, well..." Money and that maxed-out credit card she'd so generously given me was a subject I preferred to avoid. "I had a few expenses."

Her eyes trapped mine like a clairvoyant's might for one of those intense evaluations. "I've topped it up. No need to worry."

"That's good of you. I..." What could I say, that I was waiting for a piddly settlement?

Reading me well, she gave me a sympathetic smile, which only made me feel worse. "Think nothing of it." She rested her hand on my shoulder. "Why don't we marry?"

I nodded slowly, as if that idea was only just dawning on me, which wasn't the case. I'd thought of little else.

"If we marry, you can dig deep into the Lovechilde fortune."

I frowned. "I'm not here for your money, Caroline."

She gazed at me. "I will have to get you to sign a prenuptial agreement, you realize?"

I shrugged. "That's predictable." I couldn't hide my resentment at being seen as some money-grubbing layabout despite having done nothing to prove otherwise. "When do you want me to sign?"

Caroline wore a strained smile, the type a mother might give a petulant child. "Oh, Cary, please. Don't be offended. I have a family to protect. You must understand."

"Why marry then?" I asked. "Why not stay the way we are?"

She tapped her long red fingernails. Wearing a fitted floral dress and with her hair up in a bun, Caroline looked much younger than her age. I knew she'd had work done, despite her denials, but that didn't temper the effect she had on me and my libido.

"I would prefer marriage. I'm a little old-fashioned, I suppose." She looked up at me with a rare, shy smile.

"Oh, I wouldn't describe you as that." I leaned back in my chair and crossed my legs.

Scrutinizing me closely, as though trying to read deeper meaning into my words, Caroline remained silent.

"You're conservative on the outside," I continued, "but on the inside, you're anything but traditional."

"An upholder of convention is hardly priggish, my love."

"It can be construed that way. Often, the two are synonymous."

"Anyway"—she released a breath—"I get this feeling you're holding onto something. You can tell me anything. You know that, don't you?"

Her floral perfume drifted over to me, and all I wanted to do was remove that fitted dress—which emphasized an hourglass figure women half her age pined for—and make her cry out my name again.

"This is coming from the queen of secrets." I sniffed.

Turning away from my searching gaze as though my eyes were harsh sunlight, she stared down at her hands. "Isn't that something we all do? It's what keeps the world civilized. Imagine if everyone shared what really went on inside their complicated heads to all and sundry."

"That's not what I meant, Carol."

Her gaze pierced me. "Don't call me that."

I winced. "Apologies."

A faint, conciliatory smile chased away her scowl. "Getting back to earlier, I'd like to be married. To you."

I crossed my legs for the umpteenth time and nodded as if I'd forgotten all about her proposal.

"Is it the prenuptial? Or is it because you're uncertain about us as a couple?" Her gentle tone released some of the unease tensing my muscles.

"Have I told you how beautiful you look when you smile?"

"Well, yes." Her eyes softened into a honey brown.

I had her sit on my lap, and she giggled.

"Mm..." Her eyelids grew heavy with lust. "I can feel you." She slid off my lap and straightened her dress. "I can't, unfortunately. I'm waiting for Drake."

"He's doing some digging?" I knew about the bones and the detectives and how preoccupied Caroline was, but unsurprisingly, she wouldn't elaborate when I asked. "Why don't you take me into your confidence? I feel like an outsider."

She puffed. "I have a complicated past, darling."

"Don't we all." I walked over to the coffee table and picked up a magazine. "If anything, I know nothing about you, but yet here we are, about to marry."

"Are we? Is that your roundabout way of accepting?" Her face tilted slightly.

"I want to know you, Caroline. I mean, even me using your diminutive generated a barbed response."

"Now you're exaggerating. I just prefer my name spoken in long form."

I blew out a frustrated breath. "Enough of the bullshit, Caroline. If we're to marry, I need to understand you, especially our strange encounters in shoddy places."

"You seem just as aroused," she challenged.

I sighed. "That's because it's you. I'd meet you in hell if you'd ask me."

Her eyebrows rose sharply.

Sadly, it was true, and I hated how weak I suddenly sounded. I approached her and took her into my arms, kissing her warm, soft neck. "I've never felt so aroused. You're a seductress, Caroline."

"Then marry me."

I searched for a hint of irony, but she remained earnest. "Isn't marriage about two souls dancing as one?"

She sniffed dismissively. "That's the poet's version, darling. Most marriages are a business arrangement."

"Like your marriage with Harry?"

She gave a slightly sad nod. "He was my best friend, too."

"And gay."

She shrugged. "I didn't go without."

"No. You ended up with his partner."

Her smooth brow nearly creased as she studied me for a moment before softening again. "See, you know about my past." She ran her hands over my thigh and stopped short of stroking my cock.

"Not enough though." I held my ground, despite her attempt to turn me from inquisitor to ravaging lover, and took her hand away before I lost yet another round. "Why is that detective poking around? And why do you keep that snake Crisp so close?"

She wrapped her arms around my neck and drew me in close again. "Why don't we go to Como for a week? We can reveal our souls there, if you like."

I got lost in the fragrance of her silky raven hair, and as my hands traveled her contours, almost unconsciously, her suggestion suddenly registered. This time, I stepped away from her abruptly.

I bit my lip and eyed the liquor, all golden in the sun. Temptation to take a nip or two came calling, and since it was midafternoon, that's exactly what I did.

She looked hurt. "What's the matter?"

"Do you want one?" I held up the bottle before pouring myself a generous measure.

She shook her head.

I took a swallow and cleared my throat. "Como's been sold."

Her eyes widened as though I'd told her that a family member had been murdered. "I didn't even know it was on the market. Why didn't you tell me? I would have bought it."

"That would have felt odd."

"You should have told me. I would have paid you double, triple your asking price. Why didn't you?" She looked angry all of a sudden.

"But it was too small. I recall you complaining about the size of the bathroom. Not to mention the bedroom."

"I would have pulled it down and rebuilt something larger."

I gulped down my Scotch and poured another shot, frustrated at her tone and at myself for being so complacent where she was concerned. Normally, I would give as good as I got. "It was mine to do with as I pleased, Caroline."

I walked to the window and turned my back to her.

"No one's questioning that, darling. But why not tell me? It was a rare jewel." She sounded like she might cry.

I turned to face her. "It's only a villa, Caroline. It's not someone's life."

She remained lost in her thoughts, and her frown intensified before she stared up at me again. "Tell me the real reason why, Cary."

The reason, however, was more complicated than me being broke. She would have discovered Markus Reiner, and that would have opened a Pandora's box.

"Oh Cary." She fell down on the sofa. "I loved that villa. I even saw us living there part of the year."

I sighed. Yes. Our time at Como had been magical. Perfect. "It was with a heavy heart, for sure. I needed the money."

"Why didn't you talk to me?"

"The same reason you won't let me into your world, I suppose."

She paced about. "Put me in contact with your solicitor, and I will double the buyer's offer."

"I don't think that will work. It's a famous Hollywood actor who has sworn everyone to secrecy. It's too late."

She huffed loudly.

"There are more villas around."

"Not in that prime location. I've already looked." She sat on the couch and cupped her chin in one hand, looking despondent.

I joined her and placed my arm around her. It was like I was consoling her for losing a loved one. "I'm sorry, Caroline."

CHAPTER 16

Caroline

EVANGELINE'S CHRISTENING OFFERED A break from the events in my life spiraling out of control. I had two escapes in family and Cary, only the latter was rather withdrawn after that long-winded conversation about marriage.

I sensed he was holding something back. There were too many questions. So I did something radical and hired a private investigator.

I had to know what was behind Cary's mask. Maybe then, I might even share my story. A story that was growing grittier by the day and was keeping me awake. Had it not been for Cary and this all-consuming passion we shared, I would have been a total wreck, especially with Rey's preposterous demands that I hand over Elysium.

How would I explain that to my family?

I also wanted that detective gone from my life. It wasn't just the questions his shabby presence aroused but the nightmares that had returned with a vengeance. Cary had mentioned my crying out in the night.

I went to my daughter, whom I found chatting and laughing with Mirabel.

"Mother, there you are," Savanah said, kissing me on the cheeks. She looked over my shoulder and rolled her eyes. "Bethany's arrived. She knows how to make an entrance. And what is she wearing?"

"Purple, hot pink, and ripped leather. Yikes. It's rather loud," Mirabel quipped with a chuckle.

"It's called 'no amount of money buys taste,'" Savanah said. "Oh god, Mummy, she's brought him?"

I remained silent, despite the rumble in my chest. Bethany, with that scruffy boytoy in tow, had lowered the tone of the event.

"I didn't know she was dating Sweeney Knight," Mirabel said.

"You've heard of him?"

My daughter-in-law laughed at Savanah's shocked expression. "I'm not just stuck in some folksy bubble, you know. Ethan's also a fan of his band. We both are. They're refreshingly proggy."

I had no idea what that meant, and Mirabel gave me an apologetic smile of the kind a young woman might an elder who hadn't caught up with the latest trends.

"Progressive rock," she said. "You know, like..."

"I know what progressive rock is, Mirabel. I was a fan of bands like Pink Floyd. It might surprise you to know."

Savanah turned to me, looking shocked. "You're kidding. Really? I thought you only listened to classical."

"I do now. But growing up, I was exposed to Pink Floyd, Genesis, and the like, which fall under that prog-rock category, I believe." I looked at Mirabel. "As you call it."

Ethan arrived and kissed me, then his sister, before going to his wife and placing his arm around her. They made for a strange couple, but I could see they were very much in love. Genetics loved variety, as science had revealed, and Cian was a wonder to behold with his regal bearing and virtuosic skills, while Ruby could become our new Margot Fonteyn.

All my grandchildren had made me proud, and for that alone, I felt blessed. If only I could get Crisp out of my life, the heavy burden weighing me down for over thirty years would finally be lifted.

"Sweeney Knight. My god, with Bethany, can you believe it?" Ethan said.

"He looks stoned," I said.

All three turned to look at me. "Hello, he's a rock star. He's not exactly going to be sipping chamomile." Ethan laughed. He stole another glance. "I must say Bethany's lost some weight. She's almost emaciated. And tattooed."

I grimaced. "Yes, I've noticed."

"There's nothing wrong with tattoos," Savanah said.

"Oh, darling, please tell me you haven't?" I pleaded.

Savanah laughed. "I've got a little one. But not on my arm. Not like Beth. Oh. My. God. She's really gone all grungy, hasn't she? What's next, a dress held up by safety pins?"

I had to smile. "It may have worked for Liz Hurley and Versace, but that would now be seen as passe. You can't subvert what's already been subverted."

Ethan and Savanah's eyebrows rocketed up at the same time.

"Wow, I love the sound of that, despite not really understanding it," Mirabel said.

Savanah giggled. "One of her mum-isms."

I shook my head at how ridiculous that sounded, and Ethan chuckled while nodding in agreement.

"But really, what do you mean?" Mirabel asked.

"To subvert is to corrupt or in this case to shock. Once that's happened, the repeat acts are somewhat diluted at best and pretentious as worst."

"Okay, like ripped clothing that people pay ridiculous sums for," Mirabel said, giving her husband a pointed look. He held up his hands in defense.

I nodded. "The punk movement made that look famous."

"Vivian Westwood, God bless her soul," Savanah added with stars in her eyes.

"And so, these attention-seeking fashion statements are fed to the masses, and they lose shock value somewhat," I concluded.

"I do like my distressed jeans," Ethan said.

Mirabel rolled her eyes.

Ethan laughed and kissed her hair. "My darling wife thinks I'm shallow and pretentious."

Mirabel turned in protest. "I never said that."

I walked off, leaving them in their little world, and went over to Manon and Drake.

Unlike her mother, Manon had put on weight, was dressing more like me every day, and articulated her words without the slightest hint of her former cockney twang.

"Grandmother." She smiled brightly and hugged me.

The epitome of a doting father, Drake stood by her side, cradling Evangeline.

I stroked the beautiful little girl's rosy cheek, and the baby smiled back. "She's a darling."

Drake had adoration in his eyes. "She is."

Manon looked lovingly at her partner, then me. "We've set a date for next month. Do you mind if we marry here?"

"Of course. Merivale's your home." I looked from her to Drake.

Bethany's screechy laugh cut through the air, and all heads turned in her direction.

"I hope she doesn't cause a scene. She's different again." Manon sounded like she was the mother, lamenting an unruly child's behavior.

I gave her a sympathetic smile. "She wouldn't be the first to misbehave at one of our functions."

"I'll have a word with her. She's on drugs, I think." Manon leaned in and kissed Drake. "Why don't you put Evie in her crib? Our little sweetie looks sleepy."

I stretched out my arms. "Here, let me hold her." I took my great-granddaughter and rocked her. "While you're here, any news?" I asked Drake quietly about our delicate arrangement.

"He's working on it. Will let you know."

I nodded. "I'll pop Evangeline in the nursery. She looks exhausted from all this attention. Janet will be there to look over her."

He looked worried, as though his baby was about to be placed in danger. I gave him a reassuring smile. "Don't worry. Janet cared for all the children. She's a natural."

After I laid Evie down, I returned to the party, and Bethany came over with her new boyfriend by her side.

"Mother, you've put on weight," Bethany said. "Maybe you should visit that gym that Carson's running."

"Not interested in gyms. I'll stick to my walks." What Bethany would never know was that sex kept me in shape.

"I'd like to introduce Sweeney." She gestured at her young, twitchy boyfriend, who I imagined had sniffed enough cocaine to start his own party.

I nodded at him, and he leaned in and kissed me. He stank of alcohol and strong, sickening cologne that was probably some famous footballer's signature blend.

"Pleased to know you, ma'am."

He bowed, and I nearly laughed. I couldn't tell if he was having a dig at our class or if he was serious.

Bethany looked back at me. "So, you're a great-grandmother. How does that feel?"

"No different from being a mother or grandmother."

"She's too gorgeous to be a great grandmother," Sweeney added.

I returned a tight smile at his cockney-embellished compliment. "Anyway, nice meeting you. I must go over and greet some of the new arrivals."

I left them before Bethany, who was clearly drugged to the eyeballs, uttered another word. Nonsensical drug babble got on my nerves.

Cary was talking to a young, blonde, and busty woman. Her face lit up as he spoke. A sudden prick of jealousy swept over me, as I observed just how invested he was in that conversation.

Guests chatted with me, but I hardly heard what they were saying. I simply nodded and smiled on automatic, something I'd become accustomed to from years of practice.

Cary hardly acknowledged me, and when I finally caught his eye, he appeared to excuse himself and then strolled over. "You're looking lovely as always," he said in what sounded like a token pleasantry.

"Who is she?" I asked, without returning the compliment.

"Oh, she's someone's daughter. I didn't really ask."

"You looked riveted."

After holding my stare as though searching for words, he broke into a smile. "Oh, Caroline, there's only you. You know that, don't you?"

"She's pretty and kept touching your sleeve."

He tilted his head. "Are you jealous?"

"Stop playing games." I turned my back and walked away.

CHAPTER 17

Cary

THAT NIGHT, I KNOCKED on Caroline's door, something I never normally did, as her bedroom was also mine.

After giving me the cold shoulder for most of the night, Caroline absented herself from the party as soon as most of the guests had left. Her oldest daughter, along with her rock-star boyfriend, had to be thrown out after the boyfriend's drunken stumbling about nearly obliterated an entire shelf of Murano glass. The staff had to keep moving things from out of his way like they might for a curious toddler, which I found rather amusing. Their loud presence had livened things up a bit. Not that Caroline had seen it that way. Instead, she'd rolled her eyes and whispered something to security, who'd then asked them to leave. Bethany didn't go silently, either, as she'd landed a few passing shots. She'd pointed and yelled, "You're all a bunch of stuck-up, arse-licking knobs!"

I entered the bedroom and being slightly drunk, I ignored Caroline's tetchy mood. Skye, the young blonde, was harmless enough, despite her brazen flirting. And I wasn't exactly encouraging her when she invited me back to her place.

I'd cheated one time too many, and the thought of my wicked past sickened me.

With Lilly, cheating had been a necessity after her libido faded. She even turned a blind eye to my occasional dalliance, which made the act of seduction easier. Especially with the youngish Italian neighbor who, bored with her husband, had become my guilty secret.

As things were now, I didn't need to stray because Caroline fulfilled me in every sense of that word.

I found her propped up in bed, reading and wearing one of her lacy negligees. Now, if ever I needed an erotic image, there it was before me—Caroline, her full breasts barely covered by white lace, her thick raven hair loose, engrossed in Proust.

For some men, it was porn. For me, it was Caroline in lace holding a doorstopper of a novel.

"I wish I could photograph you," I said, undoing my cravat.

She peered over her reading glasses and then removed them. "I thought you might have headed out."

"Are you angry with me?"

"You humiliated me." Intense and piercing, her unblinking stare held me captive.

I removed my jacket. "Oh, Caroline, please. We're grown-ups. I couldn't exactly push the girl away."

"You were talking for a half an hour. And people noticed."

When I stripped down to my briefs, her focus left my face and headed down to my groin, which might as well have been her hands caressing my shaft because it thickened in anticipation.

"Do you want me to sleep in the guest room?" I asked.

"No. In bed. Now."

I removed my briefs and smiled as she gazed down at my growing erection. Climbing into bed, I met her gaze. "You're delectable."

Her eyes softened a little as I slid my hands over her arm to the nape of her neck.

"If you do that to me again, Cary, this time will be our last."

"I promise not to talk to young, busty blondes again."

Her frown deepened, and before she could respond, I added, "I prefer busty brunettes with a penchant for bedridden French writers."

Her chuckle inspired me to go on. "Caroline, why would I be with someone like her when I have you? No one compares."

Before she could respond, I buried my head between her thighs and showed her just how much she meant to me.

"Remind me why we're here?" I asked. "Not that I mind seeing you all gowned up. You look ravishing." I kissed Caroline's hand, and her lips curled slightly.

She suddenly looked quite uneasy in Elysium's impressive ballroom, surrounded by groups of rowdy East Europeans. It was Crisp's wedding, and the guests, who had apparently made their fortunes in questionable ways, were part of the bride's party.

The bridesmaids looked like they'd come from a Barbie convention, all clad in bright pink. Their sculptured hairdos, just like the famous doll's, gleamed under the chandeliers. Their make-up was so thick one could almost peel it off.

Meanwhile, the men huddled together, and when they weren't forcing out chuckles, they scowled.

"If a war were to break out, one would want that lot on your side," I said of the group of tall, burly men in badly fitted suits, sporting hair styles worn by World War I soldiers.

"Quite." Caroline sighed.

I took her hand. "Are you okay?"

"I'm fine. I'm just not used to a function of this nature. Not here at Elysium, at least. And in answer to your earlier question, Rey made me come. It is his wedding, after all."

I was about to say something when a piercing scream split the air, grabbing my attention. It appeared that the woman's over-the-top reaction was directed at the bride's large diamond and not some kind of imminent danger.

A server swung by with a tray of champagne, and following Caroline's lead, I took a glass. The bubbles tickled my nose as I took a sip. "At least the bubbly's top shelf."

Some man came over and whispered to Caroline, and she side-eyed me with one of those stares that spoke of disinterest. Being well-versed in niceties, she put on a fake smile, and there it remained as the voluble guest filled her ear with a lot of words.

After he left, I joined her again. "Some lord?"

"Mm... Yes, how did you guess?"

"Oh, they have a way." I exhaled, trying not to sound bored, which, of course, I was. All I wanted was to return to Merivale and sink into Ovid with a fine bottle of single malt by my side.

The bride continued to be surrounded by a bevy of gushing females, marveling at her diamond ring and stroking her skintight, sparkling wedding gown like it was some miraculous work of art.

"Back in a moment," Caroline said.

I decided to step outside for a cigar, an activity I enjoyed on occasion. As I walked to the door, Serbian phrases rang through the air. I might have been at a World Cup match. Not that I followed football. Tennis was my only interest when it came to sport.

As I lit my cigar, I heard my name, and I turned to find the groom standing by the fountain.

"That must have taken some getting used to," Reynard Crisp said. No 'How are you?' or similar pleasantry.

"What do you mean?" I stepped away from the fountain, where instead of Bach or Debussy, the Serbian national anthem blared. Caroline had been so dismayed when we arrived that she called Manon to instruct her to turn off the scratchy-sounding anthem by midnight.

"That's taking patriotism a little far, wouldn't you say?" I pointed to the fountain.

He sniffed. "My darling wife is beholden to her origins. Nothing wrong with a little nationalistic pride, wouldn't you say? Unless, of course, one is trying to escape theirs."

He shot me a piercing gaze.

Instead of walking away, which I would normally do to avoid succumbing to animal instincts and smashing a glass over his head, I couldn't help but ask, "What must take getting used to?"

"Your name."

Amidst countless colliding thoughts, I chose silence.

"So tell me about this fellow, Markus Reiner."

My legs weakened, and his grin widened.

I sucked on my cigar like a man condemned.

"I went to Australia last year," Crisp continued. "Melbourne, for the Grand Prix. An interesting place. The rabble have an almost unhealthy obsession with sport, which they consider culture." He chuckled. "But Sydney is nice. Girt by the harbor. I liked Sydney."

He also liked the sound of his own voice because I stopped listening at the mention of Australia.

My former home.

The home I ran away from.

He eyed me. "I must say, you've done away with that unfortunate accent very nicely."

"What do you want, Crisp?" I stared him in the face while the grip on my glass tightened like it was his neck.

"I know who you are, and how you charmed your way into the Lovechilde inner sanctum."

"My relationship with Caroline is none of your business."

"But it is." He wore the victorious grin of someone holding an unbeatable poker hand. "You see, I own Caroline Lovechilde. She's become weaker since you arrived. Imagine her shock at learning that she's in love with not just a poseur but also an imposter."

I grabbed him by the scruff of his collar. "Enough of your fucking insults."

He stepped away and laughed. "Ah, Markus Reiner has finally made a show in all his Teutonic brutishness. I think I like him better than the fop with all his bookish frippery."

"What do you want?" I asked gruffly.

"Leave her. Find any excuse. I'm sure you can come up with something. You're gifted when it comes to bullshit."

"And if I don't?" I challenged.

"Then Markus Reiner becomes a reality, and Carrington Lovelace will find his natural home as some two-dimensional character in one of those cheesy, unreadable airport novels." He chuckled. "What were you thinking? Carrington Lovelace? I say."

His mockery stabbed at me.

I punched him in the face just as Caroline came running over.

"What's happening?" she demanded. Her beautiful eyes were wide and filled with shock.

Crisp held his nose. "I think I'll leave it to your bargain-basement lothario to explain."

And off he stalked.

CHAPTER 18

Caroline

CARY TOOK A DEEP breath. "He made some smarmy comment, and forgetting myself, I punched him."

To escape that atrocious, warped fountain music, I led him away to the parking lot where black BMWs and Mercedes SUVs had taken the place of vintage Aston Martins, Jaguars, and the other elegant vehicles I always admired. The entire scene was alarmingly tasteless and lacking in refinement.

Elysium was never meant for such an uncouth crowd.

"I'm leaving." Cary turned and touched my arm. "You can stay. I just can't be here."

"But Cary." As I watched him leave, I debated whether to go after him, but that wasn't my way. Also, considering I'd only been there for thirty minutes, it would cause all kinds of issues for me. Alas.

I headed back inside in search of Rey and found him leaving the bathroom, holding a hanky to his nose.

"What did you say to Cary? He just left."

"I told him he wasn't good enough for you, that's all."

"Who the fuck are you to make that call?"

"Keep your voice down, Carol. You're sounding like that unrefined East End girl I once knew."

"I don't give a damn." I poked him in the chest, and his eyes darkened before softening as he looked over my shoulder at a guest.

"Oh, Damian, have you met the illustrious Caroline Lovechilde?"

I took a deep breath and turned to greet Rey's guest. The man kissed my hand and rambled about something that my brain, having its own conference, was too busy to absorb.

After he sauntered off, I turned to Rey. "I've got a headache. I have to leave."

His eyes turned dark again. "Carol."

"The name's Caroline." I left before he could taunt me with sarcasm.

As I walked away, I felt his furious glare on me.

When I arrived at Merivale, I couldn't find Cary. The hall was empty. Savanah and Carson were in France, and Manon was in London with Drake and Evangeline, visiting Drake's mother. Even the servants were tucked away.

Eventually, I found Cary outside by the pool, smoking.

"I thought you'd kicked the habit," I said, taking a seat by his side.

"I had." He turned to blow the smoke away from my face.

"What happened with Crisp?"

He took a moment to respond, stroking my face while staring deeply into my eyes. "Nothing that's worth spoiling this moment. You look so beautiful right now in the moonlight."

I couldn't help but smile, despite his evasiveness.

"Come, Caroline, let's go to bed." He rose, took me into his arms, and as his warm, soft lips met mine, that tawdry wedding reception slipped out of my consciousness.

The moon was full, the night was clear, and the bracing, salty air caressed my cheeks, reminding me that being in the arms of this mysterious, beautiful man was all that mattered.

That night, we made slow, tender love.

Cary kept stroking me and telling me how much he loved me, and that detestable wedding function became a distant memory, like a frightful illness that once healed is quickly forgotten.

The following morning, I woke from a long, sound sleep. Finding the bed empty, I assumed Cary was out and about organizing breakfast, as he often did, so that a tray would be by my side when I woke.

I smiled, thinking of his sweet words and tender lovemaking. Rey was right about the paradise I'd found. If it meant losing Elysium, that was a small price to pay for a life with Cary. The family was wealthier than ever, largely due to Declan and Ethan's efforts.

When I discovered there was no breakfast or Cary, I showered and headed downstairs.

I ran into Janet along the way.

"Have you seen, Cary?" I asked.

"Um, he left earlier. Around eight. He was carrying a suitcase."

"Oh?" I held her gaze while searching for words. "Did he say where he was going?"

"No, he just pecked me on the cheek and thanked me."

My brows contracted. "Does he normally do that?"

She shook her head. "I mean, he's normally grateful and very nice about things, but... no, I thought it odd."

I let her be and went to get my phone, which I'd left in my office. When I arrived, I found an envelope with my name on it.

I regarded that envelope like it was a bomb about to threaten my life.

Picking up the phone, I called the kitchen. "Can you bring me tea?"

"Yes, certainly. Your regular breakfast with that?"

"No. Just tea."

I took a deep breath and waited as I stared down at the envelope. My hands were shaking, and I could hardly breathe.

Janet brought the tea into my office and set it on my desk, while I held that envelope in my hand as though it was something to fear.

"Thank you. Could you close the door behind you?"

She nodded, giving me a sympathetic look. She knew. Janet had been with me for many years. She could read me well.

I took a deep breath and sipped tea, the cup trembling in my hand. I needed something stronger, so I poured a nip of whisky into the hot liquid.

It was something my foster mother used to do in anticipation of her evil husband. She'd give me one of her feeble smiles then place her finger on her mouth for me to remain nice and quiet. We both had to make ourselves invisible to avoid rousing the ire of that beastly man.

I ripped open the envelope, and the note fell out. With shaky fingers, I unfolded it and read:

Dear Caroline,

It is early, so my writer's brain hasn't quite woken, thus I will make this brief.

I leave with a heavy heart. It's like I am about to remove a vital organ and enter the world as half a man.

In you, I found a soulmate.

I never thought that would happen to someone like me: an impetuous man drawn into a world of poetry while dodging the real world.

At first, your luxurious lifestyle dazzled me. But all that faded into insignificance the moment I kissed you.

Together, our souls danced among the stars. Before I met you, I thought this kind of love only existed in fiction.

I wanted to spend my life with you.

I wanted to give you everything of myself.

But I couldn't, because you see, I am not the man you thought I was.

It was a lie.

I am a lie.

What is not a lie is that I love you with every cell in my body. Please believe that.

I leave as a man who has tasted the elixir of perfection only to be doomed to a life of memories.

Memories will never allow me to taste your lips again or feel your warm, soft body in my arms as our hearts beat as one. Memories will never listen to me speaking passionately about some book I've read. Memories will never walk with me and hold my hand while marveling at the moody ocean's ever-changing color.

I carry you with me wherever my next journey takes me.

You will always be in my heart, soul, and spirit.

Cary.

Dazed and unable to process any clear line of thought, I stared down at the handwritten note now stained with my tears.

I paced around that room that had seen it all—Harry admitting to falling in love with a man, Bethany revealing that she was my long-lost daughter, and my sons announcing their marriages to women who weren't of our class.

Only without my mask, I wasn't part of that class, either, nor was the man I'd fallen head over heels in love with. It was all just unbridled bigotry, entangling me in a network of contradictions.

Yes, that room had seen it all. But I'd always remained controlled. All seething unrest below the surface but outwardly just a stiff upper lip, showing nothing. Always in control.

I paced and paced. An eruption inside me brewed away like acid spitting into the air from a cauldron of bubbling emotion. That cool, calm, collected version of me now charred beyond recognition.

A vase ended up in my hand, and I smashed it. Water streaked the butter-yellow walls like the tears on my face. The lilies collapsed in a sad heap on the floor.

I went to the figurines Harry had so admired and smashed one at a time. That still didn't appease this violent need to vent, so I punched the wall. Stinging pain traveled up to my wrist, supplanting the suffocating squeeze in my heart.

Manon came running in. "Grandmother!"

I turned, and my mouth fell open, but only heavy breaths tumbled out.

Snapping out of my breakdown, I collapsed on the sofa, covered my face, and cried like a baby. Tears poured out of me like never before.

Torrents of poison rushed out of me as my former life flashed before my eyes.

I saw my foster father's drunken eyes awash in criminal desire then Reynard Crisp making promises for a priceless sum beyond even a billionaire's checkbook.

What is the price of a soul?

No amount could fill the black hole left in its wake.

"Oh my god, what's happened?" Manon asked, sitting close and placing her arm around my shoulders.

I slowly regained composure as the storm rocking my foundations subsided. And I studied my granddaughter, seeing myself at her age, freshly married and presiding over a dynasty.

From the ashes of desperation and indigence, this bright, beautiful girl had been born, and I couldn't have been prouder.

There was something gratifying, miraculous even, in seeing someone rise from nothing to greatness. Like a unique flower growing from a patch of grime.

Manon poured me a whisky, and after I swallowed it down, I told her about Cary's sudden departure.

Manon frowned. "Then you have to talk to Crisp and find out what he knows."

"He wants Elysium." Just saying that was like a concrete curtain slamming down on me. The thought of another struggle made me want to roll into a ball and sleep.

Her jaw dropped. "But you can't. Savvie and I are having a ball turning it upmarket and hip."

I had to smile at her determination. "I've noticed."

Pushing aside the bleakness that had fallen upon me, I regarded Manon and the ambition dancing in her eyes, a heartening reminder that the Lovechilde empire lay in excellent hands.

Welcoming any distraction, I asked, "About the techno dance club. Won't that be noisy for some of the older guests?"

"We're planning on holding it in the function room at the back, which is soundproofed. Only once a month, mind you, and Elysium gets booked out by rich, young things. We've got to think of the future, Grandmother. They won't always be young, but most will always be filthy rich and need somewhere like Elysium to visit, and they already love the spa. It's a perfect fit."

"And what about the party drugs? Cocaine?"

"Oh, that already happens. The oldies drink like fish, and I often smell weed. Not to mention the endless little white streaks everywhere."

I sighed. "Well, darling, I'm afraid Elysium will soon no longer be in our hands. You could try to secure your position there by talking to Rey."

"What?" Her face scrunched in horror, like I'd suggested we bulldoze the property.

I explained how he had me over a barrel, without going into the finer details. No one knew those.

"But that's fucked." She bit her lip. "Sorry."

"I agree. It is fucked." I puffed, wringing my hands.

"Can't you do something?"

I shook my head slowly.

Oh, I could do something, all right, but I wasn't about to air the ominous solution developing within me. A plan that, with every breath, had turned into an invasive weed, suffocating any trace of goodness.

"Sorry, I shouldn't be talking about dance clubs while you're dealing with a broken heart." Manon's doe eyes filled with sympathy.

"I'll live." I forced a smile. Rising, I ran my hands over my hair, which had lost its shape during my tirade. "I hope the staff aren't wondering what that was about." I stared at the broken ceramic bits on the floor.

"Oh, you destroyed the horses."

"Yes, Harry spent a fortune on those. One-offs." I shrugged. "They're only possessions. And it wouldn't have done to have broken something cheap."

Manon's attention shifted from the scattered pieces to me, and her lips curled. "That's so true. Even though you'd be hard-pressed to find any worthless crap at Merivale."

She went to inspect the damage. "Maybe they can be glued back together. I can see if I can fix them."

I smiled and thanked my lucky stars that I had her around. "We've got cupboards filled with pretty things." She sat down again, and I stroked her cheek. "Thanks, sweetheart. You've made me proud."

She tilted her head, and her eyes misted over. "Really? Even after all the trouble I caused?"

I stroked her long, dark, lustrous hair. "What trouble?"

Manon hugged me. "I will do anything for this family. You know that, don't you?" She stared me in the eyes, deadly serious. "Let's get rid of him."

I caught my breath. "We'd be the first suspects. The police aren't that stupid. And he has friends in high places, darling."

"Then what are you going to do?"

"I'm not sure. But everything we've spoken about, including Cary's sudden departure, remains within this room."

"But what do I say if someone asks?"

"Just tell them I didn't give details or something like that. By now, everyone's used to my circumventions."

"I don't even know what that means." She wore a sad smile.

"It means that I'm good at skirting issues."

CHAPTER 19

Cary

THE MIRROR IN MY sad flat reflected a man I'd been escaping from for thirty years. I didn't even recognize myself in the tattered tweed jacket I'd picked up long ago in some Australian charity store, its ripped lining revealing its hapless state of neglect.

Thanks to Lilly's support, followed by Caroline's considerable generosity, I hadn't needed to wear that jacket for years. Maybe because of some kind of twisted sentimentality, I'd kept it. Lucky for me I had, because, along with my heart, I left all those fine jackets I'd amassed over the past two years at Merivale.

I brushed the lint off the jacket and studied myself a little longer. I'd aged at least ten years in a month. They say money can't buy happiness—a platitude invented to placate the struggling many. In my eyes, however, an excellent wine or a visit to Venice helped ease the burden of depression.

Wealth had certainly weakened me. I'd gone from silk sheets to scratchy synthetic ones, from tender steak to its gristly inferior.

My aesthetic sensibilities had fared just as poorly. After twenty years of Lake Como, followed by the splendor of Merivale, I suddenly found myself surrounded by the manufactured ugliness of a city bursting at its seams.

Fortunately, the ten thousand euros arrived just as I'd used up the remainder of my topped-up credit limit. I couldn't keep using Caroline's money, especially now that I'd left everything behind.

The first week was the hardest. I'd used the card to stay at a three-star hotel in the heart of London, which still came at a hefty price. I'd been so spoiled in those past two years that I'd forgotten how expensive the city could be.

Then a small bedsit in the heart of Whitechapel became available, and I pounced on it to try and stretch out my money.

It wasn't the fancy jackets or the first editions I'd left behind that weighed heavily on my heart. I didn't care about those. It was Caroline I missed like mad.

I was a shadow of a man now. Almost numb, as though blood no longer pumped through me.

My spirit was so heavy that some days I could barely face myself, let alone humanity, as that mass of bodies treaded along cracked pavements like they were in a modern adaptation of a Dickens novel. More skin on display, genders somewhat undefined, but still a familiar cast of characters that, from no fault of their own or from blindly following their hearts, were on a path to a dead-end.

For me, wallowing beat facing the day, and self-pity quickly became my comforter, a kind of moth-eaten blanket that I clutched onto. My brain suddenly churned out purple prose by the ream—a death knell for any modern writer. But that didn't matter, because my 'winter of discontent' reverie remained buried inside, and like some dysfunctional friend, gloom kept me company.

Audrey, my landlady, found me a good listener and had taken a shine to me. I'd only just moved in when she recounted her life story over cups of tea and cheap port. As the days blended into each other, she'd share wholesome stews or homemade scones while talking about her life and anything else that popped into her busy head.

I didn't mind, because that sweet, kindly soul's endless chatter gave me a break from my own restless thoughts.

Within two weeks of living at Audrey's, I found work teaching literature at a college, and slowly I started to thaw out.

A week later, just as I was leaving campus for the day, I ran into Theadora. Much to my horror.

"Cary." Theadora looked perplexed, as though I was the last person she expected to see.

I matched her awkward smile with a jittery greeting. I hadn't expected to cross paths with the family, either. Whitechapel wasn't exactly
the sort of area the Lovechildes frequented—other than Caroline on
one of her strange expeditions involving me and my dick.

"What brings you here?" I asked.

"I'm teaching piano at the college." The frown hadn't faded from her
face. I sensed she had a thousand questions. "I volunteer once a month
by helping the gifted players with their theory so they can get through
their exams."

"Oh, right, of course. There's a music course here. I recall seeing a
lunchtime cello recital."

"And you?" She tilted her head.

"I'm teaching English."

She nodded. "Caroline's not the same. She's lost weight, and she
barely talks much these days. Even to Declan."

Familiar with Theadora's propensity to chat about family politics,
which was the last thing I needed at that moment, I hesitated while
searching for the right response. "I'm sad to hear that."

It was the best I could do. I couldn't exactly tell her how miserable
my world had become without Caroline warming my bed and my soul.

I touched her arm. "Must rush. Got another class to get to."

I leaned in and pecked her on the cheek. I sensed more words form-
ing, so before she said something else, I hastened off.

Chapter 20

Caroline

"Transfer that plot of land over to me, as well as Elysium, and I will share all that I know about Cary. It's a fascinating tale, I might add." Reynard grinned. "And, of course, the Alice Ponting case will also go away."

I remained deadpan, despite my gut curdling at how powerful and corrupt Rey was. Those long, bloodless fingers hovered over a button that, once pressed, could destroy me.

There I was at Pengilly, his gauche estate, where a garish interior painted in the gaudiest of colors hurt my eyes. Money had done nothing for his tastes, not least the crimson, bordello-style wallpaper of that sitting room.

In the background, his new wife, Natalia, yelled at one of the staff, and Rey wore a glib smile, as though her petulant outburst was a cute little quirk.

Natalia came storming in, dressed in skin-colored activewear that defined every contour and sinew. Wearing thick makeup, she could have been headed to a nightclub.

"You need to talk to her," she demanded, either not seeing me or choosing to ignore me.

"Okay, I'll let her go and find someone else. Now, off you scoot."

Natalia rolled her eyes and left us.

"She's proving to be a credit you," I said, my tongue in my cheek.

Rey's eyes narrowed. I'd hit a nerve. "That sarcasm's a little rich coming from someone who almost married a shyster."

I rose and smoothed out my skirt. There was nothing to be gained from this meeting other than an assault on my senses. Even the lingering, sickly floral perfume Natalia left in her wake nauseated me.

Rey was about to follow me, but I held up a hand. "No need. I can see myself out."

"We'll talk soon about the paperwork. Yes?"

After leaving Pengilly, I asked my driver to take me to Declan. Dread shadowed me. How would I break the news about the farm to my son?

Declan let me in and gave me a peck on the cheek. I rarely visited his home, a former gothic church. In sharp contrast to the busy hideousness of Rey's mansion, Declan and Theadora had created an artful and tasteful atmosphere.

"It's rare to see you here, Mum." He smiled. "Tea?"

I nodded and followed him into the kitchen that extended from the living space.

"You don't have help?" I asked, realizing that I hadn't made a cup of tea in thirty-odd years.

"I do. But Mary's taken the children to a playdate."

After he made the tea, we sat upstairs in a room with a windowed wall looking out to sea.

"Stunning room," I said.

"We like it." He smiled.

Still very handsome, if not even more so, Declan had become successful, mainly from his own efforts, which filled me with pride. That was something unusual among wealthy circles, whose offspring's only great challenges often came from juggling a busy social calendar or trying to decide what to wear.

While we had the type of wealth that could allow a large family to enjoy an idle existence, there was something admirable about my children and their drive to contribute to society.

Taking a deep breath, I began, "About the Curtis farm."

"What about it?" Declan's brows gathered. "I'm about to expand Gaia's dairy wing with Paul Curtis in charge of production."

The tightness in my chest produced a sharp pain. "Reynard wants to take over the land."

His frown deepened. "But he can't. It's our land. And over my dead body is it going to that snake."

I knitted my fingers and focused out the window at the turbulent sea, an apt reflection of my emotions.

Declan stared at me. "What the hell has he got over you, Mother? This is crazy."

Theodora entered and, before seeing me there, asked, "What's crazy?" Then she stopped in her tracks, and wearing a surprised smile, my daughter-in-law greeted me with a wave.

He shook his head and rolled his eyes. "That wanker Crisp is at it again. He's trying to grab more land."

Lost to the noise in my head, I didn't hear his wife's response.

The question kept coming up: Should I tell him what really happened that night with Alice?

But then, Declan knew how fond of Alice Harry had been. He might think I orchestrated her death in order to marry his father.

I'd lost too much already. Without my children's love and respect, I would fall apart. Family meant everything to me. It would kill me to become some sad, solitary figure.

Taking a deep breath, I kept my response as brief and manicured as possible. "He introduced me to your father, and in so doing, made me promise to pay him with land."

Declan paced and rubbed his neck. "Then it won't happen. There's no contract. Fuck him off."

"Language," I said, as though he was still a young teenage boy who was already breaking some girl's heart.

Meanwhile, Theodora had remained quiet, which was unlike her. She was always so talkative, and right then, I wouldn't have minded a bit of mindless gossip. I would have done anything to go back a month and have us all sitting around the pool, Cary holding my hand as he always did while the wives chatted about the latest trends.

As silence gripped the air, Theadora turned to me. "Um... I saw Cary the other day."

It took a moment for me to process her comment, then I pivoted sharply to face her. "Oh?"

"It was in London. I ran into him at the college where I'm volunteering. He's teaching there, he told me."

"Where? I mean, how was he?" My heart raced. I wanted to head straight to London in search of him.

But would he want that? He left me, I reminded myself.

"He looked a little drawn."

"What did he say?"

"Not much. I think he wanted to get away quickly. He didn't seem too happy to see me." She chuckled. "I mean, he didn't strike me as happy, and he'd lost a little weight."

My heart cried for the man who had stolen it.

"Why did he leave?" Declan asked.

I puffed. "It's a long, sad story. In a nutshell, he's not who he says he is."

Declan sat next to me on the sofa and took my hand. "I'm sorry, Mum. I could see he meant the world to you."

I gulped back a growing lump in my throat. Using all my inner strength, I held back the tears burning behind my eyes.

"So, who is he, then?" Theadora asked.

I shook my head. "No idea. Rey knows."

"If he can find out, you certainly can," Declan said.

"I know. But, to be honest, if Cary can't find it in his heart to tell me, then it's not really worth it, is it?"

Declan nodded pensively.

I rose. "I best be off."

Declan followed me downstairs. "Crisp's not having the farm, Mother. Is it so bad if everyone learns he introduced you into Dad's world? Or is there something more to it?"

Remaining silent, I walked out the door before my son could press me further.

I knew what I had to do.

I had to go to the police and tell them the whole unfortunate story, if only for my children's future, because Reynard Crisp was like a cancer. He wouldn't stop, and the thought of his criminal activities playing out so close to my grandchildren sliced me in half.

It was either hand myself in to the law or take a darker route, just as Manon had already spoken of.

I texted Theadora, asking for the address of that college.

She sent it back immediately.

THE FOLLOWING DAY, I was in London. It didn't take long to find Cary, who was just leaving the college at around the same time as Theadora had mentioned.

Walking with his eyes on the ground, he didn't notice me waiting at the gate. My pulse pounded. I felt like a teenager about to strike up an awkward conversation with a boy she liked.

What if he tells me to go away?

Squaring my shoulders, I took a deep breath.

Cary glanced upwards and stopped walking, looking shocked at seeing me there. His hesitant gaze held a sense of caution, as though I were someone dangerous.

After a long silence, he said, "Caroline."

I took his hand, which was bonier than I recalled. "Please, can we talk somewhere?"

He looked away, as though staring at me hurt. "I suppose Thea told you?"

I nodded.

He rubbed his jaw, which hadn't seen a razor for a while. "I know I look terrible. In this jacket and these clothes…"

"I don't care how you look. Let's go somewhere private."

He sighed and nodded. Pointing to a park, he asked, "How about we sit there? Or do you want a drink somewhere?"

"No. That's good."

We crossed the road in awkward silence and sat down on a park bench under the canopy of a willow.

After a moment, he spoke. "It's not pretty, Caroline."

"No. Neither is mine."

He turned sharply to study me, holding my gaze as though trying to read more into my words.

"Please, Cary, let me really know you."

He sniffed. "I'm not sure if I really know me, Caroline."

I sighed. "I don't mean in the philosophical sense, or what makes you tick. I have a sense of that man already."

His brow contracted. "Have you?"

"You can't fake intelligence. You can't fake sensitivity. I've known enough people to understand that. I've seen how you were with Bertie."

He sniffed dismissively. "Dogs will always bring out one's gentle side."

"That's not always the case." I thought about Reynard and how I'd seen him kick a dog on more than one occasion. "And how you treated my grandchildren. How you were with me. That type of charade is difficult to uphold."

"None of that was a charade, Carol." He gave me an apologetic smile. "Sorry."

I shook my head. "No. I'm her, all right. More than ever, I am her."

His brow pinched as he studied me. He scratched his shadowed jaw, normally clean-shaven. He looked even more attractive this way. "I've let myself go a little. Please excuse the way I look."

Taking his hand, I smiled. "You look handsome. Beautiful as always, Cary."

He removed his hand from mine gently. "The name's Markus. Markus Reiner. My friends back in Australia called me Mark."

I frowned. "Australia?"

"That's where I was born. My family immigrated from Berlin to Sydney. I left there at twenty-five and moved here."

"But you don't have an accent," I said, totally stumped.

"No. I learned how to curtail it. I was rather pretentious in my college years, a bit of an Anglophile. Detested Australia and its backward ways."

"So, no Oxford?"

He shook his head. "You discovered that, didn't you? I'm surprised you didn't have me profiled."

Taken aback, I was lost for words. A faint smile grew, and after digesting this staggering new detail, I said, "You know, I prefer Markus to Cary."

He sniffed. "You haven't met Markus yet."

"But I have. That's what I'm trying to say. I love you—the man that you are. It's just a name. And while I *am* curious about your life, it still doesn't matter."

His dark eyes drilled into mine as though searching for something. "I'm still married, Caroline."

CHAPTER 21

Markus

I STOOD. "I DON'T know about you, but I need a drink."

Poor Caroline was left with her mouth agape. "Okay. As long as you elaborate on that bewildering revelation."

"Oh, I will. You'll hear the whole shitty story of my former life." I kept my tone dry and emotionless, despite the tsunami of agitation within.

As we walked in silence, I pointed at a pub I'd already visited a few times for a lunchtime ham sandwich and beer. "Will that do? It's not pretty."

"Oh, Cary... I mean, Markus. I'm not that faint-hearted." Her lips quirked into a smirk. "I've seen worst. Which, of course, you know."

Her arched brow drew a rare smile from me in response. For, yes, we'd met in even shadier establishments.

As I fell into her dark, magnetic eyes, I almost forgot why we were there, as though those thirty years prior to our meeting never happened.

If only.

But then, there was also an ironic twist to this tale of deception.

Caroline and I would never have met.

That's what mattered most.

I held the door, and as she passed by, I breathed in her signature fragrance and indulged in memories of her lying in my arms. Nicer times, when it was just us, without that closet of skeletons I'd left behind about to burst open.

After we settled with drinks in hand at a table tucked away in a quiet corner, I gulped down a whisky before starting on my pint. Moderation could wait. I needed all the help I could get.

Thanks to the booze, my chest unknotted a little. I abstractedly watched a man and woman at the bar having a heated argument, which was not unusual for that working-class pub.

I took another gulp of ale and then slowly peeled away more of my mask. "Although I wasn't at Oxford, I completed a Masters in English Lit at Sydney University."

"I don't care about your college days. I'm more interested in learning about this wife of yours." Her eyes were wide and expectant.

I had to smile. Her impatience was justified, especially as the couple at the bar continued to swap abuse for all to hear. "Do you want to go somewhere else?"

She shook her head. "I've heard worse."

I took another slug of my pint and continued. "I met Elise while teaching English Lit."

"You met her at university?" she asked.

I shook my head. "At secondary college. She was in her last year. Eighteen at the time."

"Oh? And you were?"

"Twenty-three. I got my diploma in education before embarking on a masters, which I completed while teaching."

"Okay."

"I skipped a couple of grades as a junior," I added. "Anyway, we didn't get together while I taught, for obvious reasons. But after she graduated, we dated."

I paused. "Elise was a dancer from a wealthy background, and she also wrote poetry. I guess her creative and free-spirited nature dazzled me. Or at least I confused her bipolar disorder, which I wasn't aware of at the time, with her being a fearlessly expressive wild child. Dance was her passion. And she was talented, but she would have blowups with everyone, barely making it through a performance season."

I took another drink before continuing. "Anyway, I married her. We'd been dating for six months, and she threatened to leave me if I didn't tie the knot." Pausing for a moment, I summoned those disturbing episodes in my early adult life. "It soon became apparent that Elise wasn't well. Her mood swings were severe, and she was prone to paranoia. She turned violent towards me. I had to leave, if only for my own safety. She tried to stab me once, and another time, she set our bed alight."

Caroline frowned. "Oh my."

I nodded and sighed, recalling that dramatic night. "The house burned down. I even have the clipping from the newspaper report to prove it."

"You kept that?" She looked surprised.

"I did." I exhaled deeply.

"Did her family have her committed?"

I nodded. "She did a three-month stint at a psychiatric hospital, and after the lithium kicked in, Elise was a changed woman. She metamorphosed from someone unable to sit still, who danced instead of walked, to a sugar addict who spent most of her days slumped on a couch. As a result, Elise stacked on weight, which caused her no end of anxiety. I did my best to support her, but then she stopped her medication, and her former volatility returned. Unable to deal with her combustive temperament, and fearing for my life, I left."

I sipped my pint before continuing. "That proved a drama. Elise called the school where I was teaching and told them I'd raped her, and I lost my job."

"They believed her without further investigation?" Caroline asked.

"They suspended me with no pay while they started investigations, but the principal at the time suggested it would be easier for everyone if I resigned." I toyed with a coaster. "I went back to her because it was easier than her ringing my friends, making character-annihilating accusations about how I'd treated her."

"Her parents?"

"They were very wealthy businesspeople who really didn't have time for her. They'd always neglected her, emotionally speaking. They just saw Elise as my problem. And a problem she was."

"Why didn't you get a divorce?"

"I tried, but she cut her wrists."

"Oh my Lord." She sighed.

"It was a harrowing experience. Her parents blamed me, as did our inner circle. And for a while there, even I felt suicidal. I'd lost my job and was suddenly having to live off Elise, who had a generous stipend. I felt trapped. I took a bar job and saved as much as I could while plotting my escape, since divorce was out of the question."

"Children?"

"Fortunately, none."

"So you changed your identity and came to England?" Her lips formed a tight, sympathetic smile, the type a mother would give her child after he'd endured an injury.

"I arranged a new identity first, purchased a passport, then disappeared, so it looked like I might have drowned while on a fishing trip."

Her head tilted back. "Fishing?"

I had to smile at her surprise. "I used to fish. The sea surrounds Sydney, and I always enjoyed it. My father used to take me when I was a boy. I suppose I associated fishing with an innocent but joyful period of my life growing up by the beach. I was actually a happy child and evolved into someone who dreamed of doing great things with his life. Then Elise happened, and life changed colors."

"But you haven't expressed an interest in fishing at Bridesmere."

"I left Markus behind. Carrington didn't fish."

A faint smile touched her lips. "So, after faking your disappearance, where did you go?"

"I ended up in Asia. My disappearance was in the paper. I saw a publication at a newsstand in Thailand."

"You've got those clippings?"

"It's online in historical newspaper articles. If you wish to check."

"Go on."

"From Thailand, I travelled to the States, and while in New York, I met Lillian. Ten years my senior, she was incredibly bright." I smiled tightly. "I suppose I fell in love with her brain."

Caroline's eyebrows raised. "As a woman?"

I shook my head. "Not as much. But after Elise, I craved stability. And I was also running out of money fast."

"So you hooked onto her for survival?"

I bit into my cheek and nodded.

She nodded. "Is that why you ingratiated yourself to me?"

Despite its predictability, that question still stung.

I took her hand. "At first, maybe on a subconscious level. I knew that, with Lilly unwell, my days in Como were numbered, so to speak."

"She didn't leave you anything?"

"Lilly left me Como, but she was in debt up to her eyeballs, as you now know."

"And you knew that at the time of meeting me?"

I shook my head. "That came as a shock. In fact, I only sold Como so that I could have my own money. Before all of this blew up, I was thinking of applying for a job at a London publishing house."

"You never told me that." She looked hurt.

I shrugged. "I fell into a romantic bubble, I suppose. And life at Merivale was like being in a fairy tale. Unreal but wonderful." I played with her long, slender fingers. "From the moment we met, you dazzled me. Your beauty stole my breath. You must have known that. Men can't fake the voracious desire I felt then. And still do." I sipped my ale pensively.

The telling of that uncomfortable chapter in my life, although exhausting, had helped lift a heavy load. I felt like I'd lanced a festering boil.

Caroline smiled. "And I have a voracious appetite for you too." She arched a dark, perfectly shaped eyebrow.

"That first night, I fell in love." I stared into her eyes. "I asked to be introduced after noticing your lingering gaze."

She frowned. "Was I that obvious?"

"I think we were mutually attracted. You're a very beautiful woman, Caroline." I raised my brows. "And then, once we spoke and I discovered more about you, I became smitten. That's the truth."

Her dark eyes held mine as she digested my words.

Unlike my former identity, I wasn't faking this time. Those words held a deeper truth than any I'd ever expressed.

"So, what do you know of Elise and her life now?" Caroline finally asked.

"Not much. I mean, when you spoke of marriage, I looked up her Facebook page and thought to approach her about getting a divorce, but I just couldn't, for obvious reasons." I gulped down the last of my ale.

"And you will remain married? You don't wish to return and rectify the situation?"

"It's a quagmire." I rubbed my prickly jaw. "If I return, I'll be arrested for faking my disappearance, and then I'll have Elise to deal with."

"She's not with someone else after all these years?"

"I'm not sure. I really haven't investigated. But hopefully now you can understand why I had to leave."

She touched my hand. "You could have told me. I'm not that close-minded. And I know what it is to live a lie."

The serious glint in her gaze triggered my own questions about her past again. I knew Caroline had something dark inside her. Maybe she, too, had visited hell, and with that thought percolating again, my curiosity reignited about this woman who occupied all of me.

"So what now?" she asked. "I can live with all that you've told me."

"Can you?" I frowned. "I can't continue to bullshit though. Now that I've claimed my birth name, I want to be Mark and not Cary."

"I'm happy to have Mark in my life." She held my gaze.

"I'll do whatever you want me to do, Caroline. If you ask me to go back to Sydney and clear my name, I will."

"Even if it involves prison?"

I didn't even waste a breath. "Yes. Because without you in my life, I'm already in prison."

CHAPTER 22

Caroline

AFTER LANGUISHING IN MY own hell, missing the man I'd imagined spending my twilight years with, I allowed my heart to remain open.

I finished my drink and broke the oppressive silence by saying, "I prefer Markus to Carrington."

His brows merged. "As a name?"

My lips curved up in a real smile, which helped ease some of the tension between us. "I meant as a person. I have finally seen you. But I also prefer Markus as a name."

"Now I feel naked." He gestured. "While there you are, staring down at me in your billionaire robes."

"I'm not staring down at you, Cary... I mean, Markus."

"Call me Cary, if you like. You can call me anything. Just being here with you is everything." He wore a sad smile that pulled on my heartstrings.

I went from desiring him to wanting to hold him and stroke him. I loved this man—even more so after hearing his story. Flawed diamonds had always been my preference. I could barely feel my heart pump around perfection, despite my life seeming that way on the surface.

Markus was right. He was naked now, while I still hid behind a world of make-believe.

I took a breath. "I also have a dark past."

He rose, picking up his empty glass. "That's been obvious to me for a while." His dark eyes drilled into mine, reaching for my soul, only it was already mortgaged to Crisp.

Touching his hand, I asked, "Can we go somewhere?" My eyebrow rise said it all. He understood me better than most, especially my inflamed needs that had only grown since meeting him.

"If you like." He returned a bemused half smile as though challenged by a tough decision.

"You don't want to?"

He released a stuttering breath. "Oh, I want to. But I don't have a very nice place."

"I really don't mind," I said, dying to know where he'd been staying.

He looked embarrassed. "It's a tiny bedsit. And my landlady's chatty."

"Oh? Is she pretty?"

He rested his hand in the middle of my back as we stepped outside.

"Audrey's not that kind of woman. She's more like someone's sweet, caring aunt." He smiled and looked so ruggedly handsome that I wanted him to make love to me until it hurt.

My vibrator had proved a frustrating and inadequate replacement for him. It didn't hold me while I returned to earth after a climax that had me climbing to stratospheric heights. Nor did my vibrator kiss me, unleashing electrical impulses all over my body and flooding me with urgent desire.

I tilted my face to his. "Do you have privacy?"

He chuckled. "Why? What did you have in mind?"

"Anything that involves you being naked."

He crushed me against his tall, firm body. "As long as you let me see what's under that pretty blouse."

I laughed for the first time in weeks. "My car's parked over there."

We jumped into my Mercedes and drove only a little way up the road before arriving at a two-story red-brick terrace.

Young people, big and small, crowded the street, kicking balls, scrolling on their phones, or poking each other. It was a noisy rabble of life, stirring memories of my upbringing. I'd grown up on a very similar street.

A gang of older teenagers, dressed in hoodies and sloppy gym-wear, all turned when I pulled up, their attention riveted on my car.

"I think you might want to park somewhere else, Caroline. This is a drug beat."

"Oh? I don't care. If they take it, then so be it."

"Really? But how will you get back to Merivale?"

I laughed. "We have a fleet of cars. There are always drivers around. I'm not worried."

We stepped out of the car to a fanfare of whistles. In response, Markus gave them a wave.

"You know them?" I asked, trying not to sound judgmental.

"Not to talk to, but I see them here all the time, and smiling seems to rattle them." He chuckled. "They're probably used to cheek and the middle finger."

"That's one way to deal with a potential threat, I suppose."

"They're not a threat, Caroline. We are."

I rolled my eyes at his socialist comment. Politically, we were on opposite sides of the divide, and it made our debates rather stimulating and, at times, a little heated, which was followed by passionate sex. When it came to conversation, a rebellious mind was far more stimulating than that of a conservative, despite identifying as one myself.

That woman of substance I'd meticulously shaped had turned into a woman of contradictions. This was never more evident than at that moment as I stared at the weathered postwar home where he was staying.

"I don't have my own entrance, I'm afraid." He looked apologetic. "We can go somewhere else. Like your hotel?"

"No. I'd like to see where you've been living."

"It's not pretty."

"I can just admire your handsome face instead," I said.

He half-smiled and opened the door for me.

Audrey was there to greet us with a kindly face that lit up in surprise on seeing me. I imagined I looked a little odd to her in my designer sheath and high heels.

"Oh, you've brought a guest," she said, looking from Markus to me.

"This is Caroline." He gestured. "Caroline, meet Audrey."

Audrey's mouth fell open. "Oh my. You're Caroline Lovechilde. I read about you in Hello."

That tacky article. It had come back to haunt me.

"Really? I never saw that." Markus grinned in a way that showed the real man—Cary would never have poked fun, but Markus knew how much I hated those shallow magazines.

I held out my hand to Audrey, who, for some strange reason, was curtsying.

Markus nodded. "We're just going up for a while."

She curtsied again, and Markus's eyes shone with amusement, which nearly made me laugh.

Pointing at a set of stairs, he fluttered his arm and whispered, "After you, your highness."

He let me into his room, which was almost the size of a Merivale cupboard. At least the tiny balcony facing a yard filled with vegetables and herbs made it seem less claustrophobic.

"Tea?" He stepped into an adjoining room with a small table and a kettle. "Sorry, I wasn't expecting anyone. You're the first person who's ever been here." He held up a bottle of whisky. "It's rough." An apologetic half smile dimpled his cheek.

He sat the bottle down and stepped towards me. As we fell into each other's arms, we kissed like it was our first time. His soft, fleshy lips massaged my mouth, exploring every inch. The heat between us intensified. He nuzzled me against the wall, and I surrendered myself to him.

"Is there anything I can do for you?" he asked, pulling away.

"Yes, I want to feel your big cock inside me." I unzipped his pants and reached into his briefs, wrapping my hand around his thick shaft, which lengthened in my palm.

He pushed away my hand. "I won't last." His eyes hooded as he removed my clothes with such speed a few buttons popped.

He waltzed me to the unmade bed and pushed me gently onto it, parting my legs. He hooked his fingers into my damp lace panties.

Our mouths met in a crush of passion as his fingers explored my drenched vagina.

"I've missed you like mad." He sounded breathless.

He lowered his head between my thighs and did things with his tongue I'd never experienced from any man before. I came violently, but he kept a hold of me, as though he wanted to torment me with more orgasms.

As I shuddered and moaned, he lapped up each release like a starving person might a meal until I surrendered to a climax that nearly made me draw blood from my lip.

Then he roughly spread my legs.

"Fuck me hard," I murmured.

As he entered me, filling me to the bursting point, I groaned from the intense pleasurable stretch that ached all the way to my toes.

"Fuck, you feel nice." His teeth were on my neck, gently nipping as he kept fondling my breasts. "We might need to go a little slower."

"No. Hard. I need to feel all of you."

His stubble prickled my cheek. As our hot, sticky bodies melded, I breathed him in. He smelled of the cologne I'd gifted him and sex—a smell that affected my pheromones like the siren's song did sailors.

Escalating thrusts intensified as pain turned into pleasure. The friction sent waves of heat rippling through my body, as though his cock was a throbbing mass of electrical impulses.

I clutched onto his toned ass, pulling him deep inside as each thrust sent me closer to the edge. His ragged breath dampened my neck, and my breasts pressed against his firm, masculine chest.

"I need you to come, like, now," he murmured, as though in agony.

Tormented by pleasure, I unclenched my muscles, and in his arms, I lost myself.

Clutching onto me tightly, he growled and grunted, gushing an almost endless stream of seed while I shook through one orgasm after another.

We fell on our backs in the bed, and there we lay for quite a while. Waiting for my senses to return, I stared up at the ceiling and its network of cracks, wondering if we'd just added to them with our thunderous lovemaking.

"I hope Audrey didn't hear that," I said with a laugh. "She might not curtsy next time."

He chuckled. "From royalty to fallen woman. How scandalous."

After holding each other for a while, we made love again, slow and tender this time.

"Making up for lost time." He chuckled as I placed my head on his chest, his racing heart massaging my ear.

Later, Markus rose and fixed us a drink that wasn't easy to swallow, after which I picked up my clothes.

"I'm afraid the shower is unattached. It's down the hallway." He pulled a face. "Sorry."

I shook my head. "It's all fine. Really." I gave him a reassuring smile. Once dressed, I fixed myself up before the mirror. "You can't stay here."

Sitting on the bed wearing only a towel, he didn't respond.

"You want to stay?" I asked. "Merivale's your home. Our home."

He frowned. "You want me to return?"

"Well, yes. I want you to." I fixed my hair with my hands.

"But I can't marry you. Can I?" His mouth twitched into a mock smile. "And then there's the question of my name. I want to be Mark. I want to reclaim my true identity. Opening up to you has lifted an immense weight off me."

"My family's very understanding."

"But won't they view me as spineless? Someone who ran away in the face of adversity? It's not how I want to be seen."

I nodded slowly. No one understood that better than me. We shared that need, only I was even weaker because I'd purposely thrown away the key to my Pandora's box.

Markus buttoned up his shirt, slipped on his trousers, and stood before the mirror to smooth down his hair. Even in plain clothes, he boasted more sophistication than all the men in my privileged world put together.

"Then stay at Mayfair. It's empty, and we can find a way. My family's open-minded."

"I'll stay here for now. I want to keep working, save some money, and then return to Australia to clear my name."

"But I can't lose you again." Tears pooled in my eyes.

"We can meet here," he said, stroking my cheek.

"No. The sheets are awful. The faucets are rusty. I can't."

"You weren't thinking that when we met at Whitechapel." He gave me one of those complicated stares, the kind he wore when I dragged him into one of my seedy fantasies.

A bitter taste gathered in my mouth, not only from self-loathing, but from rising tension at the thought of not getting my way. "I need you close. I want to share meals and watch movies and have you around, reading and talking about books. And our walks. What about our walks?"

I paced about like someone who'd found something precious and was about to lose it. "What will it take for you to come with me? To Mayfair, at least. I can understand your misgivings about Merivale."

My phone sounded, and while I wanted to ignore it, I peered down and discovered that Reynard was calling.

I shook my head and fell onto the sofa, sobbing.

Markus placed his arm around me. "There's something else going on, isn't there?" he asked, pulling away to look at me.

I leaned into his warm body, if only to hide my tear-stained face.

"That's also a problem," he continued. "I'm naked, while you're wearing someone else's clothes."

I stared up at him. "Why would you say that?"

"Because you're hiding something. And there's Crisp. What's his hold on you? How can you expect me to be totally invested in this relationship if you can't confide in me?"

CHAPTER 23

Markus

HER USUALLY SHIELDED, DARK eyes were drowned in tears. Such raw emotion, that of someone adrift in despair, made her appear like a stranger and not the self-assured, guarded woman I'd fallen in love with.

Not that I was turned off. Quite to the contrary, her vulnerability drew me in deeper, intensifying our connection. I wanted to become her anchor. Offer unwavering support.

"I'm here for you, Caroline. I don't care what you've done, you have to know that. But you must let me in. Completely."

She wiped her eyes and smiled sadly. "You really have turned into another man."

"No. You're just seeing the real me. Away from the fancy jackets and jaw-dropping adornments that surround your life, I am here before you in this shabby bedsit. The real man. The only man that I can be."

"How about a cup of tea?" she asked, in a tone of surrender.

"Of course, with pleasure. I even have some fresh cake." I smiled.

"No. Tea is fine. Maybe a drop of that whisky."

"Coming right up, ma'am."

"Hey." Her brow creased. "We're equals."

"Just playing, Carol."

I held her eyes. I knew she had something against that diminutive, but this time, I was standing my ground.

As I made the tea, I noticed Caroline readjusting her position. "Sorry about the poking springs on that couch."

Her eyes followed me as I stirred the sugar in her cup.

"If I tell you, will you move to Mayfair? Or let me buy you an apartment, something more to your liking?" She sounded tentative, like me taking her money would be a favor. I almost laughed at how ridiculous that seemed. Anyone would jump at that offer, and here she was, walking on eggshells so as not to offend me.

"I'll agree to Mayfair. But I am still returning to Australia to face Elise and my past."

She nodded pensively. "You will allow me to hire you the best legal team?"

I took her hand and kissed it. "If I must go to prison, then I will. You probably won't like me after that."

"I'd love you if you were digging trenches, Mark."

I smiled. "It's nice hearing you call me by my real name."

"It suits you." She stroked my face, and I lowered my cheek to meet her soft hand.

Then she rose.

"Where are you going?"

"I'm not sure if I can do this here," she said, looking suddenly disturbed.

"And the cup of tea?"

She fell down onto the sofa and buried her head in her hands.

I knelt beside her and spoke softly. "I'm sorry if I'm being too challenging, Caroline."

"You're not. It's everything else." She huffed. "Oh, I've made a mess of things. Like you, I've been running for over thirty years, and I'm tired."

I joined her on the sofa, drew her close, and waited for her body to soften in my arms. With a start, I realized it was early evening. "Why don't we go somewhere for dinner?"

"Let's go to Mayfair, then. Just for the night. I will have a driver drop you off at work tomorrow."

Caroline's pleading smile was impossible to deny.

"Okay. But only if after dinner, you tell me everything. Yes?"

She exhaled a faltering breath and nodded warily.

I kissed her on the cheek. "There's nothing to worry about, Caroline. Nothing you do or say is going to make me stop loving you."

She smiled gently and kissed me on the lips. "Thanks."

"For what?" I had to ask.

"For letting me in."

We remained on that lumpy couch for a while longer, hands entwined, basking in the warmth of each other.

THE SUCCULENT STEAK MELTED in my mouth, and I savored it as someone eating their first meal in a week might. I'd forgotten what tender steak and quality cuisine tasted like, and it was made more enjoyable by the opulence of Mayfair and that crimson-walled dining room housing marble statues fit for a Roman museum.

As I gazed up at a Gainsborough painting of a woman who might have stepped out of a Jane Austen novel, I was reminded of the fineries and aesthetics a wealthy life provided. A lifestyle that, despite embracing it with open arms, had weakened me before, much like it was at that moment, because my determination to return to Audrey's damp bedsit diminished with each juicy bite.

After dinner, we convened to the salon, and Caroline became fidgety.

"What's up?" I asked. "You hardly ate, and that last call to Declan left you pale."

She ran through Crisp's latest demands, concluding, "Elysium, I can almost do without, but that land is substantial. It's my grandchildren's future." She released a tight breath and began pacing.

"Take Declan's advice and tell Crisp to go fuck himself."

Her eyes settled on my face. Knowing how much she hated coarse language, I returned a sheepish grin. "Sorry."

She shook her head. "That's exactly what I'd love to do. But you don't know Rey."

She poured us a drink and passed me a glass. I took an appreciative sip of that smooth, quality liquor, another fine reminder of life in the privileged lane.

"But I do know Crisp," I countered. "He's evil. One only has to look at his snaky eyes."

Seeming lost in thought, Caroline nodded.

I patted the sofa cushion. "Sit here, and I can massage your shoulders."

Her frown ironed out, and a faint smile formed. I did a sweep of that charming room and the sheer beauty surrounding me. A book about Ancient Greece sat on the coffee table, and I envisioned myself enjoying a fine single malt with that book on my lap.

It wouldn't be easy returning to Australia. I could just continue to be Carrington Lovelace and none would be the wiser, other than Caroline and Crisp. But something inside me yearned to be released. Despite the unshifting gloom that had shadowed me those past weeks, I'd also appreciated the lightness of not having to pretend.

Too keyed up for a massage, Caroline began to pace again, and this time, I waited for her to speak.

After wringing her hands while staring out the window into the moonlit night, Caroline finally turned to face me. "I killed someone."

She spoke so softly I wasn't sure if I'd heard right.

"What was that?" I asked.

"I killed someone." She looked haunted. It was a new face. Not Caroline Lovechilde, but someone else.

"When? I mean..." A mountain of questions rendered me speechless.

"I wasn't quite twenty when it happened. It was an accident. A fucking accident." She stared down at her hands. "She was meant to marry Harry."

CHAPTER 24

Caroline

I RECOUNTED TO MARK the story of the night that changed my life forever.

He frowned. "But that was just an unfortunate accident. It wasn't deliberate or premeditated in any way."

"I know." I sighed. "I was so overcome with emotion that I couldn't think straight. As I went in search of a phone, Crisp stopped me and told me he'd see to it. He then explained that no one would believe me, that I'd be convicted, that my future would be ruined."

"Was she dead?" he asked.

"Reynard told me she'd died on the spot."

"But don't you see? That's his word. For all you know, she could have been alive."

I nodded slowly. "I have thought of little else since that night. I was complicit, Mark. So I did kill her."

"From all that you've said, and knowing Crisp as I do, you can't rely on his word, darling."

I looked up at him upon hearing that endearment, and a warm blast of sunshine massaged my shivering spirit, a momentary break from troubling questions about Alice's death that wouldn't stop plaguing me. If I'd called the police, she might still be alive, because Mark was right—no one could believe Reynard Crisp.

By listening to Rey without considering the repercussions, I'd not only been handed a key to paradise but also nightly visits to hell.

"Do you hate me now?" I asked in a thin, pathetic voice.

He shook his head resolutely. "Oh no, I don't hate you. I think I love you more."

I searched his eyes. "Why?"

"Because I understand what it feels like to make decisions on the run, when your heart is pounding so loudly you can't hear yourself think. And you were young, Caroline. Crisp's the culprit here. He took advantage of your situation."

"Yes, well, Reynard took advantage of my desperation by luring me into his wealthy circle." I stopped myself there. I couldn't bring myself to tell Mark about all those rich clients and how Reynard Crisp had also become my pimp.

"You didn't intentionally murder her. That's the point. It was an accident. And I probably would have done the same thing."

"Like allow someone to clean up your mess?"

He shrugged. "Probably. At that age, we're a bundle of nerves. Often at the expense of good sense and judgement. More invested in hearing about the next party than working on some kind of twenty-year plan."

"I thought about my future as early as eighteen," I admitted, thinking of how I'd made that pact with myself never to face hunger or depraved men again. "That's why I cozied up to Harry Lovechilde."

He flinched, which made me curious.

"Does that strike you as immoral? The Pontings were certainly unimpressed when our marriage was announced."

"That I can understand." He rolled his lips as he studied me. "Did you love him?"

I nodded. "Not in the true, passionate sense. Not like how I feel about you. He didn't make my heart skip a beat like it does around you."

He smiled shyly. "I felt a little weak at the knees that first night I laid eyes on you."

"And you don't anymore?" I tilted my head, welcoming the distraction.

"I missed you like mad. Now, with you here close, I feel like I'm sitting by a warm fire after being caught in a storm out in the cold."

"But not passion?" I asked.

"I would have thought that was patently obvious." He cocked his head slightly, looking so boyish that I wanted to undress and fuck him right there on the sofa. "I love being inside you, Caroline."

Simmering desire gave me a much-needed respite as blood traveled through my veins again.

"Have you seen the forensic report?" he asked, snapping me out of that romantic interlude.

"No. Not for lack of trying." I sighed. Drake had informed me that Billy withdrew his efforts due to fear of being caught.

"Lawyers are privy to police reports, I believe," he said. "As are the family."

"Showing any kind of interest would be self-incriminating."

"True. But maybe you could talk to someone who knows her family. I take it they're still alive. It's an easier option than breaking into police systems. Now, that would be dangerous."

"You make good sense. The horror of reliving that night has clouded my judgement."

"That's understandable." Mark squeezed my hand gently.

"I have to tread carefully, since the Pontings view me as persona non grata. They're convinced I did it. That's why the police keep circling me."

I sat down on the couch and turned to Mark. "So now you know why Rey has been extorting me these years. Why he owns me."

His warm hand landed on mine. "Then we'll have to make him dispossess you, won't we?"

Frowning, I scrutinized him. "I can't resort to that, Mark. I have thought about it often enough. He loves his mushrooms."

"There, that would work for sure. None would be the wiser."

"No. The police would come crawling around. And knowing Reynard, he's probably got some hidden dossier ready to expose me should something happen."

"Then hire a professional." He looked serious.

"That's already been suggested. But there's already a stain against my name, after what happened to Harry and how the man I was having an affair with plotted his murder. I can't be involved, Mark."

He shook his head as a faint smirk grew. "You're lucky I'm a lazy, unambitious writer, because the Lovechilde Saga would make for a great story."

I contracted my brow. "You wouldn't dare."

"Don't worry, Caroline." He chuckled. "I'm still stuck in the annals of Charles II. He's an equally fascinating subject."

"That's because he was a reprobate."

"Quite so. No one wants to read about celibate fops."

I laughed. I needed this.

"So Crisp used you as his way into the Lovechilde coffers." Mark shook his head. "What a sly old prick."

"And a sleazy one, at that," I murmured.

His brow pinched. "He forced you?"

I wasn't about to admit that I once carried a torch for that deplorable man. "No. I was too old and too experienced."

He looked puzzled. "Huh?"

"He likes them young and virginal."

"Oh yes, you spoke about that vulgar venue."

Mark rose and lifted the bottle. I nodded. It was hardly the time to go easy on alcohol, and this session with the man I was determined to make mine forever had helped me beyond belief.

He handed me the glass.

"Thank you, Mark."

"You're welcome." He smiled charmingly.

"No, I mean... thank you."

He stroked my cheek. "No, I should be the one thanking you for finding me. You're far more courageous than me. I would have wallowed in self-pity while listening to Audrey talk about how her only daughter prefers the company of bad men."

I sniffed. "Does that mean you'll stay here?"

"I'd be a dumbass, as our good friends the Americans would put it, to refuse."

My world brightened anew. "We can work this out. You don't need to go to Australia. I'd hate to lose you. Or, at least, let me get the best legal team available."

"We'll see." He gulped his drink, and his mood darkened a little. "Haven't you got any dirt on Crisp? I mean, his predilection for young girls seems to suggest something untoward."

As I held his gaze, I recalled a comment made by Helmut the night I met Gregory for the first time. "I recall hearing that Rey had a thing for his stepsister. That he slept with her when she was thirteen, and that at sixteen, she disappeared."

Mark opened his hands. "There it is. Find this stepsister, and you've got your bargaining chip, so to speak."

I nodded slowly. "I can't even recall her name."

"Use a PI."

I nodded. "Only... Reynard Crisp isn't his real name."

He laughed. "Reynard Crisp. Why does that not surprise me? It seems I'm not the only one good at cooking up B-grade character names."

"Huh?" I asked.

"Oh, it's an insult Crisp tossed at me that night I punched him on the nose." He laughed. "Reynard Crisp is the title I'd give a sly cad, were I ever to write an airport thriller."

I had to laugh at that.

"You know, you really have a trump card there, Caroline. Find the sister, and you could be free."

"Brilliant idea." I kissed him. "You've given me something. I don't know why it never occurred to me."

"Sometimes an objective listener is all it takes." He gave me one of his long, perplexing gazes. "So, who is Carol?"

It had been almost too easy to expose my primary debilitating secret, but the thought of talking about my life before Rey, and the birth of Caroline, turned me to ice.

"Can't we leave it at that? Isn't that enough?" I asked.

"Of course. It's been intense. But I would like to know, one day soon, because there are still some questions."

"Some other time." I stroked his handsome face. His shadowed jaw made him even more desirable as I recalled how it had scraped gently on my thighs.

In sharing our secrets, we'd grown even closer, and I wanted this man more than my next breath. "For now, I want you to fuck me." I unbuttoned my blouse and stroked his growing cock with my other hand.

Yes, Markus was right—one couldn't fake desire.

CHAPTER 25

Mark

AFTER A NIGHT OF passionate lovemaking, I slept in, and as a result, I jumped out of bed when I woke.

"But you can't just hurry off. We haven't had breakfast," Caroline protested. "Why don't you leave this job and let me employ you?"

I paused while gathering my clothes. "You're kidding, aren't you?"

"I'm sure I can find something enjoyable for you to do." Her smile faded. "Please accept my money. I've got so much of it. I can afford to support you. Why should you put yourself through this?"

I rubbed at my thickening stubble. "I'm sorry if I scratched you with my beard."

Caroline sat up in bed, naked, her full breasts inviting my dick to unwind again. This woman had me constantly in the thrall of lust.

She flinched. "Don't tease."

I laughed. "How am I teasing?"

"By bringing up cunnilingus."

I had to smile. The contrast between this woman's well-honed public persona and her private one was immense. "I like my new job, by the way." I dressed as quickly as I could, wincing while putting on my briefs.

"You're not going to shower?" she asked, staring straight at my erection, and—whether unconsciously or not—brushing her tongue over her lips in a way guaranteed to provoke me.

"I'm running late, Caroline."

"Then let Jason drive you."

"That might be helpful." I lay down my clothes on the armchair. "I'll take that shower then."

She followed me into the turquoise bathroom with its heated floor tiles, sunken bath, and shower large enough to accommodate four people.

"Caroline, really, I need to hurry," I said, doing my utmost to avoid her curves. Caroline had a better body than women half her age.

She laughed. "What do you think I will do to you?"

"Well, swallow me whole." I raised an eyebrow. "Which I love, of course."

I turned on the faucet, and not just one jet but four gushed out water. "After Audrey's trickling shower, this is like the Rhine Falls."

She chuckled as she stepped into the large cubicle. "Can't you be sick for a day? I can write you a note."

I shook my head. "I meant it when I said I love my job."

"Why?" She scrutinized me with that prying, unblinking stare of hers. "Are there pretty young pupils with crushes on you?"

"Not that I'm aware of, and I'm not interested, anyway." I ran my hands over her curves. "They're not you."

Her eyes softened, and I took her into my arms and kissed her.

"You're not so easily replaceable, Caroline." I stroked her cheek. "I'm going to school, so now stop distracting me, you wanton woman."

Five minutes later, I stepped out of the shower, and Caroline handed me a warm towel from the heated rack.

Yes, billionaire luxury was hard to resist.

I'D FORGOTTEN HOW MUCH I loved interacting with interested and engaged mature students who were in my class purely because they loved books. I couldn't think of a better way to spend my time than dissecting masterful storytelling, effortless passages, and discussing famous characters as though they were living, breathing entities.

But I had a big decision to make that required some time alone. Tempting as moving into Mayfair was, I had to think about the future, and there were two people both Caroline and I needed to remove from the path to our forever after.

I could no longer drift around and revert to my former pampered lifestyle. Despite laughing off Caroline's offer to employ me, a profound rumbling of dissent swept through me.

I was no longer that man.

Maybe Carrington Lovelace could be that foppish yes-man, but not Markus Reiner. He was tougher than that. A man who made his own way. I wanted to be with Caroline, but on my terms, for a change.

Unsettled by the prospect of Caroline's family seeing me without my mask, I needed time to prepare myself. Had the situation been reversed, I would have been livid, especially given the way they'd accepted me into their inner sanctum. The inevitable tension alone would make family gatherings untenable. I wasn't quite ready for that. My life was complicated enough for now.

As Audrey opened the door, something she often did while I rummaged for my keys in my book-laden satchel, I contemplated my next move. Instead of choosing to bury my head in a book, I needed to make some radical changes.

It wouldn't be as simple as Caroline might have thought. And away from her, I could think a little more rationally.

CHAPTER 26

Caroline

As a function was being held at our hotel in London, I had to attend and mingle among familiar and non-familiar guests, despite it being the last thing I desired. However, I needed to support Ethan, who was about to open a new Lovechildes in Los Angeles.

I hadn't seen Marcus for three days, and my prickly mood reflected that. This attachment to him overwhelmed me, and while his reluctance to catch up with the family while wearing the guise of Cary was understandable, I still pined for him. Unaccustomed to not getting my way, I'd lost myself to this man, something I'd promised myself never to do.

We'd spoken, but his obstinacy regarding sleeping arrangements had almost sparked an argument. However, as he kept reminding me, with time and a little patience, we could make this work.

His wife in Australia had piqued my curiosity, so I had her investigated to learn more about her, something I'd kept to myself.

Ethan kissed my cheeks. "Mother."

I smiled at Mirabel, who held Cian's and Ruby's little hands. My grandchildren were so beautiful that all my worries melted away at that moment.

As the night progressed, I found myself cornered by the CEO of the new LA hotel. I forced a smile as he gushed on about how Hollywood A-listers would simply adore the classic luxury of the Lovechilde brand.

"But don't they already live in LA?" I asked.

"Not Daniel and Rachel, or Idris, or George and Amal, and besides, British actors are the flavor of the month in Hollywood."

"Haven't they always been?" All my favorite actors were Brits. But I kept that to myself and before he could rebut that nationalistic comment, I excused myself.

Mirabel, who'd been standing within earshot, followed me to the powder room. "He spoke like he knew them."

"Oh, he's just trying to impress us," I said as we stepped into the rose-scented room.

Mirabel stood at the mirror and leaned in to fix her makeup. "They have invited Cian to perform with the King's Orchestra. They have a junior section, apparently."

"Oh?" I smiled like a proud parent of a genius might. "But that's marvelous."

She nodded, mirroring my delight, her eyes beaming with anticipation. "I couldn't be happier. He's also showing an interest in jazz."

"Oh no." I pulled a face.

"You don't like jazz?"

"I'm a fan of jazz classics. But being a jazz musician? Isn't that synonymous with a drug-taking bohemian lifestyle?"

"He's only eight, Caroline."

I exhaled. "And so he is. I just love the thought of having Debussy or Bach performed at our family gatherings. And he's so talented."

"Yes. Perfect pitch, apparently." She smiled.

"That's a rare talent, I'm told."

"I've got perfect pitch as well," she said, as mildly as one would admit to having good teeth. Only perfect pitch was as impressive as possessing a high IQ. For a musician, at least.

I studied Mirabel. She had flowers in her hair and wore a green gown with pink roses, which shouldn't have worked, but she always wore her clothes well.

"I didn't know that." I looked into her beautiful face and regretted the way I'd once shunned this woman. "Then you passed it on to him."

"I must have, given that his father's tone-deaf." She laughed.

I had to smile. "Ethan has many talents, but music isn't one of them."

She nodded. "Cary's not here, I see."

"No. He's busy." Hoping there would be no further questions, I kept it short and sweet.

"I liked him."

"He's still around, Mirabel." I gave her a curt smile before walking away, as the black caviar I'd just eaten churned in my gut.

Theadora was surrounded by children, and as I passed her, she waved.

"You're the nanny, I see," I said.

"Something like that." She chuckled. "I can't really imagine this being in LA." She gestured at the sumptuous burgundy room adorned with crystal chandeliers and antiques.

Declan joined us. "Nor can I." He took his wife's hand.

"So is Cary coming?" Theadora asked.

"He's busy." I tried to remain blank-faced.

Declan's eyes shone with a hint of concern. With his typical razor-sharp perception, he must have noticed me shifting my weight from one leg to another.

As we watched Theadora take the children to the playroom, he asked, "Are you at least talking?"

"We're back together. It's just become a little complicated."

He sniffed. "Isn't it always?"

"We always manage, don't we?" I smiled tightly.

"Maybe, but what are we to do about Crisp's latest demands?"

Ethan arrived just as Declan finished that sentence. "I heard about that. Him vying for Elysium and the adjacent land." His face soured. "What the hell, Mother?"

I rolled my eyes. "I'm working on it."

"How?" Ethan spread his hands. "Savanah's gutted."

My daughter joined us. "Yes, I am," she said.

This family of mine had a good knack of arriving at key points in conversations, fitting together like a Scrabble game—perfectly timed and pressing for detail that would make even the most seasoned politician stutter.

I regarded my daughter coolly. "Suffice it to say, I'm working on it."

I kept to myself that I was trying to find the courage to hand myself in to the police.

Or find a way to get rid of Reynard.

The latter wasn't something I found easy to contemplate, because the thought of organizing anyone's demise had turned my already light sleeping patterns into insomnia.

No, surrendering myself to the law was the only way. And in so doing, I would take Crisp down with me—the only sweet spot in an otherwise grim, once inconceivable, option.

Had I not been a mother, maybe I could have lived with this Faustian curse hanging over me.

"Where's Carson?" I asked, steering the conversation elsewhere.

"He's over there, talking about gaining a security contract for the new hotel in LA." Savanah turned to Ethan. "So, you have finally realized your dream of a Lovechildes in LA. I can't wait."

Ethan glowed with pride.

Yes, he'd done well. All my children had. Despite their teenage excesses, they'd found their places in the world and had made me proud.

A FEW DAYS AFTER ordering the investigation of Mark's Australian wife, I received a report on Elise Whitely.

The dossier contained images of a young, beautiful girl with dark eyes and long brown hair. She looked a bit like I had at her age, unsurprising, given that people were often attracted to a certain type.

Harry was nothing like Mark, of course. But I married Harry for reasons other than passion, a motivation that aligned me with most women. Survival often made us choose practicality over passion. That was the beauty of wealth. One could be free to love whom they wished. Only it wasn't so easy when the type of men who made my heart pound with desire tended to come with a bevy of complexities.

As I read about Elise, I discovered Mark had been telling the truth about her battle with mental illness. I flicked through the file, pausing at a photo of Mark in his twenties, articles relating to his disappearance, and police investigations.

At fifty, Elise looked nothing of her former self. She'd let herself go and wore a blank, almost remote expression. A pang of sympathy touched me as I studied her image.

How would Mark navigate this?

I'd spoken to my lawyer by illustrating a hypothetical situation. I suspected he knew I was talking about Mark, however, since the family solicitor had suggested drafting a prenup during those heady days of our engagement.

He advised that there were two possibilities: either the abandoned wife could sue for emotional damage or, despite there being no actual law broken, the authorities could come down on him for time wasted investigating his disappearance.

That same afternoon, Mark joined me at Mayfair. After a day of teaching, he looked tired, and I quickly fixed him a drink.

"Why won't you stay?" I implored.

"Audrey needs the company," he said with a cheeky grin.

"Oh, Mark, please," I said, pacing again. This man had me doing a lot of that lately. "In any case, you do realize it's not illegal to fake your death under Australian law?"

He gave me one of his long, perplexed stares. "Who have you told?" His abrasive tone made me wince.

"No one. But I made my own enquiries, and no names were mentioned. I just want us to be together." I hated how weak I sounded.

"I want that too." He gulped down his whisky. "You know everything about me, but I know so little about you."

He stared at the blond wig on the chair as though making a point.

I regretted leaving it out, but with so many scattered thoughts tugging at neurons, I'd become careless.

"Like this, for instance." He picked up the wig, which I removed from his grip and tucked away.

"You never complained," I said.

"It's twisted, though, wouldn't you say?" His steely stare showed me yet another new face. "I need to know why."

I knitted my fingers as I gazed out the window. How could I explain something that I didn't understand myself? "We don't have to do it again."

"Have you seen someone about it?"

My face contorted. "I'm not unwell, Mark. It's just kinky role-playing—to which you responded enthusiastically, I might add."

"Everything about you turns me on, Caroline. It's not a question of arousal. I'm just trying to understand. You now see me for who I really am, but you're still a total mystery to me. And while I was wearing a mask, I had no right to ask you to remove yours, but now it feels a little unequal between us."

I sat on my bed, kicked off my shoes, and massaged my toes, my mind wandering to something as trivial as needing a pedicure.

"You promised to talk about your life before Reynard Crisp." His tone softened as he sat next to me on the bed and placed his arm around me. "I can continue to play these games. You can wear your wigs and make me pretend to force you or whatever erotic scenario makes you hot." He paused. "But I guess I'd like to know when this first started. And I know nothing about your life growing up."

A breath whooshed out of my mouth. "When this first started? Oh Mark, please, let's not turn this into psychoanalysis."

He rose from the bed, poured us another drink, and passed me the glass. "I'm not trying to get into your head. I would just like to know about your life before all of this." He pointed at the Monet on the wall. "For instance, who were your parents?"

I sipped solemnly on my drink.

My hands trembled. The only time I'd revisited my childhood was after Bethany exposed her true identity, forcing me to explain her existence to my children. The anxiety from that day and the shock on my children's faces when they learned how their half sister was conceived still sat deep in my core. Now and then, I felt a sharp pain from it, like a wound that would flare up with the weather.

Finally, I said, "I don't know my proper parents. I never have. I tried looking for them a while back, but I recently gave up. Other things, namely you and your fake identity, have distracted me, and now Crisp coming for his payment."

"His payment?"

"My Mephistophelean dues."

"Oh yes." His mouth raised at one end. "That won't happen. I'll see to it."

My brows contracted. "Mark, please. Stay away. He's too powerful and dangerous. I can't lose you."

"I know how to protect myself." He remained serious. "You were saying? About searching for your parents?"

From one ugly subject to another. I released a tight breath. "My foster mother didn't know their identities. I kept asking, but to no avail. The agency wouldn't divulge as they were sworn to secrecy. I tried investigators, even had them poring over the hospital records from around the period of my birth."

"So you knew they weren't your real parents, then?"

"I discovered that at around fifteen or so." It came flashing past me like a horror movie, the day that woman I thought was my mother told me we weren't related by blood. She'd said so after her husband raped me, as though that information somehow made things better.

"Maybe sometimes there are certain things that are meant to remain unknown."

"I've told myself often enough." I sniffed. "But at times—like now, since we've brought it up—the thought of not knowing haunts me. They must have been terrible people. Otherwise, why would they hide?"

"They may not be alive. Your mother could have been so young she wasn't able to cope. You possess an intelligent mind, enviable drive, and a fabulous family who love and rally around you."

I nodded slowly. "That family is why I guard everything so close here." I tapped my chest. "But that doesn't stop me from wondering about my predecessors."

He nodded sympathetically.

"Perhaps on a deeper level, I'm frightened of what I might find. What sort of parents, or parent, give up their children?" I rolled my eyes at that obvious hypocrisy. "Because what's even more ironic and somewhat tragic is that I gave Bethany away." I brushed my red fingernails. "That went well. Look at how she ended up."

"You can't blame yourself for her personality. It's a little of nature and nurture combined."

"Nature, for sure," I muttered under my breath, since there were aspects of Bethany that always reminded me of her father. One of several reasons I found it difficult to remain in her company for long.

Mark must have read my thoughts, and his brow lowered. "Oh? The father?"

"Do you really want to know?" I asked.

"Well, we've gotten this far, and nothing you say will truly shock me. Even if you admitted to first-degree murder, I'd probably still be looking forward to feeling your heartbeat against mine."

I had to smile. "You say the nicest things."

He sniffed at my dryness.

I welcomed the respite and, unable to remain seated, rose to go to the window, where an elderly couple walking arm in arm caught my attention. Would that be us one day?

"And Bethany's father?" he asked gently.

"Bethany's father was my foster father. He's rotting in hell, I hope."

His brows creased. "Consensual?"

I shook my head violently, like someone about to face execution for a murder they did not commit. Perhaps that was a gross exaggeration, but it was how distraught I became at the slightest suggestion I might have agreed to sleep with that monster.

"He raped me." I stared into Mark's eyes, and suddenly a flood of tears poured out of me, like I'd burst an artery of despair.

I had to turn away as I convulsed in sobs, tears gushing out. Try as I might to suck back the overflow of anguish, I couldn't. My body shuddered as I held onto the ledge and buried my face in one hand.

Not even after that detestable pretend father did the deed had I cried like this. From that day onwards, I bottled everything up, maintaining a stiff upper lip, as they always taught us English. For good reason, too, because tears made us weak.

I didn't want to face Mark. I wanted to bury myself under a blanket. I'd never felt so naked before.

But face him, I did, and saw his face twisted in horror and disgust, blinding me with pity.

Silence amplified my choking sobs, placing a wedge between us, and I felt alone.

After a long, tense gap, I wiped my nose and glared at the bewilderment frozen on his face. "Why do you keep looking at me like that?"

He showed his palms. "I'm just speechless. What an evil cunt." He bit his lip. "Sorry for being crass. But Caroline, I'm sorry."

"I don't need your pity, Mark." The words stuck to my upper palate, making them taste bitter. "You wanted to know about my life growing up, and now you do."

The tears ceased, and I cleaned up my face as he stared into space.

CHAPTER 27

Mark

IT WAS AS THOUGH some preternatural entity had turned back time, and Caroline was now that girl whose innocence had been ripped out by a demon.

"You're still looking at me like that." Her tear-soaked eyes penetrated deeply.

I rubbed my lips together. "I'm sorry."

"Why do I get this feeling you won't look at me the same anymore? Like I'm tarnished?"

I exhaled. "That's not true."

"Am I no longer attractive to you?" Her appeals made me recoil. When it came to talking about feelings, I'd somehow missed that lecture.

"That's crazy. I'm lost for words—that's all it is."

However, it was as though she'd read my mind because I couldn't bring myself to share what had jumped into my brain. Now that she'd opened up about her past, I couldn't help but wonder about that dark side to her sexuality.

By enacting those disturbing games with me, was Caroline on some subconscious level trying to normalize forced sex? And, by so doing, dilute the severity of her own violation?

Despite my efforts to push these questions aside, they kept popping up.

"Why do I keep getting this feeling that something's the matter?" she pressed.

I sucked back a breath while searching for the right words, given her delicate state. "Reflecting on what you've confided, I can't help but wonder about those intense encounters we've had at shabby hotels."

She turned away as though trying to hide again. Caroline Lovechilde didn't crumble.

But I wasn't merely a bystander—I loved her unconditionally. The more fragile and exposed she seemed, the more my unwavering affection and resolve to stand by her deepened.

Her breath broke the tense silence. "I don't know why I am the way I am. Gregory introduced me to that alter ego."

"Does she have a name?" I asked, recalling how she'd refused to give me one.

"No. I didn't want to make her a flesh-and-blood woman. Instead, she was an anonymous creature of the night, lost to herself. That's probably the best way to describe her."

"Did it always involve being taken by force?"

She nodded. "Mostly." Turning, she looked at me, that lost child facing me again. "I think you should go. I need to be alone, Mark."

I needed space, too. It had been an intense discussion, and I had my own epiphany to mull over.

We walked in silence to the door.

"I love you, Mark. Whatever you decide, I understand."

I frowned, studying her closely. "Nothing has changed. If anything, I love you even more." My mouth curved slightly. "I just needed to understand you a little better."

"And do you?" she asked, her eyes warming a little.

I nodded pensively. "I think so."

"If you don't wish to stay here, then let me buy you somewhere comfortable close to your college."

"I can't think about that now, Carol." I gave her an apologetic smile. She shrugged. "Call me what you like." She leaned in and kissed me.

I descended the stairs and stepped onto the path of that leafy street. Curvacious white Edwardian homes sat proudly across from a bright green park where everything and everyone was in their rightful place.

As I made my way back to the rough side of town, I knew what I had to do. I had to reclaim my freedom so I could marry Caroline, because I'd never wanted anything more in my life.

CHAPTER 28

Caroline

AFTER SHARING THOSE DARK secrets with Mark, I felt lighter, despite the many challenges that lay ahead. I'd even been sleeping better than usual.

Much to my chagrin, however, Mark insisted on staying at Audrey's bedsit. I couldn't understand, but I took him any way I could. As desperate as that seemed, it was either that or not see him.

And so, there we were together in that rundown room with the sickly faded floral wallpaper.

He took my hand. "Once I've sorted everything out, I'll reclaim the man-of-leisure role you so want me to embrace."

I frowned. "Is that a hint of sarcasm I'm detecting?"

He shook his handsome head and gave me one of his irresistible smiles. I fell into his arms and onto his unmade bed.

This obstinate need of Mark's for us to split our time between my opulent surroundings and his dingy ones jarred my senses. The contrast in settings was so intense that it always took some adjusting. Especially with Audrey curtsying while receiving me in her sweet but fawning manner.

"As long as you ravish me, I don't really care, I suppose," I said with the resigned sigh of a smitten woman. But as we lay on his uncomfortable bed, I couldn't help but complain. "How can you sleep like this?"

He laughed. "I know. It's pretty bad. My back's complaining. But I needed some space to think. To plan."

"So, your plan?"

"I plan to become free. And for you to become the next Mrs. Reiner."

At the reminder of his desire to marry me, my heart warmed. "Well, it might have to be Lovechilde-Reiner."

"Whatever." He took me into his arms.

I pressed my face against his neck and breathed in his intoxicating masculinity, which sent my hormones into overdrive as always. "I just wish you weren't about to leave."

A dark cloud drifted over me again, and I unraveled myself from his arms. "Why don't you let me come with you to Australia?"

"You wouldn't like it, trust me. Sydney is humid, and their idea of high tea involves a tea bag and a joint."

His drollery made me chuckle. "I'm very adaptable. If I'm with you, I don't mind where I am. Look at me here in this..." I paused, not wanting to use the word 'squalor.'

"I'll stay at Mayfair, then," he said with resignation, as though I was trying to deprive him of pleasure.

"Look, Mark, I'm not trying to force you to do anything. It's just a little uncomfortable here."

He stroked my cheek lovingly, and I instantly relaxed. This man could make me do anything when his eyes radiated such warmth and love.

Or was he just a good actor?

No, not when we fucked or made love. One couldn't fake those cataclysmic climaxes. And two years into our relationship, our lust should have become diluted, but Mark's appetite proved just as robust as always.

"With so many choice adornments competing for my attention, I couldn't think straight. Even now, when I'm at Mayfair, I keep wandering between your pretty eyes to that glorious Monet on your bedroom wall."

I laughed. "Then I'll have to have it removed so you can admire me instead."

His smile faded into a frown. "There's something that's worrying me too."

"Oh?"

"Are you still contemplating going to the authorities?"

I'd almost forgotten about that stomach-churning decision, which I'd filed away in the farthest region of my mind. "What else can I do?"

"I rather like the mushroom idea, myself," he said, nonchalant as a host discussing menu arrangements for a dinner party.

"One can't kill the devil. He's too powerful." I sighed. "And I hope you'll leave well enough alone." I gave him a pointed stare.

"But you can't go to the authorities, Caroline, noble sacrifice though it might be. Think of your family and what it will do to them."

"I've thought of little else, Mark. But to give him all that land, and to have that wretched man as a neighbor, polluting my grandchildren's future?" I shook my head. "He's a sick, ugly criminal who needs to fall on his sword."

"Yes. I agree. That's why I'm suggesting we think of some way to remove him."

Doomed whichever way I chose, I shook my head and puffed loudly.

At Elysium, Manon pointed at furniture, instructing the maid how she wanted things done. I had to smile because that had been me once.

Her face lit up on seeing me.

I smiled. "I thought I'd drop in and check out the new art acquisitions Savanah hasn't stopped talking about."

Manon chuckled. "Savanah's chuffed, and so she should be. Just wait till you see them. They're gorgeous. I can't stop looking at them." Manon crooked her finger. "Come and see."

I followed her into the main hall, which doubled as Elysium's function room.

I examined the large, marine-themed canvases portraying mermaids among fantastical sea creatures and besotted males. "They're stunning," I said, noticing how the three large paintings told a story of love with the same characters appearing in each frame.

"It was Mirabel's mermaid song that inspired Savvie, I think. I love them though. Don't you?"

"Very much. There's a little of Marc Chagall in them, although they're more representational, I believe."

Manon nodded slowly. "I don't know who that is, but I'm glad you like them. We're thinking of having an opening, like a party, to celebrate their hanging."

"That sounds colorful. It's been a while since we've had an event."

"It has," she enthused. "I thought Mirabel could perform with Theadora and even having Cian do something."

"Oh, like a family pantomime," I said.

She giggled and narrowed her eyes. "Are you making fun?"

"Maybe. But look, it's a fine idea."

The new maid entered and dusted as we sat down and chatted.

"I haven't seen Crisp around lately," Manon said.

My mood instantly soured at the sound of his name. "He's gone away. But I'm sure we'll hear from him soon." I exhaled a tight breath.

"He simply cannot have Elysium, Grandmother. You cannot give it to him. I love it here. We all do."

I cast a side glance at the maid, who was within earshot. "Let's not talk about this right now."

The maid joined us just as we were about to leave.

"Yes, Mary?" Manon asked.

"I've finished dusting," Mary said.

"Take a break. Have a cup of tea. Jonathon, who should be here soon, will show you the ropes."

Mary nodded and left the room.

"She's new," I said.

"I've had to hire again. Staff keep coming and going."

"You're doing a great job. And Elysium will remain ours. Don't worry."

"I'm making it my mission to ensure that happens."

I held her steely gaze. "Rey's not someone you mess around with. You should know that by now."

"I sure do." She flashed me a tense smirk.

After all the trauma Manon had endured because of Reynard, she'd found her footing. Instead of wallowing in depression, my granddaughter had rolled up her sleeves and got to work, learning all that she could about running Merivale and Elysium.

However, since we shared similar traits, which were becoming more evident as Manon matured, I hoped she wasn't bottling things up. I'd asked her often enough if she was faring well, and she generally declared with a sunny smile that life was great.

THE PARTY AT ELYSIUM was in full swing. Manon had made sure everything was perfect for the large gathering.

I gazed around us. "You've invited half of London, I see."

"I thought it would be a great way to showcase the resort." Manon wore a proud smile.

Drake joined her, munching on a canape. "These are delicious."

Manon rolled her eyes at me as a wife lamenting her husband's idiosyncrasies might. "He'll end up eating everything. He has such an enormous appetite."

"It must be all that running." I smiled at Drake.

"That's what I always tell her," he said.

"Anyway, don't eat everything the servers bring," Manon responded.

He laughed. "I'll try to control myself. But hey, this caterer is by far the best."

"They are, aren't they?" Manon looked at me, seeking approval, as always.

"The food is delicious, I agree." I peered over and gave Mark a little smile as he spoke with one of the older bookish guests, whose name always escaped me.

The performance started, and Mirabel sang a song accompanied by Cian. Standing next to me, Ethan looked every bit the proud husband and father.

"Cian has turned into a confident little performer," I said.

Looking all starry-eyed, Ethan nodded in agreement.

The song kept the room mesmerized as Mirabel sang in her dulcet tones, capturing the magic of the sea.

"The art and the music are gorgeous," Theadora said as she milled around with Declan by her side.

"The children are very quiet," I whispered.

Ethan chuckled. "Ruby's dying to dance."

Dressed like a fairy, my balletic granddaughter pointed her feet, practicing her barre exercises. Ruby was dressed in a pink tutu-like gown with sparkling stars and wearing a tiara that kept flashing different colors.

"Will she ever wear human clothes?" I whispered.

He laughed. "I hope not. She looks adorable, don't you think?"

I smiled. "She looks like she's stepped out of a Disney movie."

The audience cheered, and Mirabel took a bow. "Thank you for coming here to celebrate the stunning new paintings. My sister-in-law has a brilliant eye for art. I think we can all agree."

Everyone applauded. Savanah, looking rather bashful, gave a curtsy, and Carson kissed her on the cheek.

My heart warmed seeing all my children in happy marriages, full of joy. The only bone of contention was a certain red-haired figure lurking in one corner. Except for the odd gray streak, Rey's hair was exactly the same as it had been in his twenties.

I reflected that if someone had asked me back then, before I met him, what a devil looked like, I would have described him as looking like Reynard Crisp.

He'd invited himself, as always. When it came to Lovechilde functions, he had a sixth sense. I couldn't ever recall an invitation being sent out to him for any of our events, but nevertheless he always attended, as if it was his blood right.

Manon had hired a DJ, and the event soon turned into a dance party.

"It's such a great night," Savanah said. "If only he wasn't here." She gave Rey a side-glance.

"Yes, well..." I pulled a tight smile.

"You can't let him take this place," she implored. "And now Natalia's going around telling people they're about to take over."

I looked at Mark, who was standing next to me, and frowned. "She is?"

"Mummy, you've got to do something."

"I won't let it happen. Don't worry."

I stepped outside for some air, and Mark joined me. The night breeze was crisp and awakening, and to still the foreboding swirling around me as though drunk on melodrama, I meditated on the moonlit, silvery ocean.

I sighed. "This is our place."

Mark squeezed my hand.

"I have to do it." Making that confession, even under my breath, was akin to stepping into chilly water and egging oneself on despite shivering dread. I'd been stalling for a while now, but now that the word was out about Reynard's takeover, procrastination was no longer an option.

Mark's brow pinched. "I can't lose you."

"You're the one who insists on risking all of this by returning to Australia."

"I'm only risking being sued, whereas even if they find the evidence around Alice's death to be circumstantial, you'll still be charged for not reporting it."

I shook my head. "I've thought of nothing else. But I must. Can't you see?"

Just as he was about to respond, Mark looked over my shoulder, and there was Rey lighting a cigar.

Nobody knew about Mark but Reynard, of course, so he still answered to the name of Cary. That was yet another awkward conversation I would have to have with my family.

"Speak of the fucking devil," he murmured.

Rey must have heard because his face lit up with glee. He owned that moniker like the head of a criminal empire, relishing his own power.

"It's quite an event," he said. "When we take over, I might have to employ Savanah. She is proving a talented events manager."

"I don't recall sending you an invitation," I said.

He ignored that. "My lawyer has drawn up the transfer documents."

"If you'll excuse me." I walked off.

Mark followed close behind. "You can't confess, Caroline," he pleaded again. "I'll delay my trip, but you must promise not to turn yourself in."

I stretched out my hands. "But what else can I do?"

"Leave it to me." He looked determined, which made me want to run somewhere and scream.

"He's too powerful, darling. Too many friends in high places. He's untouchable."

Declan came over. "Has something happened?"

"Yes. Reynard Crisp," Mark said.

"Why's he here?" Declan asked.

"He's come for his thirty pieces of silver," Mark replied dryly.

Declan looked flummoxed and annoyed at the same time. I couldn't blame him, considering how vague my answers to his questions had been. "So what if he introduced you to our father? Surely that piece of land at the back here is more than ample recompense."

"Just give me a moment," I said, my heart racing. "And only you. No one else."

Declan glanced at Mark before returning his attention to me. "By that, you mean just us two?"

Mark touched my hand, his eyes widening ever so slightly.

I released a tight breath. "He has a right to know," I told Mark.

"Yes, I have a right to know," Declan interjected.

I turned to my son. "Just give me five minutes. We'll go somewhere, and I'll explain."

Declan nodded and left us.

Mark's frown deepened. "You can't tell him about Alice. It will complicate your relationship with your family."

"But you understood. You've forgiven me, haven't you?" I asked, hating how pathetic I'd become.

"But I love you unconditionally." His eyes burned into mine, and a tear slid down my cheek.

A combination of dread, frustration, and intense love settled over me. "They're my children. They'll have to understand."

"That you were involved in the death of a woman their father was engaged to? Don't you see? It will bring up all kinds of questions and doubt."

"But you believe me." It felt like someone had reached into my chest and squeezed my heart.

He was right. After this, how could my family ever know when I was being truthful?

He kissed my hand and his eyes penetrated mine, not in that suggestive, sexy way but in unshakable camaraderie, which at that moment, I needed far more than romantic overtures.

"Of course I believe you," he said.

As we entered inside, Natalia's screechy laugh traveled through the large room, and the guests turned their heads toward her. She was on the dance floor with her girlfriends, all waving their arms around.

"It just gets worse." I shook my head. "Elysium's descending into a nouveau riche gutter."

"I'll be back in a minute." Mark held my gaze as though he wanted to say something important before he turned. I watched him walk off, and women turned to ogle his handsome figure striding by.

As a welcome diversion from the terror of what lay ahead of me, I allowed myself to reflect on how we'd made love before arriving at the party.

I hadn't seen him for two days, and he'd hurried me into the bedroom at Merivale, virtually ripped off my new dress and entered me in one hard, deep thrust that made my eyes water. The feeling of his passion lingered, as always.

My heart was full of Mark, and for a moment, I suspended my growing angst to bask in the warmth of our deep connection, made ever so deeper now that we'd shared our dark secrets.

I took another glass of champagne as I gathered the courage to speak with Declan.

Bethany, who had been unusually quiet in the corner with her rockstar boyfriend, chose that moment to make her presence known by pushing a woman.

I'd just passed Carson on my way to talk to Declan, and Carson looked at me and shook his head. "I better go and see what's happening."

At that point, the woman, who could have been a supermodel with her good looks and long, slender frame draped in a designer dress, stumbled and fell to the ground.

Savanah rushed over to us, almost breathless. "Bethany's just punched Olivia."

"I saw that," I said.

"She's been so quiet and then kapow."

We watched in horror as Carson dragged Bethany off Olivia.

Pointing into the hapless Olivia's face, Bethany yelled, "She's a slut!"

I rolled my eyes. Luckily, the music continued.

Carson took Bethany outside, while her boyfriend Sweeney continued drinking and chatting as though this kind of violent uproar was part and parcel of partying. Maybe in his scene, but had I not been weighed down with my own burdens, I would have taken Bethany aside myself.

After Carson returned, Bethany tried to re-enter, but security blocked her.

"You better have a word with her boy," I told Carson.

He nodded. "Apparently, Olivia was flirting with him."

Savanah shook her head. "How clichéd." She looked around the room, where people continued to party, laughing and dancing, as though nothing had happened. "Have you seen Manon?"

I shook my head. Mark also seemed to be taking a while coming back.

Declan arrived at my side. He rolled his eyes at the uproar. While Bethany continued to rant and rave, Natalia and her suburban girlfriends huddled around Bethany's rockstar boyfriend.

"It's descending into a common nightclub," Declan said, sounding more like me than usual, which made me smile. "Let's leave them to it, shall we?" He cocked his head.

We entered a smaller reception room away from the crowd.

I sat on the sofa and ran my thumb over my fingernail as nausea danced anew in my belly.

"I met Reynard when I was extremely poor," I began. "He helped me get through my studies, and I would accompany him to parties where he introduced me to some of London's elite."

Declan frowned. "Did he make you sell yourself?"

I shook my head. "I wasn't forced into doing anything I didn't want to do."

He huffed. "I just need to know why he owns you and how we can stop him from extorting our family."

Sweat slid between my shoulder blades. There was no way out.

While I searched for the right words, a loud, gut-wrenching scream rang in the air.

Declan's shoulders slumped. "What now?"

THE POLICE STATION HAD that cold, unfriendly atmosphere I'd unfortunately grown accustomed to by now. I'd been called in yet again to give another statement about what had happened at the Elysium function. And without Mark, I had no one who could share my angst. I'd grown so dependent on his wisdom and support.

The morning after that fateful party, Mark left for Australia, although I begged him not to.

"I was always going to go, Caroline," he responded as he packed his overnight bag.

"Where did you disappear to last night?"

"I couldn't have police looking into my life while my identity is in question," he said.

"But don't you see that running to Australia implicates you?"

"I have to go. I'll miss my flight otherwise." He squeezed my hand. "At least he's gone. You're free now, Caroline."

A tense breath left my lips. "But at what cost? I'm about to lose you."

"I had nothing to do with it." He stared deeply into my eyes.

I searched his gaze for answers, only to find his dark, beautiful eyes shining with heartwarming affection. Whether I believed Mark was immaterial, because I couldn't imagine my life without him.

He kissed me passionately. "I love you."

"What do I say to the police when they ask me why you hurried off to Australia? Someone will tell them you were at the function."

"Tell them the truth."

"The truth? How you faked your disappearance all those years ago?"

"If you like." His mouth curled up at one end. He seemed so easy about it all. While, in sharp contrast, I was tied in knots.

On a deeper level, I admired his determination and forbearance. Unlike me and my hand-wringing self-pity, Mark accepted humiliation with poise and calmness.

He smiled. "This time, I mean to stare my bad choices in the face."

"Bad choices that brought us together."

He nodded slowly. "Life's full of strange twists." Then he left.

A detective in a suit snapped me out of my reflections, beckoning me to come with him just as my lawyer arrived.

We followed him into a nondescript room that was as frigid as the man in the ill-fitting suit, who gestured at me to sit.

My lawyer whispered, "You don't have to say anything."

"I have nothing to hide." I squared my shoulders, channeling that tough version of myself I rolled out when confronted by adversity.

Only I wasn't sure where this interrogation would lead. It had spared me the almost impossible task of admitting to Alice's death, given the extraordinary events that unfolded as though someone had deliberately timed it, coming to my rescue in the grisliest of ways and saving me from having to tell my son. That was now a secret that I could take to my grave, despite the festering scar burdening my conscience.

"Can you please give me an account of the night?" the detective asked.

"I have already given my statement to the police," I said.

"This will be a smoother process if you just answer my question."

I flinched at his gruff tone. "I was at a function at Elysium when my distressed granddaughter came to me with the news that Reynard Crisp had been stabbed."

Realizing how suspicious it would all look—Declan and I arriving to find Mark and Manon standing over Reynard's lifeless body—Declan had agreed we should say that Manon approached us first.

"Where were you at the time?"

"I was with my son, Declan."

"Can anyone corroborate that?"

"I'm not sure whether anyone saw us enter the conference room."

"Why were alone with your son?"

My spine creaked slightly as I adjusted my position. "I wished to discuss family business away from the noise."

"I believe the victim owned some of the adjoining land, and he ran a casino that had its own history of crime."

"Salon Soir was never something the family signed off on. All the activities there related to Rey and no one else."

He stared me in the eyes, apparently trying to read deeper into my words, then he took notes. "So your granddaughter alerted you, and what happened then? Was she the first person to find him? Were there others around the body?"

I'd discussed this with Manon and Declan at length that night while we waited for the police to arrive. Knowing how it looked for both of them, I quickly came up with a passable version of events. I'd asked Manon not to mention Mark as being there because of his sudden disappearance. Declan, thank goodness, could see that no good would come from implicating either of them.

Manon remained coolheaded and assured me she'd stick to our story.

Could she have done it?

I inclined my head. "I believe my granddaughter was the first person to find him."

"It was her scream you heard? After which she came to you?"

I nodded.

"And then what happened?"

"We found Reynard on the ground, bleeding. Declan checked for a pulse only to discover he was dead, and I called the police."

"I know it's not a pleasant task recalling the gruesome state of his body, but can you tell me exactly what you saw?"

"He was on his back, blood pouring from around his heart, I believe." I took a deep breath, reliving how I'd found Rey in a dark-red puddle, redolent with the nauseating stench of blood—an iron-like smell.

"He sustained multiple stab wounds to the chest, yes." The man made another note. "We will need a full list of your guests for questioning."

"My granddaughter, who organized the event, can supply you with that."

I went to rise when the detective said, "You were also implicated in the Alice Ponting case."

A jagged breath scraped my throat as I tried to maintain a blank face.

My lawyer whispered, "You don't have to talk about that."

I nodded. "As I have said repeatedly, I had nothing to do with her disappearance."

The detective's stare penetrated so deeply that I felt like he could read the anxiety swirling within, making me dizzy. He opened another file.

"I'm sorry, but wasn't this about Reynard?" I asked.

"I believe it's linked. Her family's aware of his connection to the victim."

My palms dampened. Stifling silence followed as the detective studied the report. I had to remind myself to breathe.

I wanted to have a long, hot bath, then take two sedatives and sleep. The pain of not having Mark there to lean on hurt more than I'd imagined.

Had he done this? And why go to such brutal lengths?

The detective looked at me. "The report here shows that she was murdered."

I flinched. "How?"

My lawyer tapped my arm and shook his head slightly.

For sanity's sake, however, I needed to know.

"Strangulation, it would seem, going on the coroner's report." He looked at me with a slight smile, the warmest he'd been so far. "You didn't hear that from me."

Strangulation?

Finally, I asked, "Oh, they can deduce that from skeletal remains?"

"They can deduce lots of things these days."

Again, he eyeballed me, and as I tried to remain outwardly neutral, thoughts and emotions tumbled and collided inside me.

Then came relief.

Knowing I hadn't killed Alice was like unlacing a suffocating corset I'd been wearing all my life. I could breathe again. I hadn't noticed until that moment, but I had never really breathed properly. It had always been short, sharp breaths or long, held ones, but never even regular breathing.

The detective closed his notebook. "That's all for now."

CHAPTER 29

Mark

ELISE WAS ALMOST UNRECOGNIZABLE. She'd had lots of work done on her face, but instead of reversing the ravages of time, the surgery had given her an unshifting visage that made it difficult to look into her aging eyes. The smoother the skin, the older the eyes looked.

Freakish was the best way to describe her. I sensed she was taking potent drugs, given her almost lifeless state. Although sad, her border-line catatonia meant that we could have a mostly civil conversation.

"So, you faked your disappearance to get away from me?" she slurred.

Wearing a tight smile, I nodded. Sunshine streamed through her floor-to-ceiling window, and outside, the blue harbor glistened.

"Then why are you here?" She struggled off the couch and picked up her languid cat from where it was sunning itself.

I removed my jacket. Accustomed to the cool London air, I'd over-dressed. Most of the men there went around in knee-length shorts, T-shirts, and baseball caps, interchangeable and indistinguishable in their casual uniforms. That easy, sporting attitude was now as alien to me as golf might be to a poet.

"You still look good," Elise said with a hint of resentment.

I searched her countenance for the pretty, free-spirited dancer I'd fallen for thirty-odd years back and instead found a complete stranger.

"Thanks." I stroked the cat, who'd jumped off the couch and returned to the sunny window.

"And why now, after all these years?"

"I want a divorce. I plan to marry again."

My phone sounded, and when I saw it was Caroline, I gave Elise an apologetic smile. "Can you excuse me a moment?'

"Knock yourself out." She lit a cigarette.

I headed outside onto the Manly balcony. In the distance, I saw ships, boats, yachts, paddle-surfers, and swimmers. It was more active in the water than out, despite the endless stream of joggers. Life was in full swing. Nothing sleepy about that city.

I answered her call. "Hello."

"Oh, Mark." She sighed.

Caroline's attractive voice worked wonders for my mood, which up to now had been stuck somewhere between dread and bemusement.

"Is something the matter?" I asked.

She exhaled loudly. "Why aren't you here?"

"Have the police been around?"

"I've just left the station."

"More questioning over Crisp's death?"

"Yes. However, I discovered something that has elevated me somewhat. I just wish you were here."

"What was that?"

"I prefer not to speak of it over the phone. But suffice it to say, a heavy weight has just been lifted. When are you coming home?"

"Soon. I promise, my love."

"Am I that?" she asked, sounding girlish and arousing at the same time.

"You're more than that, Caroline." I paused. "I'm here now with Elise."

"Oh?" A long pause followed. "Is she still attractive?"

"Not to me. There's only you. There will only ever be you. I want to be with you forever, and I hope you still want that."

"I want to be buried with you, Mark."

Tears pricked my eyes. It had been an intense week. "I better go. We can talk tonight on Zoom?"

"Oh, I would love that. Send me the time, as your night is my day."

"I will."

"They won't lock you up, I hope," she said.

"No. They've got nothing on me."

She huffed a bit. "We are talking about Australian authorities here, aren't we?"

"What else?"

"Let's talk later."

"Okay, my love." I ended the call and took a deep breath, drawing in the sea air, as the afternoon sun burned my face.

I knew how leaving England the morning after Reynard was found dead looked. The police had called and left a message, but I hadn't been able to bring myself to call them back.

CHAPTER 30

Caroline

"THE POLICE HAVE TAKEN my fingerprints, and they think I did it," Manon said, pacing around in my office.

I fluttered my hand. "Sit down. You're making me nervous."

She fell into the armchair. "It's freaking me out. I'm still dealing with the aftershocks of seeing him lying in that pool of blood."

Drake, who was sitting on the sofa, said, "You should talk to that counsellor I told you about." He looked at me. "I've been trying to talk her into seeing one."

Manon frowned. "No. I hate them. They'll ask about my past, and I'm over talking about that. Grandmother's better. And so are you." She gave him a loving smile.

"They took my fingerprints too," I said soberly.

"Really? But you were with Declan at the time," Manon said.

I shrugged. "It's a standard procedure, darling. It helps them isolate DNA."

"But my DNA might be there. The knife came from the kitchen. Anyone could have touched it."

I nodded. This case was far from over, despite my relief at learning I hadn't been responsible for Alice's death. Not directly, at least. But with the police circling and growing questions over Mark, I was back to not sleeping.

"Natalia didn't even shed a tear," Manon continued. "She's making noises about being the rightful owner of Salon Soir, though."

Yes, I had Rey's young, fiery widow to deal with. I recalled with great distaste the tacky naked dress that showed off her collagen-rounded bum she'd worn to Elysium that night.

However, while Rey had enjoyed protection for his many illegal activities, Natalia wouldn't, I imagined. Once the air had cleared, removing that unsightly casino—and its trashy, uncultivated patrons that spilled into Elysium—sat at the top of my list.

I turned to Drake. "What did you find out about Natalia's brothers?"

"They're all legal. The authorities are aware of drug-smuggling, but it's down to catching them red-handed. I believe it's only a matter of time."

"Good. I want that place gone."

"I can't believe they've allowed it to operate for so long," Drake said.

"What has?" Declan had arrived, followed by Ethan and Savanah.

I rose. "Why don't we go into the family room and have some afternoon tea?"

As I left the room, Declan took me aside. "Did you arrange it or did Mark?"

I studied him closely. "You know him as Mark?"

"He told us the whole story."

"By 'us,' you mean Ethan, Savanah, and Manon?"

"All of us." His brow raised.

"I hope you won't hold it against him."

"If you're happy to accept him despite the lies, then who are we to judge?"

I noted a hint of condemnation in his tone. "That's not what it sounds like."

He exhaled. "Mother, it's been a roller coaster with you. First, Will is implicated in our father's murder, and then Cary turns into Mark, a man who faked his identity. What do you think?"

"I know." I sighed. "Life has never been a straight road for me. Obstacles sometimes turn into advantages and vice versa."

"Are you talking about that mysterious debt you owed Crisp?"

"Come. Let's have some tea." A tight smile quivered on my lips.

Does my family need to know everything?

Just as that question percolated in my thoughts, a tornado in the shape of Natalia tore through the hall. Waving a letter, she pushed through Janet and nearly bowled the poor woman over.

"Hey," Declan snapped with authority. "Calm down."

"I won't calm down until I've spoken to her." Natalia pointed her finger at me.

"Then you better step in there and lower your tone," I said. After directing the agitated woman into my office, I turned to Declan. "Stay."

Manon, standing close by, came in as well.

"Not her," Natalia demanded.

I nodded at my granddaughter, who rolled her eyes and left.

"Won't you sit?" I gestured at the armchair by my desk.

Natalia sat and crossed her legs, which were somewhat constricted in a skintight skirt. While she might have just inherited an empire, Natalia had yet to learn about the dress code of the super-rich.

She slammed a letter down on my desk. "I'm sure you had him murdered," she announced.

"I think that's for law enforcement to decide," Declan said.

She turned and gave him a pointed look before returning her attention to me. "He wrote this, which I'm sure the police will be interested in. I've made copies."

She'd brought the original, which wasn't smart, but I wasn't about to educate her on how to run an empire.

The letter read:

To whom it may concern.

Should I be murdered, as I imagine there are some that want to see me dead, this posthumous letter reveals some hidden truths about Caroline Lovechilde.

I took a breath and paused. That bastard had apparently decided to take me with him.

Caroline Lovechilde, or Carol Lamb, as she was known, killed Alice Ponting. I just cleaned up her mess. This tragic event enabled her to marry into one of the UK's richest families. Alice was Harry Lovechilde's fiancé.

As someone who didn't miss opportunities, I made a pact with the newly married Caroline Lovechilde that I would take a parcel of land, namely the ground where Elysium resort now sits, and the adjoining farmland, in return for my silence.

I pledge that the transfer should continue accordingly into the name of my lawful wife. Or, as the bearer of this letter, which contains dates and necessary details as proof, Natalia Crisp has enough evidence to see that Caroline Lovechilde be charged with the murder of Harry Lovechilde's intended wife.

I set the letter down and stared Natalia in the face. "It will be his word against mine."

Natalia rose and stood over my desk. "That's bullshit and you know it. You did it, just as he said."

"Calm down," Declan said, before looking at me with a question in his eyes.

Natalia scowled. "You're no better than any of us. Even worse, because you murdered your dead husband's fiancé and that's why you've been living the highlife here in Downton Abbey all these years."

Her words acted like a whip on naked skin. I winced as she exposed my long-held secret and unleashed a monster despite Reynard Crisp's fake version of events. The self-confessed atheist clearly didn't believe in judgement by taking his lies with him to the grave.

Declan had gone pale. He turned to Natalia. "I need a word with my mother. Alone."

Lifting her chin with insolence, she tottered in her skyscraper heels to the door. "The transfer will go ahead, and then I will destroy the letter."

I slumped back in my chair, fixated on the letter before me, scrawled by a man educated on the streets rather than at school where clean handwriting was as fundamental as the basic alphabet.

All kinds of thoughts flooded my brain, like how I'd been duped as a teenager into believing the man was suave and sophisticated when his only talent was masquerading as a man of the world.

"Is it true?" Declan asked.

"I didn't kill Alice." I went to the window, where a menacing sky revealed nature's unrest. Gulls struggled through turbulent winds, just like the gale-force emotions pushing me around.

I took a deep breath and faced my son. "I was twenty. She'd been drinking and accused me of flirting with Harry. Alice was pointing in my face and acting aggressively, and I pushed her off me. She stumbled and fell onto the ground and lost consciousness."

"Why didn't you call an ambulance?"

"Rey made me believe she was dead. I've only just discovered that he lied to me." I caught my breath. "I thought she was dead, Declan."

"If you'd called the police, as you should have, she'd still be alive."

"And you wouldn't be," I returned.

Our eyes locked. Yes, it was a tangled web of contradictions.

Manon knocked on the door and entered.

"Not now," Declan said.

I sighed. "No, let her stay."

"It's all in that letter, I take it?" he asked.

I nodded, squirming, in the hope he wouldn't ask to read it.

"Then it's incriminating. It will be your word against a dead man's."

"A dead man who was running a criminal empire." My mouth formed a tight line. "She brought the original letter, which I'm now in possession of."

"Then burn it and tell her to go fuck herself." Manon's mouth curled slightly. "Sorry."

"No. It's probably not a bad idea." Declan sighed. "I don't know what to think. We always suspected something, but not this."

I couldn't stand the idea of my son seeing me as a scheming murderer. "Alice was strangled," I said at last.

"How would you know that?" He frowned.

"The detective that interviewed me revealed the coroner's findings. I'm not a murderer, Declan. It was just a terrible accident." I shook my head. "I trusted Reynard when he said Alice was dead. I was young and scared. He convinced me that walking away was my only option. That my name and reputation would be stained forever otherwise."

A long, aching silence followed.

"You do believe me?" My voice cracked. "I've made some terrible calls in my life, but I've never resorted to murder."

"I believe you, Grandmother." Manon put her arm around me. "We can work this out. Destroy the letter. I'm sure we can find dirt on Natalia." Her face lit up. "I just thought of something. The underage girls. I was there. I have footage."

"But won't that implicate you?" Declan asked.

The breath trapped in my chest exited at this welcome shift away from Alice's death.

Manon frowned. "I don't care. If it brings Natalia and her brothers down, then it's worth going to court. And the brothers are running drugs. Drake's still got that footage of that shooting—I can't understand how Crisp got away with that."

"Rey had an extensive network of powerful men on his side," I said.

"Then we'll have to get as much dirt on them as we can because there's no way in hell they're getting any more land," Declan said, rising. "I think it's best we keep this to ourselves for now."

I turned to face my son. "Please say you believe me." My mouth trembled as tears burned at the back of my eyes.

His very slight nod helped unlock some of the tension in my shoulders. I'd created a moral conundrum, and I couldn't blame Declan for having to grapple with this new conflict.

Declan added, "I think we need to convene a meeting with Drake and Carson to find a way to catch the brothers red-handed."

"What about Natalia? She's heir to a massive fortune. She won't go away so easily," I said.

"Leave her to me," Manon said. "I've got some ideas. I remember a couple of girls who were underage. I'll go through my records."

"You kept notes?" I asked, impressed by my granddaughter's eye for detail.

"I kept everything." She smiled. "As insurance."

"Why didn't you use that against Crisp when everything blew up with Drake?" Declan asked.

Manon shrugged. "It's only just occurred to me. And I didn't want to deal with the law. But now, I don't care. I'll do anything to keep Grandmother safe and to get rid of that scum."

Declan nodded. "Let's have a meeting tomorrow. Bring what you've got, and we'll work on how to rid ourselves of that family." He looked at me. "Any info on who murdered him?"

I shook my head.

"They questioned me," Manon said. "I wish I had."

"And Cary... I mean, Mark?" Declan looked at me.

I pursed my lips. "He wouldn't have used a knife. He can't even watch violent movies without recoiling."

"I see." Declan rubbed his neck. "A hit man?"

"I don't know, Declan. I'm sure he had many enemies."

A FAMILY DINNER WAS arranged to celebrate Carson's birthday, and the dining room resounded with chatter, laughter, energetic children, and curious toddlers. Life continued on, despite police investigations and blackmail hanging over my head.

As I watched my family talking over each other and poking fun as they always did, one could almost believe that the last month hadn't happened.

It had all been swept away for one night, at least.

If only I had a way of telling that to the dissonance buzzing within that not even quality wine could quash. In fact, nothing seemed to vanquish my relentless squirming, exacerbated by Mark's absence.

"Who fed the kids sugary drinks?" Savanah asked, racing after her waddling son to stop him from destroying an oriental vase.

"When's Mark coming back?" Ethan asked.

"Not sure." I kept it short. My family didn't need to know how much I missed him. These few weeks of his absence had felt like a year.

I'd even contemplated a trip to Sydney. Had I not been so consumed with police enquiries, solicitors, and plots to see the back of Natalia and her brothers, I would have done so.

"What's he doing in Australia?" Theadora asked.

"He's reclaiming his identity."

Mirabel nodded. "That's so radical, disappearing like that."

"It happens more than you think," Ethan said. "I only read recently that after major disasters, some people, mainly men, escape their lives by feigning death."

"I suppose it's the chicken's way out," Savanah added.

I remained silent. Yes, I knew how it looked, but as I'd discovered, decisions made in the heat of the moment out of sheer despair rarely seemed as clear-cut when one reflected on the reasons behind them.

The following day, I arranged a meeting to discuss round-the-clock surveillance of Salon Soir and what steps we could take to bring in the law.

"Did you see the material I sent you?" Manon asked.

I nodded and directed my attention to Declan, to whom I had passed it on.

"The authorities will ask why you didn't inform them at the time," he said, looking at Manon.

Drake took her hand, as though showing his support. She gave him a reassuring nod. "I have decided to clear my conscience, haven't I?"

"It could get you into trouble," Declan reiterated.

"I don't care." She squared her shoulders and showed me what courage looked like.

Drake didn't share her determination, it seemed, going by his frown.

Carson joined in. "Savvie mentioned the cops were sniffing around at Elysium. They've been talking to all the staff."

"That's to be expected," I said.

After we discussed at length the different methods of surveillance, everyone left but Manon, whom I'd asked to remain. Drake whispered something to his wife, likely expressing his concerns, before he left.

"You really don't have to implicate yourself like that," I told her.

"I'm determined to. I contacted one of the illegals, who is no longer that." She half-smiled.

I fidgeted with my gold pen. "How did you locate her?"

"I remembered she'd told me something about working at a nail parlor in London."

"Oh? That was quite a long time ago, though."

"I know. Anyway, I contacted every nail place in and around London and found her."

Impressed by Manon's tenacity, I smiled. "You missed your calling as a sleuth."

"I actually enjoyed it." She shrugged. "Anyway, I found Tania. Natalia's brothers had smuggled her into England. Natalia knew her back in Serbia and promised her a safe passage and a new life here. She told her that some friend had a nail business. Which was true." She paused. "But then Tania was forced to auction her virginity at Rouge. She became legal but at an enormous cost. She's still scarred emotionally—she can't go near men. Although he paid for her, the man raped her repeatedly."

"And she will testify after all that?" I asked, disturbed by what I'd heard.

"I offered to set her up in her own nail business."

"But if Natalia gets wind of that, it might become inadmissible."

"She won't hear about it. Tania promised to wait until Natalia's been kicked out."

"Kicked out? She's Rey's widow. The authorities won't kick her out."

"She's a criminal, Grandmother. Her brothers are not only smuggling drugs but also people, it would seem. And what's more, Tania's keen to report them."

"Why hadn't she earlier?" I asked.

"She was scared she'd be deported."

"Mightn't she?"

"I spoke to an immigration solicitor, and apparently if she's been granted citizenship through the proper channels, she cannot unless a crime is committed."

"And she received hers how? I thought the man who bought her facilitated that."

"No. The nail-business proprietor sponsored her and got it on her own merits."

"Well then, she's safe." I nodded slowly. "Good work. Only... are you sure you want to drag yourself through this?"

"I do."

I went to her and gave her a warm hug. "You're an impressive woman, Manon. Sharp, dependable, and smarter than most your age."

She broke away, her eyes shining with emotion. "Thanks, Grandmother. You're my hero."

We shared a touching smile, and I took her hand. Yes, she'd become my favorite, all right.

CHAPTER 31

Mark

THE POLICE STATION IN Sydney overlooked the harbor, which wasn't unusual for the city. At least the panoramic sea views were one pleasure I'd extracted from that trip, along with clean air, sunny skies, and soft sand to sink my feet into.

Nevertheless, I missed England like I would an erudite, occasionally cantankerous, and witty friend. I also missed Caroline like I could never have imagined possible. Before meeting her, I'd always identified as self-contained and comfortable alone.

The constable directed me into a room. "Step in there, please."

A man in a suit arrived, mumbled his name, turned on a tape, and charged straight into it. "You left England when you were expressly advised not to."

I looked into his eyes. "I'm not charged with anything."

"No. But you were present on the night of a murder." He glanced down at his notes. "At an event hosted by the Lovechilde family, of which you are affiliated as a partner to Caroline Lovechilde. That is correct?"

I nodded.

"You were required to provide DNA samples and have your fingerprints taken, but you fled for Australia the following morning, I believe."

"The ticket was booked. I wasn't about to lose my seat."

"It's a red flag for the authorities, you leaving in such a hurry."

"As I explained, I booked the ticket prior to the event."

"I've been instructed by the London authorities to arrange DNA and fingerprints." He pinned me with a lingering stare, looking to profile me, I imagined.

I scratched my arm where I'd been ravaged by mosquitoes. Humidity and mosquitoes were other things I didn't miss about Sydney.

"You are a prime suspect, you realize?"

Shrugging it off as if he'd just accused me of a traffic infringement, I opened my hands. "I imagine there were many guests in attendance who qualify as potential suspects. Reynard Crisp wasn't exactly well-liked around there."

The detective eyeballed me again, another long and hard stare, hoping I'd show something. I didn't. The only thing making me antsy was Elise playing games with me by refusing to sign the divorce papers.

Finally, he said, "Okay, that will be all for now. You'll have those samples taken in a moment, after which you must report your movements."

"I plan to return to England at the end of the week," I said.

He nodded. "That will be all for now."

After having a cheek swab taken and my fingerprints stamped, I left with a head full of drama.

Elise had demanded I see her in person, despite my suggestion that from this point on, I would communicate via a solicitor.

The legal bill was another matter. Caroline had insisted I use that generous credit line she'd extended. While my former identity might have been able to bury his head in a book, now that I'd divested myself of that charade, this whole kept-man arrangement didn't sit so well.

I stepped into a pub, bought myself a cold pint of beer, and sat on the balcony so I could soak in some sun and enjoy the postcard view of the rippling harbor.

A huge cruise ship was heading toward the port, and I fantasized about being on it.

When did life become so complicated?

Just as that thought drifted over me like the gliding yacht on the water, a couple of heavily tattooed men pulled up at the table next to mine.

As I continued to sip on my beer, lost in my thoughts, I heard one of them say, "So, mate, do you think he'll get three weeks? I mean, it was barely a fucking tackle."

And there it was, Australia and its football-mad obsessives. Londoners had a similar fixation with their own football code, but the fans were louder in my former home.

"Dunno, mate. It's a fucking joke, if ya ask me."

I could have moved and really wanted to, but they were big, burly fellows. Their necks were as thick as their heads, and I wasn't about to offend anyone.

A couple of girls joined them. They also sported tattoos and smelled like a cheap perfume counter. With their plumped lips, tiny shorts, and crop tops, they were an advertisement to the cosmetic-enhancing industry. I suspected they'd buried themselves in so much product that even their souls were coated in polymer.

But then, that was my inner cynic. And I had a lot to feel dark about. Elise.

Why wouldn't she just sign the fucking papers? She just had to drag this out by persecuting me as some form of retaliatory punishment.

The girls squealed with laughter. "That's so fucking true. And he's not even straight."

I had to stop eavesdropping, but how could I not when in earshot of such larger-than-life characters? Everyone in that town seemed to go around with a neon sign over them. At night, the place had a sense of danger about it, like the football game had left the stadium and was playing out on the streets.

For now, I had to tackle Elise. Not literally, as physical contact was the furthest thing from my mind. There was only one woman I wouldn't have minded tackling—in the friendliest of ways—and that was Caroline.

"She's marrying him. Can you believe it?" the blonde girl said. "After that restraining order? He put her in fucking hospital."

"He's kinda hot though," the other girl said.

I had to leave before my day grew bleaker, despite the shining sun.

From one dysfunction to another, I made my way to Elise's Manly home. The ferry ride was pleasant as I sipped on another beer.

My phone rang. Caroline.

"Oh, Mark, it's crazy here."

"It's always crazy there. That's one of Merivale's many charms." I chuckled.

"Police are circling like vultures on a carcass."

"Okay, fair metaphor. I take it we're not talking about the funeral?"

"That's Saturday. I don't want to go, but I must. There's someone there I'm hoping to see."

"Oh?"

"An old acquaintance who's coming from Germany to attend the funeral."

"Okay. And what does that mean?"

"It means he might have an answer to a question that could lead the police in another direction, or at least, I hope."

"Speaking of which, I've just had my fingerprints taken. I'm a suspect, it would seem."

"We all are, darling." She sighed.

"It's nice to hear your voice." Her refined tone was music to my ears. "After listening to mangled English these past days, hearing you is like listening to a blackbird's nocturnal song."

"You say the nicest things." She chuckled. "I miss you, Mark. Are the divorce papers signed?"

"Not quite."

"She's not cooperating?"

"Not sure. I'm off to visit her now."

"You will be back by Saturday? Even if she doesn't sign?"

"I'll be back. I'll leave it in the hands of the solicitor."

"I raised your credit limit, darling."

Resigned to taking her money despite my misgivings, I sighed. "Thank you, Caroline. I don't know how I'm going to repay you."

"Oh, I can think of a few ways." A smile shone through her words.

I chuckled. "I'm a little too old to be your plaything."

"I don't know about that. You're more virile than men half your age."

"Oh, and you know that how?" I asked.

"Is that a note of jealousy?"

"I'm not normally jealous, but I'd hate another man touching you."

"Then you better get back."

Caroline and her considerable sexual appetite. I couldn't imagine her doing without for long. "Or else?" I had to ask.

"Or else nothing, sweetheart. After you, I can't imagine any man making me feel the way you do."

I exhaled. I felt the same. "Yes, we fit well together, don't we?"

"Oh, we do. In a very big way."

I laughed.

"Please hurry back."

"Until Saturday."

"I cannot wait."

I couldn't resist adding, "Be sure to wear that lacy red ensemble you wore before I left." My pants grew a little snugger, thinking of her in the skimpy lingerie.

"I've got something even better."

"Now you're making me all hot."

"And you me."

I blew a kiss into the phone and smiled for the first time that day.

ELISE ANSWERED THE DOOR in a kimono.

I glanced at my watch. It was six in the afternoon. "You've just gotten out of bed."

"No. But I plan to go there." She gave me a teasing smirk, and I got a sinking feeling.

I didn't need to be overly perceptive to read her intent.

"So, you wanted to see me?" I asked.

Elise lit a joint, took a deep puff, and passed it to me. I shook my head.

She looked disappointed. "You never used to knock it back in the past."

"No, I didn't. But I don't partake anymore."

"From memory, you were one hungry hedonist."

I laughed at that ridiculous exaggeration. "Yes, I recall having to go without food often."

"I didn't mean food. I meant pussies, drugs, alcohol. You couldn't get enough. Remember that night I sucked you off under the table at that swish club?"

We were about to do this? Skip down memory lane?

I shrugged. "Well, we were young and wild."

"But it was fun. We had fun, didn't we?"

"Sure."

She continued to puff on her joint, lost in thought for a moment.

"What do you want, Elise?" I got straight to the point. I meant for this to be my last visit.

"I wanted to see you again. Chat. You know, talk about the fun times."

Her eyes held a hint of mischief. I recognized that same look as the one she wore when she was in one of her episodes. When she could go from laughing and dancing and offering her body to me any which way to throwing a tantrum within a breath.

She rose. "Can I offer you anything?"

"No. I'm good. Why am I here, Elise?"

She pulled down her lips and pouted like a child being scolded. "Aren't you happy to see me?"

I rolled my eyes. "Elise, will you sign the divorce papers?"

"Maybe I will, maybe I won't."

I sighed. "Okay, I get it. I didn't leave under good circumstances."

She laughed sarcastically. "Um... yeah. You could say that. Faking your death. I fucking cried."

"I'm really sorry. What can I do to atone?" If ever I regretted speaking, it was then. What was I thinking, asking that?

She dropped her kimono and stood stark naked before me. "You can start by fucking me, I suppose."

I rolled my eyes. "I'm with someone."

Her scraping laugh raked over me. "That never stopped you before. Remember the night I found you fondling Belinda's tits? And then in bed with my seventeen-year-old cousin? Remember that?"

"I know. Not my finest hour."

"You were a fucking sex maniac. So, fuck me. Or doesn't that big dick of yours work anymore?"

Before I could say anything, she fell on her knees and pulled down my zip, rubbing my penis.

I pushed her away. "Hey. No."

"Oh. You have turned all frigid."

I walked to the door. "I'm leaving."

"Then I won't sign."

"Fine."

When I reached the front gate, Elise yelled from her balcony, "I'm going to sue for emotional damages."

A nearby couple, having stepped into their front gate, looked at me as though I had a set of horns.

I gave them a timid smile and strode off.

I'd tried and failed. I would just have to pay her. Handsomely, I imagined, in cash.

CHAPTER 32

Caroline

As it was a Sunday, I'd arranged a lunch by the pool for the family to celebrate Mark's return. A necessary diversion, given the tension surrounding us.

Detectives continued to circle the family, prolonging the agony of media scrutiny this case had attracted. And now that Mark had come back to England, the police had an annoying tendency to arrive unannounced for more questioning.

There would be no divorce, but I could live with that. What was marriage, anyway?

"I could try inducements," Mark said as we dressed for lunch.

"No. She sounds unhinged, and you'd only continue to stir her up."

"She's suing, you know? I got the email when I arrived." He bit his lip, and all I wanted to do was attack it with my mouth. This man had my hormones boiling over. Even with all the drama around us, my body had gone into overdrive at having him here.

"Don't let it concern you." I smiled. "It's just nice to have you back."

"Now that I'm back, I'd like to teach again."

I frowned. "Really, you want to go back to living in London?" My heart sank at the thought of him not being at Merivale.

As though reading my mind, he added, "I thought I could apply for a teaching position at a college close to Bridesmere."

"You don't have to, Mark. Why don't you finish that book? I loved what I read. Truly."

"You really read it? I thought you were just trying to impress me. To lure me into your bed."

I caught the playful glint in his eyes and returned it with a smile. "I believe it was you who initiated the seduction."

He took me into his arms and kissed me. "So it was."

Manon and the family were already in the large sunny room when we joined them. The children were running all over the place with the dogs chasing them. Bertie was busy acquainting himself with Carson's new border collie puppy, Charlie. The cute pup had made everyone clucky, including Mark, who bent down and tickled the black-and-white canine's belly.

"Is he house-trained yet?" I asked.

"He sure is," Carson said. "Charlie worked it out himself. This is one of the smartest breeds."

The children had taken a liking to the cute creature as Freddie and Bertie looked on.

All in all, it was a hectic but heartening scene, and I wouldn't have asked for anything else. There was lightness in the air, especially with Rey gone.

Manon held her beautiful daughter and rocked her, tickling the stunning baby's nose and making her giggle. Lilly and Gabriel, Savanah's twins, waddled around as mother and father watched on with bright smiles. Cian and Julian kicked a ball around, and Theadora and Mirabel chatted about clothes and music as they often did, while Mark described Australia to Drake.

Declan drew me aside. "Anything from Natalia?"

"No. I did, however, destroy the letter."

"I'm sure we'll hear more. She's not going anywhere."

Manon must have sensed we were talking about Salon Soir and joined us. "I've got a statement from Tania ready to go."

I nodded. "Well done."

As a welcome distraction, for I really wasn't in the mood to talk about Rey's widow, Ruby did a cartwheel. That fired up Bertie and Freddie, while Charlie tumbled about underfoot.

"It's a circus," Mark said with a chuckle.

I laughed. "Yes. A glorious, bustling family." I turned to him. "Is it too much for you?"

He shook his head. "No. I've grown rather attached to this lot. Children, canines, and adults alike."

We shared a warm smile.

It was a perfect day. The sun blazed over a thriving garden filled with colorful blooms, surrounding a pond with water lilies that resembled a Monet.

We all watched in wonder as Ruby performed impressive dance moves.

"She's really showing some progress," I said, turning to Ethan, who had stars in his eyes.

"We went to a school concert, and she was luminous." He looked at his wife.

Mirabel nodded, equally proud. "There's no turning back. She's totally dance-obsessed."

"Every family should have a Terpsichore," Mark said.

"Explain," Theadora said, joining us as we watched Ruby spinning endlessly. "She's making me dizzy." She chuckled.

"Terpsichore was the muse of dance in the Greek pantheon."

After lunch, we sat outside by the pool so that the children could run with abandon with the dogs. Janet arrived, looking worried.

"What now?" I puffed. I'd had enough drama to last me a lifetime.

The women were screaming with laughter at something, while Declan and Ethan tossed a ball and Mark lounged back with the *Guardian*.

Before Janet could speak, a pair of constables strode in.

Everyone froze, and my head went into a spin. I quickly assumed they were there for Mark, who looked up from the newspaper. His eyes darkened, and my spine grew stiff.

Everything became blurry, so when the police officer spoke, it took me some time to register that what he said was, "We're looking for Manon Winter."

Manon glanced at me with fear in her eyes then grabbed her baby and hugged her like a mother trying to hide her newborn from danger.

"You're being arrested for the suspected murder of Reynard Crisp."

Drake looked like he was about to explode. Clearly in shock, he looked dazed before removing Evangeline from her mother's arms.

"What's this about?" he asked, switching his attention from Manon to the police officer, but the officer only read Manon her rights as the other constable led her away.

"I didn't do it, Grandmother." She looked back at me as we followed them.

"Don't say anything," I said. "I'm calling our lawyer right now."

ONCE BAIL WAS GRANTED, Manon was released. Shivering and looking drawn, she hugged Drake, who'd spent hours pacing around at the police station.

"Are you okay?" I asked. I hadn't slept for two nights, worried sick.

"I am fine. But it was awful. I can't go back in." Her voice cracked. "And I could really do with a cup of tea and something sweet."

Drake gave her a sad smile and wrapped his arm around her waist.

We went to a café close by, and after we'd received our orders, I asked, "What exactly happened, Manon?"

She was about to answer when a photo was snapped.

"The fucking media haven't wasted time," Drake said, looking ruffled and exhausted.

"I called my lawyer to see what could be done. Nothing, apparently, according to him." I sighed. "One downside to being a Lovechilde."

We drank our tea quickly and prepared to leave through the crowd of reporters outside.

"Great." Manon buried her head in her hands. "I look terrible."

"Don't show any emotion," I said as we pushed out into the crowd. "Look dignified. Now, let's make haste."

We fought through the media scrum, with Drake acting like a bodyguard as he shoved past eager reporters, pushing away their cameras and clearing a path for us.

Once we were in the car, Manon cried on Drake's shoulder all the way back to Bridesmere.

Despite my internal deluge of questions, I gave her the space she needed.

The moment we arrived home, Manon ran to the nursery where Janet was caring for Evangeline. She came out hugging her daughter while continuing to sob, and Drake placed his arm around her, trying to reassure her that everything would be okay.

I left them alone and went in search of Mark, who often favored the family room, also known as the yellow room. When I entered, I was met by the entire family, all looking up at me at the same time and obviously eager for news.

"What happened?" Declan asked.

"She's been granted bail. The media's swarming. Some even followed us back here."

"Oh shit," Ethan said. "Here we go. There'll be a feeding frenzy for the media."

"Where's Manon now?" Savanah asked.

"She's gone to her room with Drake and Evie."

"Poor thing."

"Has she made a statement?" Declan asked.

I nodded, and a jagged breath left my mouth. Mark arrived and came to sit by my side, holding my hand. "She insists she didn't do it."

"What have they got on her?" Ethan asked.

"They found the weapon in a skip with her fingerprints and another set of prints."

"Well, that says something," Savanah said.

"The kitchen staff?" Declan asked.

"They've been ruled out. It was a foreign weapon, apparently."

"Have they taken everyone's prints from the event?"

"They're working through it."

Mark shifted a little, and I glanced at him, noticing the tight line of his mouth.

I returned my attention to the rest of the family. "In her statement, Manon said that when she found Reynard bleeding on the ground, she pulled out the knife without thinking. Realizing what she'd done, she ran outside and tossed it in the rubbish."

"But that's crazy," Declan said.

"It was the shock of seeing him like that. Her instincts told her to remove the knife."

"But why not tell us? I mean, it just doesn't add up. She'll be slayed in court," Declan said.

Mark rose and paced. "I was there."

Everyone's attention turned sharply to him.

"What?" I asked.

"I saw her holding the knife."

"Did you see her do it?" Declan demanded.

He shook his head. "When I arrived, she was standing over the body, pale as a ghost and holding the weapon. I told her to get rid of it and to act like nothing had happened."

"But she could have come to me," I said, hurt that he hadn't told me. "I would've understood."

Mark shrugged. "I think she was hoping it would all just go away, and she didn't want to implicate you."

"But it implicates you. You're an accessory after the fact," Declan said.

Mark nodded. "I'll hand myself in and give a statement."

"Is that necessary?" I asked.

He sighed. "If we want to help Manon's case, I think it is."

Back to paddling for my life in a stormy sea. I shook my head in frustration.

CHAPTER 33

Mark

THE MEDIA SCRUTINY HAD become unbearable, especially for Caroline, who protected her privacy as a bird guarded an egg.

I was out on bail, and as we sat in the library, looking morose, Manon arrived with Drake and passed a file to Caroline.

Caroline toyed with the folder.

"What's that about?" I asked.

Caroline flicked through the pages in a desultory manner. "Information about Natalia and her brother's smuggling ring of underage girls."

"This is becoming quite a saga," I said, attempting to make light of a heavy situation that kept growing weightier by the minute.

Carson knocked on the door and came in, looking at me and nodding. "We've got something interesting."

She frowned. "Oh?"

"Footage of vans arriving, delivering filled sports bags."

"They need to be caught red-handed," she said.

He nodded. "At least we know operations are on again. I can pass this material to Scotland Yard."

MEDIA HAD DECIDED TO call Bridesmere home all week, parking outside Merivale. All we could do was make ourselves as unrecognizable as possible when we left the house.

I toyed with my baseball cap and looked at myself in the mirror. "I hate these things."

Caroline gave me a sympathetic smile. "I know. I just wish I could get rid of them."

We headed out for a walk through Chatting Wood with Bertie scrambling at our feet.

Upon our return, a detective, looking as conspicuous as we did in our dark glasses and hats, waited in the red room.

In happier times, that room had entertained a plethora of guests from elite circles. Whether that kind of breezy mirth fed on quality champagne and food would return to Merivale seemed unlikely, given recent dark events.

"What now?" Caroline muttered.

After showing the detective into her office, Caroline turned to me. "Call Manon, if you wouldn't mind. She's probably in the nursery."

That's where I found her, holding her daughter with Janet close by. "You're being summoned. Caroline wants to see you."

The poor girl looked pale and forlorn.

"Are you okay?" I asked.

"Not really. Look at that bullshit out there."

I gave her a sympathetic nod and headed out to the yellow room for a coffee and the Times new-release book reviews. Despite an impending hearing, I wasn't thinking beyond that day. That live-in-the-moment approach was keeping me sane, and the last thing Caroline needed was both of us wringing our hands in synch.

Caroline needed me to stay strong and positive. She seemed more concerned about me doing time than I was. Perhaps I could finally write, and I had plenty of first editions to keep me going for years. Not that I imagined that would be the length of my stay.

At least, I hoped not.

Caroline joined me half an hour later, and instead of sitting, she adjusted a painting. It was something she often did. Her dislike for slightly askew paintings that sometimes weren't even noticeable was close to an OCD affliction.

However, she kept staring at the still life as though it was about to tell her something.

Aware that a turned back meant trouble where Caroline's body language was concerned, I asked, "What's happened now?"

She spoke without moving. "Someone's come forward and admitted to murdering Reynard Crisp."

CHAPTER 34

Caroline

"Tell me exactly what happened that night," I asked Manon, who'd caught my hand-wringing habit.

Drake was with her, looking just as bewildered as I felt. The police had announced that someone had come forward and admitted to the murder.

"Did he say who it was?" Manon asked.

I shook my head. "I'm guessing you have some idea."

Manon looked at Drake, whose slight nod told me he knew something more.

I continued. "You'll still face charges for accessory after the fact, but hopefully we can commute that with good lawyers. But you have to tell us everything."

Manon kept fidgeting with her cardigan button. We'd been there for at least an hour, and all she'd done was shake her head, expressing incredulity that the actual murderer had surrendered.

"It's almost as if you're not pleased to be exonerated," I said.

"No. I'm relieved."

"Then why? You have a child. A reputation."

"You've got me," Drake interjected as he turned to his wife.

She stroked his cheek lovingly as a mother, because he looked more distraught than she did. Then Manon took a deep breath and said, "I'm sorry, Grandmother. I did it for you."

"What do you mean?" I asked.

"I tried to stop her from admitting to doing it, because I thought it might dredge up your past."

I shook my head. "Who's she?"

Manon continued to fidget as she walked around the room. Another habit she'd no doubt contracted from me.

"Manon, sit down and tell us exactly what happened," Drake said gently.

"Okay, this is what happened." Her eyes shone with apprehension, which had me on the edge of my seat, preparing myself for anything.

"When I left the powder room, I heard Crisp in the back room, crying for help. I ran in, and he was being stabbed continuously in the chest." Looking haunted, she paused. "I froze. I could have stopped her, but I didn't."

She sobbed. "I watched her kill him. She dropped the knife, and, staring me in the eyes, she said, 'He raped me. I've wanted to do this for forty years.'"

Manon wept, and Drake took her hand as tears streamed down her face. "It was fucking awful. All that blood. I'm still having nightmares. I should've stopped her, shouldn't I?"

"You were in shock. And she might have stabbed you, had you tried," Drake said.

"I agree," I added. "Why did you handle the weapon?"

She puffed and rolled her eyes. "I don't know. I guess I didn't want her being caught."

"So you incriminated yourself instead?" Drake asked, spreading his hands.

"I wasn't thinking straight. It was such a shock. I just told her to run. And she did, and there I was with this knife, and... well, I tossed it out."

"You should have wiped it, Mannie," Drake said.

"I should have done a lot of things." She sounded annoyed. "As I said, I don't know why I did it."

"Okay. It's happened. Let's not dwell on that. What have you told the authorities now that this has come to light?"

Manon frowned. "They haven't spoken to me yet."

I nodded, pondering the best course of action. "You have to tell them what you told us."

"But then she'll be convicted for withholding information and disrupting the investigation," Drake said.

"True." I sighed. "Let me talk to the lawyer. He must be present if you are questioned again."

She nodded, staring down at her tangled fingers.

I hesitated. "Who was it, Manon?"

Yelling disrupted that tense moment of waiting, and before I knew it, Natalia had stormed into my office.

She pointed at Manon. "You're a fucking bitch. You were there, too, with the girls."

"Calm down." Drake blocked Natalia as she lunged for Manon.

"I'll get you for this, bitch!" Natalia pointed at Manon's bewildered face, while Drake took the widow by the arm as she continued to shout abuse, leading her out.

Declan and Theadora arrived just as Natalia wiggled out of Drake's hold.

"Let me go. I'm leaving." Natalia paused and pointed again. "But you haven't heard the last of this."

"What's happening?" Declan asked.

Manon spoke at last. "I gave the authorities information and photos about our time at the Cherry bar. One of the underage girls has testified. And now Natalia's charged with smuggling illegals and aiding and abetting pedophiles."

"Does that mean she has no claim on the land?" Declan looked hopeful.

"I'd say so. It will be a lawyer's banquet, no doubt," I said.

"But won't that implicate you?" Theadora asked Manon.

Manon shrugged. "I wasn't the one bussing them in, was I?"

"We can sort that out," I said. "Our lawyer's got a lot on his plate right now."

Declan put his arm around Manon. "Good work."

She nodded, looking a little exhausted. Poor girl. It was only just occurring to me the intense shock she must have experienced at seeing Rey murdered.

"Carson's got some quality footage also. I think we'll get them this time, Mother," Declan said.

"I think so."

He frowned. "Are you okay?"

"There's a lot to deal with. But that's a question you should ask Manon. The poor girl has been subjected to a harrowing situation." Manon had snuck out, leaving us to discuss the situation.

As we sat for afternoon tea, Declan asked, "So, did she tell you who did it?"

"Manon hasn't told me yet. I think she's trying to protect the victim."

"The victim? You mean the murderer?" Declan asked.

"Evidently, Crisp raped her."

His face scrunched in horror. "Hell."

I sighed. "That's where he belongs. If only Dante's nine rings of Hell were real, he'd be burning there right now."

CHAPTER 35

Mark

CAROLINE AND I WALKED up to the cliffs, holding hands, with Bertie scampering beside us. For me, it didn't get much better. Maybe it was a sign of my age, but the simple pleasures had become the most poignant. Those vertiginous cliffs, the soaring wind, and a restless sea, plus Caroline's warm, soft hand in mine as we shared nature's splendor.

"They've offered me a post," I said.

"If it's what you want, then I'm happy for you. At least it's close to Merivale." She paused. "You really want this? You know you don't need to work."

"I know. But I really enjoyed my stint in London." I stopped walking and turned to face her. "I'm sorry I can't offer the whole marriage thing. I'll have to pay Elise that ridiculous sum of money."

"I settled it," Caroline said in a matter-of-fact tone.

"You did?" I frowned.

"Let's not mention it again. Just hold me."

I kissed her cool cheek and breathed in her rose fragrance that always mingled perfectly with the salty air. If I could describe the smell of paradise, that would be it. The sea air and Caroline. "I'll find a way to repay you."

"Oh, Mark, let's not talk about money anymore. With that horrid casino shut down and our land reclaimed, the family is wealthier than ever."

"Then why the heavy heart?"

"What I learned about Rey's murderer has affected me profoundly."

"You are bringing in the best lawyers, though."

"Of course. She needs that sentence reduced to a bare minimum. The man was a monster."

"Has she agreed to testify?"

"I'm trying to convince her. I'm going to London in the morning."

"Caroline, you paid her bail. You've done all you can. Maybe let her decide."

"I'm not certain she's in the right psychological state to decide. I want to assure her I'll support her through this. If not, she'll be facing a long spell in jail. I couldn't live with that."

"It's affecting you that profoundly?"

She sighed and nodded slowly.

It suddenly occurred to me that Caroline shared that poor woman's experience. "She was a victim, like you were."

The sudden remote glint in her eyes made me regret dredging up that violent chapter in her young life.

"I'm sorry," I said. "I shouldn't have mentioned that."

She shook her head. "No. You're right. When I heard what happened to Meghan—or Mary, as she calls herself now—it was like a knife twisted in my gut."

"Then visit her and share your experience. It might help her."

Caroline nodded. A sad smile touched her lips. "Thank you."

"For what?" I asked.

"For understanding. And for being the love of my life. I thought I was too damaged for a soul mate."

An eagle soared above, and the timing couldn't have been more perfect. I pointed at the magnificent creature. "That's how I feel. I've never been happier. I feel free for the first time in thirty-odd years, and I, too, never expected to feel this way about anyone. I thought love was just some Hollywoodesque idyll crafted to entice us into a complacent subservient existence."

She laughed. "That's rather cynical." She held my gaze and became earnest again. "To connect to someone on a deep level, we need to know ourselves first and be brave enough to remove our masks."

I nodded pensively. "Thanks for helping me do just that."

Caroline squeezed my hand. "Likewise."

Our eyes met in a kind of profound acknowledgement that defied words.

"And you're quite the philosopher," I added. "A very sexy one. Come on, let's go back. I've got a call to make."

She wrapped her arms around me, holding me tightly. "I'm so glad you're here. Please don't leave again."

"I have no reason to," I said. "We know everything about each other, don't we?"

"Oh, we do." Her eyes filled with suggestion. "How about a little afternoon nap after that call?"

I smiled. "I think I can manage that."

CHAPTER 36

Caroline

THE FLAT WAS DARK and depressing, as I sat on the tattered armchair with a spring poking into my back.

Mary handed me a cup of tea. "Sorry, it's not the whole tea service."

I smiled. "It's fine."

"You really don't have to do this. You've done enough. I'd be rotting in prison right now if you hadn't bailed me out." She gave a bitter chuckle. "Just delaying the inevitable, I guess."

I shook my head. "I've been speaking to some experts who have defended and won cases like yours. At the very least, you stand a good chance of having your sentence reduced to five years."

"All I want is for Manon to be spared a conviction." Mary sighed. "The poor girl covered for me, and I feel like shit for dragging her into this. I shouldn't have dropped that fucking knife." She bit her lip. "Pardon the language."

"I don't mind."

She held my gaze. Although she was mid-fifties, she'd gone gray and bore a face of wrinkles that spoke of a tough life.

"You knew Duncan well, didn't you?" she asked.

An icy finger stroked my spine. "Yes." I was still coming to terms with the name Duncan Marwood. Reynard's real name. A name he'd shared with Meghan, his stepsister and murderer.

"You realize he murdered a boy when he was ten?"

My heart lurched. "Oh?"

She nodded. "He was a dark, twisted character back then too. When our parents got together and I moved in with him, he used to find frogs and trample on them. He would laugh and say that was what he'd do with anyone that got in his way."

"How old were you then?"

"My dad got with his mother when I was six, and we moved in together when I turned seven. He was three years older."

"And who did he kill?" I asked.

"Ewen, a boy at school. He used to bully Duncan, always making fun of his bright red hair." She paused. "Ewen drowned in a local pond. When we heard about it, Duncan stared at me and gave me one of those looks someone gives when they've done something they're proud of."

"So you never really knew for sure?"

"Oh no, he admitted it to me. After he raped me. He told me all about it."

I winced at her matter-of-fact tone. "Your mother didn't try to stop it? Did you tell your parents?"

"He threatened to kill me." She knitted her fingers. "He raped me for three years. Every Saturday night, my parents would go out. He'd be left there to mind me. I'd tried to run away, but he always found me."

"What of your family? Why didn't you tell them?"

"They passed away shortly after I left home at sixteen. I changed my name to Mary and became Mary Childs when I married. I lived in Scotland for a good part of thirty years."

Her mouth went hard. "But then I returned here to kill him. I'd wanted to kill him for forty years. I carried it like a devil on my back. You see, he robbed me of a good life. I couldn't stay married. I tried, but I would have nightmares. I made a terrible wife. I hated me husband even touching me."

"And children?"

"None." She sighed. "I saw you were hiring at Elysium, and once I was there, I waited for the right time. Saw an opportunity and took it."

What I didn't tell Mary was that I'd been looking for Meghan Marwood myself. At Reynard's funeral, I saw Helmut and asked him about Rey's stepsister.

Helmut had given me the name and, wearing a frown, asked, "Why go there? The man's dead."

Snapping out of that thought, I added, "I want to give you all the support I can. You see..." I tangled my hands. "I went through a similar experience."

Mary, whose face had stayed blank even in the telling of her troubling childhood, winced.

As I told her my story, she shook her head. "Did ya kill him?"

I shook my head. "No, he died of cancer, I believe."

"Mm. Hope it was slow and painful."

We stared at each other and smiled, bleak as that sentiment was.

"I want to support you all the way," I said. "And by that, I mean to buy you a nice place and set up an account."

Her brow creased. "You don't have to do that, Mrs. Lovechilde."

"Let's not talk about that again. Now, will you speak to my legal team?"

She gave me a sad smile and nodded.

Como was as pristine, sun-drenched, and splendid as always, the lake calm and oblivious to the roller coaster of life. As I ambled by that fairytale lake with Mark's arm linked in mine, I felt complete.

I'd bought back the house that Mark had lived in with his former partner.

"How did you wangle it?" he asked as we walked back to our new home.

"I just made them an offer they couldn't refuse."

He stopped. "It doesn't worry you that I lived here with Lilly all those years?"

I shook my head. "Ghosts don't worry me anymore."

"And you really think you want to live here? Away from Merivale?" he pressed.

"We can mix it up a little. There's a nice big family yacht moored at Cannes that I've not been on for years." I tilted my head. "Maybe a trip to Venice. A slow trip. What do you think?"

A wide smile grew on his handsome face. "I'm happy anywhere you are, Caroline, really. If you wanted to live at Audrey's bedsit for a year, I would be happy there, too."

I scrunched my face. "No chance of that."

He took my hand, and we went inside.

"I could use a siesta," he said with that suggestive grin of his.

My body fired up, burning with the anticipation of making slow, beautiful love.

THREE MONTHS LATER

A gondolier paddled by, belting out a tune to an amused pair of tourists, as I sat outside enjoying the sun on a balcony overlooking the Grande Canale.

Just as I closed Mark's book, he joined me, and I gave him an appreciative nod. "It's marvelous."

One of those rare creatures who found compliments tricky to navigate, Mark frowned and smiled tightly at the same time. His eyes in the sunlight were the color of honey. "You're not just saying that?" He hadn't even wanted me to read his book in the end, fearing I'd hate it.

"Mark, I genuinely enjoyed it." I smiled. "I couldn't put it down."

He laughed. "The ultimate compliment for a writer, I suppose."

"You captured the excitement and extravagance of Charles II's reign so well. What a shameless hedonist he was, reveling in excesses that even by today's standards would raise eyebrows."

"That was his charm, I suppose. Although the exchequer wouldn't have agreed."

I chuckled and felt the kind of pride one feels when a loved one achieves something out of the ordinary. "It was truly great."

He sat down next to me. "You're my inspiration." He paused. "You read my dedication?"

Our eyes locked with that profound understanding that only soul-connected lovers could have. I never experienced that before Mark.

"How could I miss it?" I went to the front page and read:

To my wife and the love of my life, Caroline, without whom this book could never have materialized. Her belief in me gave me that push I needed to reach the end.

I laid the book down and stroked his handsome face. "You've made me so proud."

He gave me one of his sexy smiles. "Why don't we go inside?" He cocked his head toward the bed.

Later, as we sat basking in the afterglow of lovemaking, I asked, "So, husband, what should we do today?"

"It's warm. The Lido for a swim?"

"Why don't we spend a night or two at the Excelsior?" I suggested.

My phone pinged, and seeing it was Declan, I took the call. "Darling."

"Mother. Sorry to call on your honeymoon, but I thought you'd want to know that Mary Childs got two years."

I released a breath of relief. "That's better than we could have hoped. Don't you think?"

"I do. I was there on your behalf. She appreciated that."

"I'm so glad you called. That's taken a weight off my shoulders." I sighed. "I thought it might be five years, but that is truly a great result."

"Mary asked me to thank you for everything."

"I'll make sure she's comfortable and will stay in touch so that when she's released, she has her own home and all she needs to lead a comfortable life."

I ended the call and smiled.

I'd never felt so light and happy. My family was well. My grandchildren were healthy and flourishing. Married to the love of my life, I was free at last, no longer owned by a villainous billionaire.

THE END

MORE BOOKS BY J J SOREL

DARK DESCENT INTO DESIRE

BILLIONAIRE Blake Sinclair is a deeply complex man who always gets what he wants.

A Steamy Romance set in London featuring a billionaire smeared by a scandalous past and an impoverished sassy artist whose innocence becomes his obsession. She not only becomes his object of desire but goes somewhere no one has ever been: to the heart and soul of this damaged man.

UNCOVERING LOVE

An age-gap romance about an older woman and a younger man set in an isolated sprawling estate by the sea.

At 40, Scarlet Black's life is a series of mistakes, featuring a dangerous ex on her trail. A unique acting gig in an English coastal mansion becomes her lifeline. Her mission? To unmask Daniel Love, the enigmatic billionaire who's as tempting as he is secretive.

Scarlet falls for Daniel's irresistible charm, despite her covert agenda. Yet Daniel has his own hidden layers.

The heat between them is inescapable, but so are their secrets. The question is, who will spill first? And can trust blossom when the truth comes crashing down?

Or if you're in the mood for a Steamy Rags-to-riches romance set in glamorous Malibu then sexy billionaire, Aidan Thornhill might just

become your next book boyfriend, or at least a figure of fascination!
ENTRANCE
This Steamy Billionaire Trilogy blends fairy-tale settings with dangerous desire. Described by readers as full of raw emotion and intrigue, Entrance is the ultimate tale of two soulmates, drawn together by an intense attraction that transcends all obstacles as they battle past baggage and outside forces threatening to unravel their relationship.

jjsorel.com

THORNHILL TRILOGY

Book One Entrance

Book Two Enlighten

Book Three Enfold

SIZZLING STEAMY NIGHTS SERIES

A Taste of Peace

Devoured by Peace

It Started in Venice

LOVECHILDE SAGA

Awakened by a Billionaire

Tamed by a Billionaire

Chased by a Billionaire

Corrupted by a Billionaire

Owned by a Billionaire

The Importance of Being Wild

The Importance of Being Bella

In League with Ivy

Take My Heart

Dark Descent into Desire

Uncovering Love

BEAUTIFUL BUT STRANGE SERIES

Flooded

Flirted

Flourished